Charity

What's in a name?

By Bradly Williams

Charity - What's in a name? Copyright© 2014 by Bradly Williams

ISBN 978-0-9909147-0-9

Edited by Cesirys Espaillat

Learn more about Books and Appearances by Bradly Williams at www.bradlywilliams.com

Other books by Bradly Williams include:

Love Redefined Copyright© 2009 by Bradly Williams
ISBN 978-0-57803651-9

The Art of Ivan Tirado Copyright© 2014 from
The Art of Ivan Tirado, LLC. ISBN 978-0-9909147-1-6
--A shared work with Art by Dr. Ivan Tirado, www.ivantirado.com
and Poetry by Bradly Williams

Published by Bradly Williams

Table of Contents

Chapter 1 – This is who I am

My name is Jonathan Harris. I'm 35. Today that is, I turned 35. In 5 years I'll be forty, 10 years following that I'll be 50. I have suddenly realized that it is not the past 35 years that will determine the rest of my life, but it is the next 15 that will.

I grew up in a small town in Iowa. Don't ask. You wouldn't know it. It's actually a bit more complicated than that. I grew up in several small towns in the middle of nowhere, of many disrespected, lesser than appealing states. Maybe that is partially why I am who I am.

Growing up I watched shows like *The Love Boat, Fantasy Island, Knight Rider, The A-Team* and so many others. From an early age this was my understanding of reality. I liked the idea of fantastical adventures, heroes, epic stories. And maybe, that's why I am where I am.

I live in New York City. The West Village to be exact. I work in the Financial District. Oh yea, I'm that guy. "I work hard all day. I play hard all night." Weekends? Ah, weekends are a blur. Weekends are just a vicious cycle of women, nightclubs, trading, and the bar scene of the week.

But today, everything in my being wants something different, something better.

**

Jonathan steps out of the musty cab onto a Wall Street corner. The stampede of humans, all speed walking in unison covering every inch of the sidewalk, while Jonathan makes his delicate dance to the trading floor.

"Jon! Going to kill it on the floor again today?" a voice calls after him.

"Again!" then Jon mutterers under his breath, "Just like every day."

A vibration shakes the inside of his pocket. The answering is an instinct. A thick southern accent greets him on the other end.

"Jon, my boy, these other losers are eatin' my lunch."
"I know Bill."

**

Bill was a modern day JR Ewing. He made his money through a variety of endeavors; all from the little bit of oil money his daddy had left him. He was a suits and boots kind of guy with a cowboy hat and all.

He spoke in a booming voice. A large belly resting over his belt buckle, he leaned back in a leather tub-like chair in the biggest office on the 70th floor of Dallas Main Center.

"No, really, I like a good lunch. But honestly, the way I'm losing money with these kids in this economy, I'm happy if I can afford the dollar menu!" Bill's belly followed in motion with his laugh.

"I know Bill, and they're not kids..."

"Sounds worse if I refer to them as well trained seasoned pros that are losing my money doesn't it?"

"Good point. Look Bill your money isn't lost."

"It's not? Well, where is it? Cause, me and my accountant have been lookin' and lookin' and—"

"I have it, I have it right here and here and oh, there."

The sound of the keys on a keyboard drowned his rambling, while Jon tried following the screen scrolling numbers and trading symbols.

"That's good Son you find it and you get it for me. Oh and once you do, let's see if we can do a little something extra for you. Like maybe a chain of fast food joints... with a dollar menu, you can decide what—"

Jon cut him off in his typical way.

"All right, Bill we'll talk. Save up those favors ok. I'll give you a chance to pay me back someday."

**

You see it's the summer of 2010. We've had quite the economic downturn. I'm one of the lucky ones. I not only came out unscathed, I came out on top. I call it luck, some call it skill. Others call it destiny or fate while some say it's Karma. Karma! Ha, if only they knew me… the real me, what's underneath the surface. They only see me at work.

Yes, I work hard and yes, I do a lot of hard work for others so they can succeed. But ultimately to get what I want, to do what I want. Don't we all?

When I least expect it, it's 4pm. The end of the day comes with the ringing of a bell. May as well be a cow bell. The bulls are leaving the market, as are the bears. I go for a cab but another hand goes out as well, a woman's hand.

"Headed up town?" It's what I'm saying to her, but I'm a combination of startled and mystified.

Then she responds, something I'm sure the cab driver can hear.

"We're on Wall Street. There's not a lot of options."

I'm stuck in my thoughts, going through the routine of Fridays in my head. Fridays are drinks up town, typically followed with taking a woman back to her place. Just maybe this Friday things can be flipped around. I'm lost in the possibilities of this moment for what seems seconds, but it must be longer. The lash of her words whips me back to reality.

"Are you getting in?" She snapped. Terse, yet clear, she was being inviting as well.

This is one of those moments. You know the moments where time has a way of freezing around you. The mind analyzes the now and the past in an effort to pre-determine the future. I knew all the games. I've played them. Heck, I invented some of them. It's often just a question of if I want to play, not if I'll win.

"Why not?" I say as I get into the cab.

There was something a little different about this young, striking woman. She definitely didn't work in the market. I couldn't quite figure her out. The silence seemed to be a requirement I dare not break. We pulled up to Penn station.

"Have a nice--" I started and she was gone. We went our separate ways. Today, as I mentioned, was different. Today I wasn't interested in the same old game.

Heading for one of my favorite spots with a rooftop garden bar near Penn Station, I could see an old friend heading home.

"Jon! Hey man, how's the market treating you?" a voice burst through the streets

"Hey Adam, you know me… and I believe what you should be asking is, how am I treating the market?"

I have to laugh; one of the keys is to always exude confidence regardless of whether it really represents the truth underneath.

"Well, either way, the answer is, very well."

"Of course," Adam responds. "Well, where ya headed?"

"I was going to get a drink but--something, well I was just about to change my mind and was going to head home instead."

"Wanna go ahead and grab that drink and join me to let off some steam from the long week?"

It'd been a while since I had seen Adam. "Yeah, is that an invite?"

"You bet, whatcha got in mind?" I had to ask before fully agreeing.

"O'Hannigans on 52nd off 9th?"

"Perfect."

**

Jon's hand goes in the air for a cab, along with a whistle. Immediately a cab pulls up, and for a moment he swears he sees the girl from before. He pauses. As his mind goes back to the thought of the woman from earlier in the day, the cabbie yells. *Hey Buddy, ya in or ya out? I got fares all over ready to get some place!*

"Jon", Adam steps in, "You ok?"

Then he looks toward the cab driver.

Go ahead, grab another one, we're gonna walk, Adam whispers to the driver.

"Jon, what'd ya say? Walk it? Or have you become driver spoiled?"

"Sure", Jon said, "let's go."

**

On the way, I couldn't get the image out of my mind. It was more than déjà vu. I wasn't quite ready to open myself up to this friend whom I hadn't seen in months. So, small talk ensued. We talked about the usual things. Work, and plans for the weekend.

Moments later we're at the pub with pints in hand and a "*Cheers,*" kick off the evening.

It wasn't much longer and it came out--drinks have a way of doing that. It's already in my mind and the drinks just sort of helped the thoughts make their way to my tongue.

"Adam, what do you think of déjà vu?"

"I don't know, I guess our mind connects different memories and when we have an experience that triggers any connection to our past it will seem as if we are reliving it all over again."

Shrink! I say both jokingly and accusingly of Adam

"It's what I do," Adam replies. "Seriously what's going on Jon?"

Somehow several pints later things became extremely sobering. Adam dealt with people who struggled every day with battles of the heart and mind. He worked with celebrities and the financial gurus of the city. However, he also volunteered his services to a local non-profit in the Bowery. They focused on meeting more than just the physical but also the mental needs of the homeless and hurting of the city.

"It's just… this girl."

"Jon, you never change."

"No, I'm serious."

"So am I Jon. C'mon man, it's always about a woman. She's twenty two and she drives me crazy and we had a great night but I really don't want to call her back and—"

"Forget you. Adam, when was the last time you even saw me?"

"Jon I've known you for years. Does it matter, what do you expect?"

"A friend, and a professional, that's what I expect. She's not twenty two, actually I don't even know. Actually, I don't even know her, it's dumb, and really it's crazy. I've got the last round. Let's catch up again."

"Jon, I'm sorry. If you need to talk…"

A moment passes. I took a deep breath as I dropped the cash on the bar and head for the door. I stop and turn my head, "I get it. I really do Adam. Another time, maybe, another time."

**

The sun has burned its way through the curtains and right into Jon's bedroom. His cell phone blinked the time, 7:00 AM. The radio filled the room with music.

Every day is a new day, I'm thankful for every breath I take, I won't take it for granted. So, I learn from my mistakes. It's beyond my control, sometimes it's best to let go.

Ugh, as he sits up. The scent in the room, creped into his senses, he immediately turned his head trying to recognize it. He could see her, again.

His phone alarm goes off, buzzing. The dream is destroyed and he wakes shaking his head.

Still entranced he quickly rises up and begins to search out her scent. He starts to call out her name, and quickly realizes he still doesn't know her name. But, strangely she is living side by side with him. His mind runs with thoughts of her.

I don't even know who this woman is. Yet, it is as if she is now everywhere I am. She's in the seat next to me on the train, at the same table when I am out to eat!

Jon begins to ask himself, *Is this what happens when you don't go back to her place? Is this what happens when you don't play the game. Does the game haunt you, the other player, living amongst you until you embrace the game and play?* He shakes his head again and get's up.

Jon brushes his teeth, throws on some Gym shorts and a T-Shirt. And, he's out the door for a run.

Jon glances at his watch/heart rate monitor unit, as his run slows to a walk. He makes his way into his local coffee shop, Earth Brew, around the corner of Greenwich and Horatio Streets.

"Double shot Canadian skim latte with a shot of caramel and whip, please."

"Here or to go?"

"Here," he mutters, *I got no where else to be, no place I gotta go.*

"Anything else?"

"Yeah, wheat bagel, butter, thanks."

He swiftly drops cash on the counter, and moves slightly to the side as he waits.

**

In the corner of the cafe, a woman sat with her computer. She stood out from the rest, who were intently typing away. She was almost a glitch of silent disturbance surrounded by the sea of moving humans in and out with their espressos. Others busy in only their mind sitting relaxed around her. All writing, studying, accompanied by cups of coffee, a typical Saturday morning crowd.

**

From the waiting bar of the coffee-shop he could see her. The mysterious woman that had been haunting his dreams sat right there, in the corner, of his favorite cafe. Jon determined he could not go to her. What would he say? He asked himself, *who am I becoming? Who is this woman that has the best of me? Why can I not find words to speak and why do our paths continue to cross like this?* Confused and a bit taken back, he began rushing the barista for his coffee and bagel to-go, in an almost simultaneous moment he turned his head, and noticed she was gone.

"Never, Mind, I think I will stay after all," he told the cheeky girl behind the counter.

Was she there at all? Am I going crazy? I have to find a way to engage her. I have to engage whatever this is. This isn't anything I'm used to.

Jon took a seat, the very seat where he had seen her moments earlier, or so he thought. He slid back, set his bagel down, and then looked to his left. A book sitting just slightly out from the edge of the shelf, "Theorists- A book on those who believe in what we don't want to"

Seriously?

Next to him laid several religion books as well.

He finally reached for the bagel he had sat on the table in front of him as he sipped from his cup, leaning back, looking around, in a combination of paranoia and anticipation.

One thing is for sure, I may not be crazy but I am living in a different state of mind.

The next bite he took, he notices two books on the table among others. One called, "Love – The Truth…"

Love, what does anyone know about love? Have I loved anyone? For that matter has anyone ever really loved me? In this city, in my life it's about an exchange of services. That's how love has always worked, that's all I've ever known. Then, he saw them.

A couple walked in the door, they were a few years older, laughing and enjoying themselves. At least this is how he saw them.

The man was carrying their baby in one of those carriers on his chest. He asked his wife what she'd like, and pointed her towards the restroom. "I'll grab our coffees and a table." He watched as this guy prepped their coffee and moved to a table playing with his daughter the entire time. Jon noticed the glances to the bathroom the man made. Not watching out of frustration but with waiting, this man was not in a rush, he was concerned. He had even returned to ask for her coffee to be slightly re-heated. His wife appeared relieved when she returned. They sat and laughed as they talked. If they didn't have a child with them, you would have thought they were newlyweds. The child seemed to add joy and be a part of this 'team'. Jon glanced back at the book on the table.

You want to know the truth? That's love, he thought as he recapped what he had witnessed from the family.

The care, concern, and joy in the family who was now sliding out the door.

Love was not a word Jon was familiar with or had explored much of his time. A man to his right sipping from a cup glanced up and with a heavy Hungarian accent said to him, "Romans 12:2"

"Excuse me?"

"I'm sorry, I couldn't help but notice. You seem distracted, you seem, distraught and between the book on the table and the way you watched that family a moment ago. I just thought it might be a place to go."

"Um, ok thanks."

"You could say, that is just one of my favorites to read. Take care."

"You too."

Jon took another bite and another sip. Then he dropped his head. *Crazy fool, peaking into my world from a table away! What is happening? I suddenly feel like I've been thwarted into an alternate universe of some sort. I can't keep doing this. I'm a man of action, not a coward. It's why I'm successful at what I do. It's why I get what I want, how I want, when I want. I confront, I do not run. I inquire, I am not complacent. I will no longer be still about this matter!*

He sipped his last sip, grabbed the last of his bagel and

headed out the door, but the man who spoke to him a moment before was nowhere in sight. *I let it happen again. This is not going to keep getting away from me.*

Jon stretched and casually headed back to his apartment. He continued to have visions. He began to see this woman in every woman he passed, little girls, old ladies, homeless women. They all wore her face.

A beautiful woman jogged by, "Good morning Jon."

Jon saw her, but again it isn't her he sees. He remained silent as he stared past her, as if he was blind in some way to anything but the images his mind was projecting.

"Uh, Jon?"

"Sorry, morning Liz."

"You ok?"

He stuttered trying to respond. "Yeah, doing great, how about you?"

"Good, just finish your run? Wanna join me for a shower and some brunch?"

Jon was clearly distracted. "I think I'm going to have to take a rain check Liz. Great seeing you, have a good run. Oh, and enjoy your brunch."

"Ok Jon," She said it with a slightly confused look as she jogged away and then quietly speaking her thought. "That's a first."

Jon rushed home, rid his clothing and ran into the bathroom for a hot shower. Steam bellowing over the glass and he was washing himself intensely, with the idea that he was trying to wash off something that was more than external. It's as if he was trying to wash off, 'who he was.'

Jon heard his own thoughts scatter through his mind.

Who am I? What have I become? Is this all I am. Why do I suddenly feel so dirty? Why can't I get it off?

On the outside we see his disgust and frustration as he worked to keep his composure.

In his robe he stepped out and sat at his laptop and began to write.

A new thing consumes me. I am not sure what it is. I can not seem to even hold face to the outside world. While I am able to hold back the tears, I cry out on the inside. I want to be a new man. I want--

He stopped. He realized he didn't know. For the first time in his life, he realized.

I want... I want... I don't know. I don't know what it is, or how to get there.

He shook his head slightly. He walked to the kitchen and poured a drink. He moved quickly and went to his table, looking, searching, and then to his book shelf.

A quick glance up and he went to his nightstand, pulled out the bottom drawer. Tearing through some papers and brochures he pulled a book out.

"Romans, Romans, Romans," he said it again and again as he searched through it.

"There! Now what was it? Ah come on! I have to remember numbers all day, and I can't remember... wait, twelve, yes twelve, twelve two."

Romans 12:2

Do not conform any longer to the pattern of this world, but be transformed by the renewing of your mind.

"Renewing of your mind? I feel like my mind is spinning. Is that what happens at this age? Does the mind just begin to reset or renew itself?

Maybe that's it. Maybe it is time to change?

Maybe it is time for me to renew Jonathan Thomas Harris."

Then he fell back into bed. The mental exhaustion has overcome him.

Sunday morning looks a lot like Saturday. A morning run, then time to grab coffee, again. Would he see her again? Was she even there yesterday?

He ran with more than anticipation. Instead, today his run was with actual expectation. He stopped at Earth Brew again, same coffee, same wheat bagel. He looked over. She was not there.

Did I get my hopes up too much?

He went to the couch. Dropped down and slowly began to enjoy his bagel and coffee. He made mental notes of the differences again and again.

It's Sunday not Saturday. I did get here early. Maybe I missed my 'run in' opportunity.

Ending his breakfast, Jon removed all the residue of his stay at the coffee shop. He stepped into the hectic city once more, eyes downward in a typical New York pace. At the door he spotted a little girl, a baby in a stroller, she resembled the woman he'd been searching. Or maybe that was just his mind projecting this woman in his head.

Will this ever stop? I really am seeing her in every woman I pass.

He bumped the lady who appeared to be the little girl's mother.

"Excuse me miss," he said and then looked up. *It's her.*

She smiled. He had thought of a hundred things to say to her. Now he was lost all over again. *Who's the little girl? Is it her daughter? Maybe she was watching her for a friend.*

Then she helped him. "Good morning."

He detected a light French accent and responded.

"Bonjour mademoiselle." Then in his mind, *that's the best I could come up with.*

She responded well, with another smile. Then he saw a Bible under her arm. *Finally, an in.*

He said very assuredly and intently, "Romans 12:2."

"Pardon?"

"I like Romans 12:2,"

"Oh that's nice. Which one is that, what does it say?"

"Roughly, you must renew your mind. We have to change how we think."

"Oh, and are you?"

Lost in her eyes, he responded. "Am I what?"

She smiled and before she could answer, Jon caught himself. "Yes, yes I believe I am. Better yet, I believe somehow from somewhere, I believe I'm even getting a little help. Believing in that which before I didn't want to. Maybe I am theorist."

"Maybe. Maybe you seek the truth."

"Yes, truth, I guess it's all about truth. Once you know the truth."

"Eileena, mochacinno," a shout from the barista interrupts the conversation.

"Thank you," she responds.

"To go?" Jon asked, noticing the paper cup

"Yes, it's a beautiful day. We're going for a walk."

"Could I join you?"

"Join us? What's your name?" She asked with a smile and a slight tilt of the head

"Jon."

"This is Charity Jon, I'm Elieena. If you want to join us, then do so. Here, each morning this week. 8am?"

"Why not today?"

"Jon, renew your mind."

"Ok, ok. Have a nice walk. Enjoy the day."

"You too Jon."

She's never coming back here again. I know that face. I've seen it when friends of mine get shot down all the time. I think I remember it from a couple times in my early twenties from when I first came to New York. Thought I was big time. They could see right through me. And so could she. I bet she knows exactly the kind of guy I am. Only, only, I'm not that guy. Am I?

At that moment Jon could sense a change. Not just an emotional feeling, but also a deep sense of something shifting in his life. It wasn't about this woman. It was deeper than that. Though he couldn't explain it, he was excited about this world he had entered and what it might have to offer.

Jon took a stroll down the streets of New York for the rest of the day. Watching people, feeling their pains and their joys. He could almost hear their thoughts, their conversations, he realized how many lives you are a part of in this city. Even, when no one realized it.

He laid down on a rock in Central Park and dosed off. When he awoke he reminisced to naps at his grandmother's home. His mom was often running around with many men and her girlfriends and such, dropping him off for the day or days at a time

"One day, in a single moment it will be clear, out of your control, life will choose you. How you respond will reflect how you will forever be defined," Grandmother's shaky voice echoed in his head. *Could I be living that moment she spoke of?*

**

Monday

The alarm went off in Jon's dark room. He hustled out of bed in a rush and then it hit him, he couldn't go into work, he had to meet her.

He jumped on his Smartphone sent a few emails, threw his laptop in a bag with a few files and rushed to the coffee shop.

It's 7:49, plenty of time. He walked in, ordered a cup of something stronger than normal. "Quad skim latte."

He sat down, ripped open his bag, pulled out his files and laptop and began working. He didn't look up again until suddenly.

It's eleven? She never came? Did I miss her? Maybe she missed me?

He went back to his apartment and finished the day working from home constantly distracted by the thought of the woman and even more so the little girl that had been with her the day before.

This time he tried to look up from time to time a bit more but the intensity of following the stocks, working his Smartphone and laptop made it difficult to watch for this woman.

That afternoon Jon prepared an early dinner and sat down to his table where books on love laid neatly. *What am I missing?*

He continued to think on this question as he read, relaxed, listened to music and watched some TV.

Suddenly he thought back, to what his grandmother had said. He realized he had not renewed anything. His life had not changed. When Monday came he went back to the same Jon as before, just sitting at a table in a coffee shop versus being in an office on Wall Street. Location didn't depict change, and Jon knew it.

How could I not see this? He went to a specialty store nearby and bought a small turtle chew toy that made fun sounds when you squeezed it. He had remembered she had her daughter in little turtle socks. Then he returned home, read a little and due to the anticipation along with the faith and the hope he still held onto, he turned in early.

Jon awoke at 7. Opting out of working for the day, he dressed comfortably and left his work bag at home by his desk. He strolled through the village and made his way through the doors, "Half-caf caramel misto please."

The girl looked at him a bit funny, "Half-caf?"

"Yes, thank you," he sat down and began to soak up the scene around him, taking time to look at the art that hung on the brick walls.

She walked in, "Jonathan?"

At first he thought it must be the Barista, then he realized, they were still working through orders ahead of him. Suddenly, as if on a delay his mind clicked. It was *her* voice! He quickly turned his head. Was he imagining things? He rushed out the door and is sure he sees her get in a cab as it pulls away.

This is crazy. He saw another cab sitting there on Greenwich and rushed for it.

"Jonathan?" The cab driver asked.

"Yeah."

"Get in. Quick. This is for you."

The cab driver passes him an envelope and he gets in the car. The little baby girl he had seen with Eileena just days before sat next to him in the back seat. He opened the card. On the outside it had his name. Under the lip of the opening, it said 'Renova,' which translated loosely to, 'Renew your self. Seek the truth'

He pulls out the note and begins to read it.

The cab driver insists that there was a woman that hailed his cab but as he came back from the nearby hot dog vendor she was walking away. "I get in and find this envelope with the name Jonathan on it and see a baby in the back. Next thing I know there you are. I didn't even have a chance to get out before I had lost her in the sea of people and you walked up."

Jonathan determines to take her and call someone he knows who worked with social services to see what to do next. First, to determine who the woman was in relation to this little girl and if she had no family then possibly... *Possibly what? Give her to someone who will determine her life for her? No, if she has no family, I'll be her family. I will do whatever it takes to care for her, to love her, to adopt her.*

He knew all those that knew him would challenge the idea; he makes the decision not to share the information.

Chapter 2 – Flashback

Approximately two years ago-- Maria is a nurse, three months pregnant. She was nearing the end of a shift.

"Maria, I know you're on the clock, but, well um, the test results are back."

"Doctor Phillips, I was sure you were gone for the night."

"I had a patient that coded. He's stable but it was close. I thought I'd check in on you on my way out."

"Thanks, I've been trying to stay relaxed like you told me to. Not, easy."

"Well, do you want to go for a walk? Grab a cup of coffee in the cafeteria?"

"That'd be great. I have one more break, and I just need to drop this off at the nurses' station."

The two headed out the doors and down the hall to the cafeteria. "Maria, I know how much this baby means to you. I know what some of my fellow doctors would tell you to do but I've known you for way to long to suggest some of the things they would."

Maria's head dropped and tears kissed her cheeks. She knew whatever Doctor Phillips was leading to, it was not good. "Doctor, you know I respect you in the field, as my doctor and as my friend. What is it and what has to be done?"

"Your daughter's heart is not developing properly. Her chances of survival are minimal. We're talking less than five percent."

Maria pulled back her tears. Each of them nod to staff they passed by, and then before they sat, she took Dr. Phillips by the arm. He looked toward her then gazed away as to avoid eye contact.

"Wait, there's more. You can save her! You know something."

"Maria-"

"Is it that new, trial? Do you think it could work?"

"Maria, I…I just don't know if it's a good idea."

"Michael! Could it work?"

"There might be a way. With this particular deformity and with what she is getting from you we could use your heart to jumpstart the serum so that it is more likely to take. Until now we've used only much older test patients. I don't think the usual method of initiating it once introduced to her heart is safe."

"What do I have to lose? You already said she has less than a five percent chance to live."

"There is one more thing you have to consider. The radiation that is in the liquid could get drawn back and if introduced into your body… well."

"What, wouldn't I just flush it?"

"It's designed very specifically? If for any reason it doesn't take, there's a chance both of you could reject it, and we could lose you both."

"Is there also a chance for her to survive even if I do not?"

"That's the thing Maria. That is very likely a possibility if it is not fully captured by her little heart. If not contained anything that seeps out presents a slight threat to her, but an even greater threat to you, due to the design and focus of how it will be prepared and placed."

"I need to know the facts Michael, if that happens, how long would I have?"

"We have no idea Maria. As I said, this is something that is still new and has never even been considered for what we are talking about right now."

She looked outside the cafeteria window and up at the stars. "You see those stars?"

"Sure, it's Orion".

"I always loved Orion, a warrior, a fighter, protecting the skies at night. I always imagined Pegasus was his horse and the Big and Little Bears were actually Bears that stood by his side."

Dr. Phillips took in a deep breath and slowly let it out, he looked at her, "Maria, there's one more thing we've found. It seems the defect is genetic. Though it has never caused you an issue, your heart has the same defect. It's like a weak seam on clothing. Yours has held together much longer than one would have expected. Using your heart to help your daughters' could tear it apart. It could at least weaken it shortening your life. Or, if we're lucky, somehow it could strengthen it. There is no way at all to even speculate."

"Michael, just tell me what you believe will happen."

"Best case scenario is, her heart receives it, grows strong, and no one will likely ever know a thing. However, while I think there is a strong possibility to save her, I'm worried some of the liquid will come back through the cord, somehow enter your system and slowly tear your cells apart.

It would be like inserting a cancer with, in part, exactly what we often use to cure it. I don't think we could save you and in the weeks and months to come…anything could…" Dr. Phillips filled his lungs once more before he slowly continued, "again, it's unlikely we could reverse it."

Maria counted her heartbeats and looked Dr. Phillips in the eyes, then stared back at the skies.

"Maria, you have to understand. The risk you are taking, means, even if we could save you in such a circumstance, it would mean revealing what we did to save your daughter. Much more would be at stake than your life."

"I understand. I have to finish my shift. Can we talk tomorrow?"

"Yes, we can do this as soon as you wish but I'd suggest not waiting too much longer. It'd be best for it to develop while she is still able to gain what she can in the womb for as long as possible."

"Thanks Michael," Maria turned, she could see a man jump in a cab by the ER doors and watched as it sped away. He looked familiar, but she didn't get a good enough look to tell for sure.

There's a man on the gurney. A doctor begins pushing it and Maria is called on for help.

"Who dropped this man off? Was he on his own? Where's his family?

An ER tech heard her questions and spoke in her direction, "Some guy just brought him in, said he was on his way home and saw him grab his chest and go down on the sidewalk. He jumped from his taxi, and then brought him here. Then he just took back off in his cab.

All I heard him say as he left was how sad it is when a single life can be lost on a street often walked by so many, and that no one should ever be alone here. He shook his head and was gone before we could turn around with a clip board."

Maria shook her head, a bit lost in her thoughts and a bit bewildered. She heard the distant call of a doctor, "nurse! Nurse!"

"Sorry, I, I thought…"

The doctor shouted some quick instructions and sent Maria off to tend to the new patient.

**

Maria walked into her usual stop and ordered her usual, "Grande latte with a little whip cream please… Oh…" as she looked down and rubbed her belly, "--decaf"

"Coming right up," the girl behind the counter pleasantly said.

Maria walked over to the 'pick-up' area of the bar, got her coffee. She slid over to a seat in the back under the lamp setting her coffee on the table and dropping her bag on a chair. Browsing the books on the shelf she noticed an old Bible. Clearly it had just been left there. Wrinkled and torn it was bent on every edge. She grinned, her eyes twinkled, and her mind went to a place long past when she was just a child.

**

A younger Maria and her mother sit on a couch together. "Maria, remember you can always come here. This book has been around for a very long time. There is a reason for that that you may not understand, for a very long time."

Maria let out a heavy breath and thought of how tired she was of being told she's 'too young to understand' and how 'it'll make sense when she's older.'

"That's ok. Just remember what I have taught you. Remember, God is everlasting. If you need Him, He is here," she laid her hand on the Bible and then took Maria's little hand and gave it to her.

Only a few years older, Maria watched her house burn to the ground. A fireman has carried her out and is kneeled next to her. "Mommy, my Mommy!" she said in between cries.

"Where is your daddy?" The fireman asked.

Maria yelled, "I don't-" then her voice dropped to a near whisper "-have a daddy." She ran off into the legs of a police officer. She looked up and she saw a woman in uniform.

"Honey," the officer said, "it's going to be ok."

Maria hugged the officer's legs; her crying joined the smoke filled air.

The officer picked her up and they stepped away and around the other side of the chaos. The officer knelt down to her, "Hon, I'm sorry about your mother. I can't bring her back. I don't know what to say."

"I know. My mom taught me about death. I just never expected...this."

"I know. I know."

**

A couple walked into a state building, where the officer and Maria are waiting. "Hi, we're James and Deborah Smith"

"Maria, this nice couple is going to be taking care of you. They have two other children about your age. I think you'll enjoy spending time with them."

Maria's eyes filled with tears.

"Maria, I do have something for you. They found it when they were cleaning up after the fire." The officer holds the Bible that her mom had placed her hand on, with very little damage to it, and she hands it to Maria.

Immediately, Maria heard her mother's voice, "He is here."

"NO! You can keep it!" Then, quickly she turned, "let's go."

After walking the stage, Maria hugged her adoptive family and friends in celebration for her high school graduation. In the corner the officer stood watching in admiration, "Maria?"

"Yes?"

"I think she was right, and I think she's still here too. And I and I'm sure she, is very proud of you."

"You're... but you can't be? You can't be much older than me?"

The officer handed her the Bible from her youth, the cover and a couple pages with burnt edges.

Maria opened it and inside, on the front of the cover, the inscription: "He is here and I will always be with you as well," signed by her mother.

"My Mom couldn't make it. But she said it was important that this got to you... today. I'm in a college program sponsored by the academy."

Maria looked closely and saw that the uniform wasn't a standard NYPD uniform, but just a grey academy uniform. "Wow, you look just like her. I don't, I don't know what to say. Thank you. So much has happened since that day."

**

In the corner cafe a pregnant Maria, sat looking out the window. She could see the same man from the scene at the hospital getting up with his paper and leaving. She gathered her things and chased after him, but he was gone.

She dashed around the corner but with the rushing multitude of workers; he was lost.

The following day at the hospital Dr. Phillips approached Maria. Hanging her head, she looked past the clipboard in her hand. "Maria. Are you ok?"

"Yes Michael, thank you. It's time Michael. I've decided to move forward with the surgery."

"Are you sure?"

"Yes. If I don't, I know I'll likely die anyway from the

condition that not only is affecting her but me as well, and be of no good to my daughter or to anyone. If I do this, it could be a breakthrough, it could save me and it could be a decision that gives my daughter, her mother."

Lost in a rush of thoughts and the knowledge that her daughter would never know her father she slowly said, "Lord knows she deserves to at least have that."

"Ok Maria, we'll do it. Let's move quickly. I have a night shift coming up in a couple nights. I noticed you're on call just before then. We'll set it up so it looks like a natural procedure, a check up on the baby as if something doesn't look quite right. No one will even know the difference. We'll just admit you on a 'sick stomach' with concerns."

"Ok," Maria replied with shakiness in her voice, "thank you."

Fear, nervousness, anxiety were just a few of the emotions that Maria was entangled in those next few days.

Doctor Phillips reminded Maria of typical pre-surgery procedures and precautions to take especially since she was pregnant. Luckily it was short with very little invasiveness.

The two depart, headed back to work caring for others. Dr. Phillips and Maria lost in thoughts about her baby's life.

It's different when your work is to take care of strangers. You do care; however, it is part of your work to keep it, just work. When it's personal, everything is different. When it's you, well let's just say it can be hard, on the other side.

**

Jon was on Wall Street, the bell had rung and suits owned the streets. It was even busier than on prior days. After all, it was 2008 and just prior to the financial crash that lied just ahead.

Everyone was making his or her way to their favorite happy hour spot. Jon decided to do something different. He dropped by his apartment for a quick change and dropped off his briefcase then headed to the Lower East Side. Mid-Town and Up-Town were just not what this night called for.

He made his way into a casual, yet still somewhat trendy and hip kind of a place. Simple with nice lighting where you could see the person next to you yet the lights are low enough to relax and connect, making it easy on the eyes as you took in a cocktail.

Not long afterward, she came along and took a seat.

Game on. First, a survey: she's very European but of what decent, hard to tell, professional but not too professional. Local too. You can tell if you've been here long enough. Looks like the type who grew up here and made the most of a little, to do okay with her self. He catches a glimpse of a badge in her purse as she opens it to get to her wallet. Must work some place with security access of some type. He didn't catch enough of it to tell for sure where she worked though.

The bartender shouted her name, and went for a draft and a pint glass. *Yep, local! Just as I expected.*

She reached for her wallet and the bartender said, "You know on Friday I always get your first one."

Jon wore his best smile and kept it simple. He had learned that worked best.

"Well, that's a great way to start off a Friday."

"Not you!" the bartender said, "Six bucks or would you like to start a tab?"

"Um, a tab."

The woman smiled and chuckled under her breath.

"You like that huh?

He smiled and with a laugh, "if you're having a second, let me get that one."

"How do you know we'll still be talking after I finish this one?"

"I don't. But, I'm an investor, I invest millions every day on what I hope might happen."

"Oh, a man of faith I see."

"I think of myself more a man of risk… evaluated risk."

"Oh?"

"Well, I look at it like this. Either way I do better than I would with the market."

"How do you see that?"

"Well, if you do not continue talking with me at least you still have something of value," he nodded his head toward the beer taps, "if we do develop this conversation into more than introductory banter, then I surely will have received something of value and I hope in that case you would feel you doubled your investment."

There's a lot to be said for a good line, one of intrigue and mystery. One that says I'm educated but I don't know everything. Importantly, Jon was saying, "either way, one of us will bring value to the other, so no one really loses here."
She recognized the ball was in her court. He'd given it to her. Would she play on?

**

Jon awoke in a sweat. He looked left and saw that the woman that lied beside him was the same as from the night before. He got up and walked to the window.
Once more he looked toward his bed and didn't see her. Thinking he saw the door to the bathroom swing slightly, he shook his head, opened a curtain, made his way to the kitchen for a cup of coffee and looked again. She was there. He took a sip and decided to lie back down. Unusual for Jon, he dosed back off.
His mind was in that middle state, not quite awake or asleep. He sipped coffee again in the kitchen. As he returned to the bed he glances in the mirror and saw himself but he was years older.
Again, he jerked up out of bed dripping in sweat. The girl was gone. *Was she ever really here?* He reached for his cup of coffee. As he lifted it from his end table to his lips, he noticed the rim of the near empty cup and the light red lipstick.
Strange, usually they stay. Maybe I just forgot to wash the cup off from the day before? Either way, it's time for my morning jog.
Jon moved through his usual motions, throughout the day he reflected on the evening, considering the combination of reality and his dream from the night before and morning of.
Exhausted he laid his head and muttered, "Suddenly it's as if

my mind is in two places, awake and dreaming at the same time."
Living two lives will do that to a man.

**

We return to Maria at the time when she sat in the cafeteria talking with Dr. Phillips.

They were discussing the date and time of the procedure, and what she could do to prepare her and her baby. He wanted to be sure she would be ready for the various possibilities and since it would not be authorized, how they would handle each of them.

**

The next few days went by quickly. Jon awoke, ran, went into the office or to the market floor, trading, drinking and with a new woman each night, sometimes there was dinner, other times it was just a short night at their place and nothing else.

**

Maria took care of others. Helping others to live, knowing inside, she may not live much longer.

Chapter 3 – The Surgery

"Alright Maria, You know everyone in the room. I have filled them in on everything, exactly as we discussed regarding the procedures we're taking. Marcos is handling anesthesia, Sarah will assist me, and as an added precaution I've asked Dr. Lucas to watch over the procedure as a second set of eyes so to speak. Are you ready Maria?"

"Yes," Maria replied quickly without even a blink. She had thought this through. She had searched deep about this and knew exactly what may and may not happen. They say for some things you can never truly be ready, but for this at least mentally, Maria had prepared herself in everyway she knew possible. She had even found herself praying. She was searching and reaching out to anything she knew to help make sure this was the right decision. After all, other than Dr. Phillips, there had been no one else she felt she could trust to even bring up such an idea.

Dr. Phillips gave Marcos the nod, ran his hand over Maria's head sliding back her hair and smiled. "Let's get started. Sarah, go ahead with the ultrasound."

Night has fallen; it was perfect. A slow late Tuesday night, well now into the early morning hours of the next day, Maria faded quickly as the anesthesia took effect.

"Her vitals all look good. She seems very healthy, in great shape." Sarah said.

"She's always taken very good care of herself, as long as I've known her." Michael followed. He surveyed her chest and stomach.

Sarah looked up, "The baby also appears to be doing well, healthy heartbeat, sitting well in her stomach. Actually she's in a great position for the procedure. It's as if she knows and is scooting right over, saying: 'Ok, go ahead.'"

Dr. Phillips looked over the ultrasound and listened closely to both the heartbeats.

"Do you see that? There it is. And, there, can you see that as well?" He asked the questions about what he already knew. Every single one of them had to buy into not only what they were about to take part in but also why they had to do it. "Look, you can see two sections of the heart that are not developing properly. It's as if they aren't growing at the rate of the rest of the heart and body. Listen closely," he amplified the sound and the room was silenced by the beating of this child's heart. "Listen."

There was a strange whistling sound. "What is it?" Marcos asked. "I've never heard anything like that. How did you even discover it?"

Amazed, after all no one else had seen what he'd seen or heard, until now.

"The whistling sound is the result of two things. As blood is flowing to and from the heart there seems to be a leak in the heart."

"A leak? But wouldn't that be a problem that could be addressed with known surgical methods?" asked Dr. Lucas.

"No, Luke, you see, this is different. This seems to be almost a leak going in, where oxygen is not entirely being pulled in. It's so thin we can't even be 100% sure of where it is. I believe it's also what is hindering the growth in the lower aortas. That of course, is causing an issue with total growth. This could cause an issue with blood and oxygen flow to the entire body and brain. We don't know how it could result because, frankly, I've never seen something exactly like this. The other part is it could be like a tire with a bubble or a balloon where all the air is pushed to one side, eventually it pops."

He turned the sound down and the room remained silent as everyone began to realize what they were dealing with, the unknown.

"Scalpel," Dr. Phillips made the smallest incision possible into the stomach watching the ultrasound. Next they would utilize a new machine along with a combination of laser technology and focused radiation.

He looked around the room and explained. "The concept is to be able to both charge growth in the part of the heart that isn't growing, while helping it heal and patch itself where the oxygen loss is happening.

Once I begin, I cannot stop, I need to know we're in this together. We've all known Maria for a long time. We've watched her save lives and I for one am willing to risk mine to help save her child's by her request."

The tension thickened the air in the room. Heads began dropping and simultaneously looking back up each nod. Sarah moved the machine into a precise position. Dr. Lucas moved to a place where he could be the second set of eyes. Marcos watched over the vitals of the two patients in hand.

Carefully, Dr. Phillips began, utilizing the laser to make pin point cuts with precision while releasing the exact, prior calculated amount of charged radiation. The heart seemed to jump a beat shortly after each time he did so.

Over the next couple of hours each of those involved broke into a slow steady sweat. The scene no longer showed any fear or gloom instead began to reveal anticipation, hope.

"That's it."

"How does she look?"

Each person checked the appropriate equipment readings and nodded in agreement.

"She's doing great. I expected the stress to show through more. Blood pressure, heart rate, oxygen levels, actually... oxygen levels have improved slightly. Could it take effect so quickly?"

"Possibly, it's a prototype serum and procedure. We can only hope from here. Let's sew her up and make sure everything is clean. Most important, let's get her someplace where she can rest."

Arrangements had already been made with a friend of Maria, who drove an ambulance to get her home. The team would take turns the next 48 hours in her home watching over her. It would be crucial that those that took care of her were familiar with the surgery, and that they would keep it confidential.

Slowly Maria began waking up, she took a moment to get a drink, have a nibble of some food, and take in a protein shake or better to provide both her and the baby with what they need.

By the second day she was sitting up, asking questions about the procedure. "How did it go? How did she look?

How's her heart? How's my heart? How were my vitals?"

She knew which questions to ask. She'd seen complicated procedures. She'd been around and knew what it was like for doctors to perform a new surgery for the first time.

In a strange way, while this was new to them it seemed like something she'd lived through again and again. She'd played through it in her mind over and over based on the experiences she'd been a part of over the years. Standing over the beds of so many patients, only this time she was in the bed, she was the one who had been on the operating table.

Finally, she let out a deep long sigh, as the last person she went through all the questions with was Michael himself. As he stood in agreement with his co-worker he had validated each of her concerns, she grew stronger. Her eyes lit up. As she rested, as she recovered, as she regained her strength and spoke to each person on the team, more than this strange substance they had injected her heart with, hope filled her heart as well.

Truth be told though, hope was almost as strange to her heart as the liquid and lasers were. After all, she'd seen so much hurt. She'd been through her own and she'd held the hands of many as they lost others. She wasn't sure if it was her body reacting positively to what had been done or if was simply her mind beginning to believe once again that maybe, just maybe, there was a reason to believe in good things.

One thing she knew for sure. If this saved the life of her child, if she lived to see her smile, and smile back, if they were able to run and play, hold hands, if to simply know the touch and love of one another, mother and child... that would surely be good. Her faith would be restored. Now though she'd had quite a long day, full of emotion and conversation. Now it was time again, to rest. In a couple days she'd have to return to work.

Only a few days later she would have her first follow up with Michael to see how both she and the baby were responding.

**

Five days after the surgery Maria is doing well. Back to doing what she is best at, serving others. Not even knowing how much she loved them. She provided a service above and beyond the need they had, touching them deeply. Now it seems she was doing it with more passion than just responsibility. It meant more now. Everything meant more now.

Sometimes she'd realize the difference. She could feel it. She stopped in the hallway a few steps away from the nurse's station, first placing her hand on her stomach then on her heart. She peered down the hallway of doors, each with someone needing to be healed and each with a clipboard filled of what ails them.

While the hallways were silent, she heard the cries of each person hurting, scared, and in need. Some had loved ones by their side while others were all alone. She intended to make sure each of those, knew that they were *not* alone. She would go in, touch their hand and assure them of this.

She stepped into room 408. Mr. Crosby, "You are not alone. I am here. We are all here, to stand by you and to help you stand again."

The man smiled and just then a lady of nearly the same age, wrinkled and grey walked in, smiled and said, "thank you dear."

Maria didn't know if this was his sister, his wife or just a friend. What she did know was that, she was sharing what she was given. Hope. And often, she was realizing, hope itself gave life.

Dr. Phillips saw her as she walked down the hallway. "Hey day dreamer."

Maria was dazing off looking ahead to her next patient.

"Hey, day dreamer," he said again with a little more enthusiasm, a chuckle and a bit of boom in his voice.

"Sorry Doctor," she replied. "I was, I was…"

"It's ok," he said. "I can only imagine the many thoughts in motion these days. How are you feeling today? Taking it easy I hope. Giving everything time to heal properly, or, at the very least doing so as much as you possibly can to reduce the stress."

"Yes, I haven't been pulling double shifts if that's what you're asking. I've been doing some yoga and meditation each day and also the two-a-day breathing exercises you prescribed."

"Very good, and how's the baby?"

"She's kicking now. Actually, I feel better right now than I've felt in ages. But, I haven't forgotten what you told me, that the procedure could give me a sort of, charged feeling. At times, I feel like I can take on the world. I'm glad you warned me to be aware of it otherwise I just might try to!"

Doctor Phillips smiled. He looked at her, laid his hand on her shoulder and said with a caring tone, "I'll see you tomorrow night."

As Michael walked away, Maria glances at her watch and realized her shift was ending soon and she had a few more patients to visit. Then it would be time to get home and take care of herself and well, and her daughter.

I'm having a daughter. What a crazy feeling it is to have a life inside of you, to know you're about to give life to another and be responsible for it entirely from this point forward. She felt both overwhelmed and excited, she continued on with her duties.

Over the months ahead, Maria excitedly moved toward the time when she would give birth. Every time she found she was lost in the idea, she thought, birth, this was a rebirth of sorts. *I feel I've been born and born again.*

She couldn't help but feel the many emotions of joy and pain that came from the life she had lived. Over and over she recounted her childhood, the events that came, and the hurt. She considered the surgery and considered the dangers knowing much like her own mother she could bring the same fate on her daughter.

"No!" she shouted out loud, awkwardly looking around as her co-workers and strangers both looked at her.

She glanced in a room and said, "No, for the third time, you can't have another pudding Mr. Johnson." She smiled at everyone, forced a chuckle and said to the next closest person to her, "he loves his pudding."

Wow, I really have to control myself, she muttered, feeling now as if all eyes were watching her everywhere she went. She looked forward to getting home, having her one glass a day of red wine, sitting down with a good book, something, maybe less dramatic than the life she lived. The life she was living. Nothing better than to move on to a good nights sleep, and sleep had a healing factor that was in its own way, immeasurable.

"Ahhh, whoa, whoa," the pain interrupted Maria's sleep. *So much for the healing factor of sleep,* she thought groggy and half awake.

"Ahhh, ouch," she was hurting but she was smiling. She knew what lied just ahead. These were pains of a child that was ready to enter the world. The contractions seemed to come and go at first but then seemed to be a little more regular.

She knew what to expect. She had seen it at the hospital time and time again. She quickly glanced at the clock, careful to remain calm and make sure this was the real thing.

Yawning, about to fall back asleep a little later, another one came, "Ohh boy."

Looks like I'm not going to sleep anytime soon, may as well watch some late night TV. Late night stand up?

"And did you hear in the news today," the late night host said before she clicked on her remote once more.

"In all the places, in all the world," another voice said before being cut off by the click of her remote.

"There it is. What are you gonna do when you get up there? Spit off the top? No, I'm gonna meet my new mother." Maria smiled; she had found the perfect movie to pass the time. She knew it could be a short time; all night or soon she could be headed back to bed if these were nothing more than Braxton Hicks.

She laughed, and at times cried from the contractions, other times from the movie. As the movie was coming to an end and the credits began to roll she had one more. She glanced at the clock, she looked down at her phone where she had been using her 'labor tracker app' to chart the timing. She reached for the remote, turned off the television and her head dropped. She took just a moment, a moment of silence; a deep breath and she brought her head up looked toward a photo of her Mom she had on her shelf alongside another of her adopted parents. Her head then fell back, her eyes closed. She spoke out to herself, "It's time."

Her bag was packed. Her hand reached for the phone, and with one touch she called Dr. Phillips. Within a few minutes later there was a car waiting outside. Maria walked out, down the stairs of her brownstone, and rolled into the back seat.

"Maria?"

"Yes."

"I spoke with Dr. Philips. My name is James. Let me know if you need anything. The ride is taken care of."

James sped off toward the hospital. Along the way, Maria's head was racing through the thoughts of what was in her future. She wanted badly to hold back the emotions and the excitement but couldn't help but imagine a baby in her arms, a child growing up, graduation, her wedding and all the learning along the way. Then she sensed the fear, a fear of what could be, what might happen. Her body shook from the pain of another contraction. "Ahhhh."

"Miss Saint-Clare, are you ok?"

It was odd hearing her biological father's last name used to refer to her. But Michael had insisted he have a different name to refer to her when those less involved in the situation came into the mix, specifically cases such as this, a livery car service driver.

"I'm fine." She took a deep breath, and another. Continuing with the breathing exercises, she followed the time on her watch. She continued to time the contractions and the time between them. They were getting closer together and longer.

As they pulled up in front of the hospital, James was at Maria's door before her hand could reach the handle. As it opened a nurse, pulled up with a wheelchair. "Are you ready?"

That's when it hit her. Maria was suddenly struck with the fact that she was about to have this child due to the help of some folks who deeply love her. She had not even realized it before that moment. She also realized the secret that they, like her, would have to carry with them for the rest of their lives. "Yes," she answered.

Chapter 4 – The Arrival

Maria realized once again she was on the outside looking in. She knew what was happening and why, but now and more publicly than when she had her surgery a few months earlier.

It was as if she could hear the voices of each person's mind speaking aloud as she was wheeled through the hospital. It never seemed as noisy as it did now, early on a Sunday morning. With the noise of those arriving for their next shift and others heading out. That combined with the late night crowd of homeless and sobering individuals being released as the sun came up. There was also the usual emergency patients and regular ongoing business.

She began to practice meditation while she waited. The nurses knew her and handed her the paperwork she had filled out in advance for her to review and sign. She looked it over, signed it and returned to clearing her mind. Soon she began to silence her thoughts, relaxing while the contractions were getting closer together and somehow feeling better regardless of them getting stronger as the morning continued to evolve.

"Maria. Maria," a soft soothing yet strong voice came through. She opened her eyes and looked up to see Dr. Phillips with half a smile, before he could finish asking, "How far..."

She interrupted, "5 minutes 45 second."

"Well then, it looks like you timed it perfectly."

Again, her lips half smiled she gave a slight nod and looked toward her stomach. Rubbing it, she said, "it's going to be ok," a tear rolled down her left cheek, "it's going to be... ok."

"Ok, let's meet her," Michael said.

Usually he'd call a nurse over. Instead, he began to roll her toward the delivery room. Glancing over to the nurse who brought her in, she came over, handed him a clipboard and took over the drive. They began discussing things.

Suddenly, they got to the part about others being in the room. Others such as family or friends and just as they got to the room, they stopped.

"Maria, we never talked about..."

Realizing what he was about to say, knowing her history and the pain it had caused, Michael struggled to complete the sentence he began. He knew the father would not be a part of this child's life and wasn't sure if Maria even knew him or if so where he was.

Maria tilted her head, looked toward Michael and with an I.V. in her right hand used her left hand to pull her hair over her ear. "It's ok. I have all the people who love me right here."

"Right." He choked a little and then with the strength of a friend and a man who's led many in difficult times he responded, "That's right, you do."

At that moment the others involved arrived to be with her and assist depending on which direction the delivery went.

"Let's go." Dr. Phillips spoke in a commanding voice. He'd taken part in assisting hundreds of deliveries in this hospital but none as personal, as risky and as important as this one.

The group came together and prepared Maria for the delivery. Ready for anything they had a number of instruments and high tech pieces of equipment to deal with whatever came their way. There was hope that this would be a simple and normal delivery however, everyone in the room knew this child would be unlike anyone else.

Only those in the room would ever really know exactly how true that was.

Maria got on the bed with the help of those around her; laying her head back she smiled. Everyone surrounded her in what felt like a circle of unity, support and smiles in return.

A comfort she couldn't quite explain had overcame her mind and her body. Her heart that was racing with anxiety and nerves was now steady.

Michael began all the tests and checked both her and the baby not just once but twice. He administered some additional fluids that would work with what was given to each of them in the previous surgery. This began to attach itself and provide an additional charge for the baby's heart in hopes that as she separated from her mother she could continue to be self sustaining.

Once again, much like a battery getting a jump start, if she had enough power, soon the Doctor would be able to take the cables off.

Maria began to receive a small dose of anesthesia as they had a light amount of repeat work to do providing another dose of the same medication used earlier on in her pregnancy.

No cuts would be needed. They used a long bending tube with a tiny needle and camera on the end to work its way toward the baby. They used it to insert the medicine similarly into the baby's heart near the area where it had shown to have an issue.

Michael wanted to make sure that the adaption of coming into this world and away from her mother didn't put any unforeseen stress on her small heart. He had no idea how strong or weak the tissue really was. His hope was that the light additional dose would help complete the work he'd begun.

"Emily, quick! Suction… gauze! Everyone, it's seeping."

A small amount of the radiation filled fluid began to seep outside of the point of entry. Quickly contained everything seemed to be fine. No readings were off scale. All seemed to be in order and in line, and so they continued with sweat on their foreheads and a little less of a steady hand.

Michael overwhelmed with the procedure asked the team to watch over her, record the vitals, and stepped out into the viewing room next door. In the room to the side he looked in, head hung pulling his mask down and catching his breath. After a few deep breaths he washed his face, his hands, and went back in.

"All right, remember this is just a normal delivery. Is everyone ready?"

"Yes." Maria, whom everyone thought had actually fallen asleep, was fully awake and aware.

"All right Maria, it's time to push. You're ready. She's ready and we're ready."

Watching the readings of heart rate and blood pressure closely Maria went through the process they'd all seen so many times. When the baby began to appear, she did so healthily. She appeared and appeared strong. Upon the last push Maria gave, it was as if the little girl was not only ready to come into this world but as if she was pulling herself into this world ready to take on whatever came her way.

Michael had already been given the go ahead by Maria to

step away and turn things completely over to the gynecologist that he had referred her to prior. Everything looked good. She'd asked him to cut the cord. But after that, somehow he knew, he'd likely never see either of them again.

Immediately he held her up so Maria could see, he handed her to Maria to hold. "You're in good hands," then looking toward the baby, "And, welcome."

As Dr. Phillips, stepped out, she whispered, "yes, welcome to the world, my love, my---."
Dr. Phillips would never hear her name.

The baby cried. In her cries you heard them count one through five, four times over. Soon everyone was crying along with her. She was weighed and measured and taken away however in every place someone was assigned internally to keep a close eye on this little girl. There would be no mistaking, she was to be kept safe and watched over.

The next morning, Maria took her little girl and they went home, a home that no longer seemed so lonely. Her home no longer held bottles of wine. She had a new type of bottle to hold. The home had been baby proofed in every facet. She grinned and said to herself, "Michael…" she knew he'd been a part of this too.

Everything she needed was there. She had no baby shower yet there was a pile of gifts lying there by her couch, cards on the table and a sign hanging that said, 'Welcome Home Maria and Baby!'

Amazing, she thought. Nearly overwhelmed she remembered she was a mom now and she had a baby to feed, then she smelled something. *And it appears I have a baby who needs a diaper change!*

The days ahead were amazing. In all actuality the months ahead were even more than amazing. Not even words could truly describe this new joy that Maria was feeling from this gift, this responsibility, this relationship.

They had days in the park, making tents in the living room, teaching her, watching her grow and documenting every moment in photos along the way. She had put in a request for a transfer as she'd heard there were some budget cuts coming anyhow. Then a few months later, Dr. Phillips moved as well, and all for the best she figured if she didn't call on him if she didn't need to. It had been risky enough dragging him into this. Her new hospital was in Queens and so she'd hired movers to handle everything and soon was living a full and happy yet restless life.

It was this joy, fulfillment, and responsibility that drove Maria. It kept her disciplined and her strong will was further built. She had to raise this little girl nearly on her own. Sleepless nights between work and care for her, she was constantly surprised by how she didn't collapse in either case. She didn't though and so, she kept going.

**

Jon was up to his usual ways, buying and selling, stocks, drinks and even women. Or he may as well have been buying them.

"This is fantastic!" A woman yelled as her head rose out of a convertible Tesla. Her blonde hair whipping in the wind, a string of pearls for a smile she leaned over and left a permanent mark from her ruby red lipstick on Jon's cheek. Jon simply smiled.

"It's just a typical Saturday afternoon." He pulled into his country home for the night, the next morning a car arrived for her, however he had already gone. He had other business to attend to. Big bold beautiful business from Japan.

"Cai, how are you?" Jon pulled up in front of a store upstate in a village of New York, between his country home and the city. Filled with incredible and expensive pieces of work from all around the world out came a woman, a tall Japanese woman with long black hair, the kind of black that made one think of the night sky when it is nearly a midnight blue. When she smiled it was as if stars aligned on every corner and a breeze ensued when she passed by him.

"This is it Jon. What do you think?"
"Words do not describe its beauty, just like you Cai."
"Nor do they describe its value Jon."
"Just like you as well." He responded giving his best to penetrate this woman's strong exterior. A woman of business and

clearly of a class he could only imagine being in line with. She was not one to play games with and he knew it. However, like any hunter, the bigger and deadlier the prey, the more exciting the pursuit.

"Jon, follow me, let's do business." And business they did. To Jon's surprise her office much resembled his apartment. She'd been expecting him. His favorite drinks sat on a table along with a plate of light and expensive snacks. More than just wine and cheese however that was on the table as well. Smooth Jazz, and low lights gave the final touch.

She had been wearing a long, light, shimmering and thin covering that draped over her, not a coat yet it was something that would keep her covered from neck to toe.

Then, it came off.

Jon was speechless and he was rarely a man with a loss of words. This woman had done just that. All that remained on her was a deep blue outfit that only magnified every inch of her. A little taken back, he found himself still in a mind for business.

"And, the piece?"

"Jon, the piece is as we discussed, one hundred thousand."

"And you?"

"You don't understand, I'm not selling you anything else, I'm not giving you anything either. Jon, you know me well enough to know--" she stopped as she drew herself close, wrapping her arms around him and staring deep into his eyes.

"Cai, I thought I knew where we stood, but this."

"Oh… are you speechless? Jon, I'm not giving, as I always do I take exactly what I want, how I want, when I want. Did you think you were the only one capable of that?"

**

Several hours later, Jon found himself home and in bed.

"Wow! What a dream!" He was madly thirsty. He thought to himself.

I never dream about women, not women I know, not like that. He opened his eyes more fully; the sunlight came through the windows. He saw a stunning piece of a woman and a dragon entwined

standing on a pedestal. *Wait. That's, that's the piece. Is that a note?*
He walked over, and opened it.

From Cai,

I enjoyed you. Enjoy this. I had you taken home, you were,
too say the least, less than conscious after our... transaction.

Your car should be in the garage. Keys are on the table.

----

*I'd think I was in love if I believed in that sort of thing. Instead, I feel
more like a prior defending champion and I just lost to my first opponent.* In
this case she had a KO on her scoreboard and Jon had been handed
one in the L column.

Well, if you can call such an event a loss, he thought.

He smiled again, even bigger with a slight chuckle and
moved on. Always living in the moment, this moment had come
and gone and there were others that lay not far ahead in the future.
He knew this, because it was always the case. This is how he lived.
The next day was Monday, he'd be back on Wall Street
making deals and moving at his usual pace that matched that of
everything else he did. How he walked, how he drove, how he did
everything. Fast and loose and with intention
Throughout the week and the months and years to come,
that one day kept coming back to mind. Each time he looked at the
woman and the dragon, he asked himself if he was the dragon, or
had the dragon captivated him? When he was in bed with a woman
and looked over, that question seemed even more daunting.
He ran, he went out, he ate, well, he ordered in. He drank
alone. He drank with others, and at times drifted back dreaming of
only two women. Both women, who in their own rights seemed a
bit unreal, more dream than reality. Most of the ladies he'd been

with he couldn't tell you anything about. He couldn't even recall them by name, much less tell you when he had met them. He had no real memory about how they looked or what they did. At the time it only mattered that they did what they both desired.

However, Cai was a woman of wealth and independence that were equaled only by the very artwork of her body.

One day something changed, there was no one with cake. There was no party. There was no one who wanted to celebrate. For all the people he had helped even those he had hurt, Jon, realized he knew no one and no one knew him.

On that day Jon realized it was time for change, on that day Jon had arrived. The arrival of a new state of mind was coming. Suddenly Jon realized more than the desire for a single serving relationship that lasted for a night. Instead he realized the deep need for a relationship that would require him to do something he had never done. He didn't know how to define it. However it was then that it hit him.

It is not the last 35 years that will determine the rest of my life, but it is the next 15 that will.

Chapter 5 – Adopting a New Life

Sitting in the cab this little girl of, only at his best guess, just about 1 year of age sat next to him. Jon continued to go through what to do.

He thought through what had just happened. The cab driver continued to have his internal conversation, confused and bewildered as to how the little girl ended up in his cab. Muttering to himself, he was still insisting that the woman who went to get in his cab when he stepped away had all but disappeared when he came back from getting a hotdog from the nearby street vendor, "she was just there. She was just there, not there, then there, not there then there."

"A funny little man and distracting," Jon glanced his way. *Okay,* he realized he's dealt with stock market crashes that should have lost his clients millions. *This is like any other high stress moment. Right? Isn't it?*

"Drive. That's what you do right?" John said in a calmed voice.

"Yes sir, where to?"

"Good question." *Home? Social Services? The police? This couldn't be a coincidence. One. Step. At. A. Time. When things happen in such a way that coincidence could not be a part of it, then there must be purpose. What if that purpose was not what it first appears to be?* "The park and take it slow. I need some time to think."

"Slow… in New York? I guess I could go up through the village and maybe up the east side…"

"Yes, please. Feel free to enjoy the sound of the meter clicking."

Again after repeating through each of his thoughts Jon determined to take her and call someone he knew who worked with social services to see what to do next.

First, to determine who the woman was in relation to this little girl and if she had no family, then possibly…

Possibly what? Give her to someone who will determine her life for her? No. If she had no family I will be her family.

I will do whatever it takes to care for her, to love her, to adopt her.

Jon made some calls and within 10 minutes had the week ahead covered. He placed most of his client's investments and stocks into reserve and stable accounts. He may have been filled with emotion yet deep down he needed some time to figure things out and couldn't risk burning multi-million dollar bridges along the way.

Where do I start, where do I even begin? I don't know what to do! Diapers! Is she still in diapers?

Again and again his emotions and the voices in his head were slowly overtaking him.

What am I thinking? I can't do this! I can't, I don't know how. But I have to. Then again as he would do over and over, he took a deep breath reminding himself it was like any other situation he'd encountered. *Problem solving is… problem solving.* He'd gotten a good start and his clients would be fine.

So what next?

I'm going to need help. Who can I call? Who do I know who would even remotely know what they are doing with a child? More so, who do I know who can help a man who is completely clueless about what they are doing with that child?

Slowly, a number of names went through Jon's mind. He thought again of the Social Services contact he'd made. Sure, he helped her out and she seemed nice enough, but he needed more than nice, he needed someone he could trust with the life of this child.

More than that he needed someone with whom he could entrust his very own life as well. He acknowledged he was about to risk everything for her to pull this off. Every few names that went by in his thoughts he would continue to only see the little girl's mom, thinking, *Well yeah, ideally!*

"Wait, what if that's it," he said aloud.

"What if what is it sir?"

"Oh, just thinking aloud."

That'd be a great start. Maybe I can retrace her steps.

He had come to know them well.

That is, if this woman was even for sure her mom. What kind of mother would do this? What could she possibly be thinking?

He knew she had a way about her, a way of knowing him unlike anyone else. He had chased her, but he began to wonder if she had been near to him the entire time. After all, it is very difficult to chase someone when they follow close behind you. Meanwhile he needed another option. If she didn't surface he needed to have the ball rolling on a back up plan. That worked in his business, and he was going to tackle this the same way.

It was all he knew in order to achieve success, to win, to accomplish the good thing for his client. And this he realized in this moment would be the most important person he ever cared for. In this way these would become the most important decisions he would ever make. No matter the millions, a life, an actual life had never been put into his hands.

I need someone! He yelled in his head but shuttered under his breath. He shook his head. He paused for a long moment of silence. He said it again, *I need someone*, as he just sat there with his head in his hands.

Then it hit him, a friend he'd made on the force. She'd worked her way up to Detective and was always there for him. He knew he could trust her. How? Cause she never cut him a break. She held him accountable. When he decided he could schmooze her into helping fix some parking tickets from a few late nights he ended up leaving his car on the street in the sweeping zone for the following day. Or when he got into the altercation in the early part of his career before he learned a little bit about priorities and that going to bars at night was ok, being behind bars for a night can make it a little difficult to get to the trading floor the next day. Then he smiled thinking back.

**

"Officer, I um…"

"Don't. I see it all the time, what are you 24 she asked? New to the city huh? A Lower East side Bar isn't the neighborhood for young and up and coming Wall Street hot shots. Why don't you go get a cocktail at a nice French spot, say in Hell's Kitchen or Midtown? That'd be more fitting."

"Officer… Ruth is it?"

He remembered snickering at her name.

"Nice, that's an excellent way to improve your already bad situation."

"Sorry Officer."

"Let me help you out, Jonathan."

How does she know my name?

"I have your license," shaking her head knowing his thoughts. "Jonathan, you're going with me. One night won't kill you or anyone's money you manage, but let me give you a little piece of advice, let this be the last time I see you-- the very last time I see you, here, like this. Make good use of your phone call. If you need out sooner than later, I'm betting there's someone out there who can help you out, and if not, if you're good at what you do, here's a card for someone who can."

He didn't know anyone, and he did call the man whose name was on the card, a lawyer. He had the money for bond, but needed a little help going though the process. The next morning by 10 o'clock he was out. He went to work, on his Smartphone in the cab ride and then on his computer from home after a quick shower. She was right. It didn't kill anyone. It did however teach him an excellent lesson.

**

Wow, I haven't talked to her in a while. I wonder if she'll even remember me. Of course she will, quit procrastinating and call her.

Jon reached for his phone. Under the name Ruth he hesitated once more to call, and then quickly pressed for a text message.

Ruth, it's J. Ruth, I need some help. I need some advice. Please call me. Please let me know if we can meet in the park, soon. Or somewhere. But somewhere soon.

His head hit the back of the seat and he looked out the window. *A baby store! Clothes, diapers... women who have kids!*

Stop here! Stop here! He thought, *stop thinking and speak man,* he had to tell himself. Then he exclaimed with anxiety and excitement all wrapped into one.

"STOP! Stop here! I'll be right back. Wait for me, pull around the block, anything, but don't leave. I'll be right back," he repeated, as he started to get out.

The driver stopped him. "Whoa, I will not be left with this little girl two times. And it's not a trade for cash."

Jon handed the man his credit card and grabbed the little girl. He had no time to argue.

**

"Hello Sir, how can we help you?" Another associate stepped up as well.

"Aw, look at your daughter, she's drooling. Where is your baby bag? Wipes, um stroller?"

To each question he just shook his head. *Great, how to explain? Do I explain? In all of New York I just came across the nicest most helpful person, which I both need and do not need all at once.*

"Um, um..."

"It's ok, let me guess! Daddy day, right."

"Huh?"

"Daddy day! I know most parents have an agreement in the city when the dad's are the bread winners the dad has to do a day off with their daughters every now and then. Mom is off getting her Pedi/Mani and Cut n' Style. Am I right?"

"Huh," shaking his head, "yeah, sure, I guess."

She began to talk and walk.

"Follow me," but under his breath he heard her say, "Man, don't even know where his woman is or what she's doing, great, poor kid."

As Jon caught pieces of her commentary, he chimed in.

"Um yes, that's it. Gotta give her a break from time to time right?"

"Once a week? No, you're in a suit, Wall Street or

advertising type I'm betting. Maybe, once a month? Wait you'd be more prepared. No ring. Ah, she dumped her on you didn't she. No notice, changed plans and said here, take her, I need a break! Oh, I know the type. No respect for a working man. Honey, you do not have to play along with my comments, I'm so sorry for my attitude.

Well, that is unless you don't help at all. You do help, don't you?"

Jon was completely stunned by this woman.

"Um, yes of course I mean yes, I help, no we don't, I mean yes we…"

"Oh, let's just take care of that little girl."

Completely taken back by the conversation he'd just been involved in he followed her as they moved through the store. As they went along she was pulling items from shelves. The first of which was a bag. A bag that she filled with the basics: first wipes, then diapers, then lotions, soap, and a variety of things. Most of which he somewhat recognized, others, not so much.

"You do help, DON'T YOU?" She repeated with more intensity.

"Why yes, of course! And yes, she did but it's fine. Things come up. I'm her dad. I mean what was I to do? I try to make myself available anytime I'm needed."

Hmm, that sounded good. Eighth grade drama had finally paid off.

"Well, here you go. Would you like a couple changes of clothes or do you keep some at home?"

Jon improvised, which at this point he'd become quite good at. "Oh, you know, it never hurts to buy a couple new things, and honestly she's gone through a bit of a recent growth spurt."

"Well, let's get you taken care of. Looks like she's about to wake up from her nap."

The girl was starting to move around and rub her eyes. So far he had been lucky. He couldn't imagine if she were to wake up and start crying or needing something. He wasn't quite ready for that.

Jon checked out and quickly headed out to jump back in the taxi. *Where is it, where is it?*

Then he spotted him at a nearby taxi stand. Back in, he

placed the child into the seat.

"Thanks, can I have my card?"

He handed the driver a $100 bucks. 'Please, keep driving, same route." Thinking through his next steps and not yet having heard from Ruth, he told the driver to stop in the 70's. "I'm going to take her for a walk."

"A walk?"

"Yes, a walk." It was a nice day, fitting for a walk.

The driver dropped Jon off on the park side. And he walked. Bag over the shoulder with her in her carrier and realizing his running wasn't enough. He needed to find a way back to the gym. *Ha, who am I kidding, this IS my exercise now.*

He began to use the bag and carrier to alternate curls. After a couple on each side he realized that that was a good idea… in theory.

Then as he chuckled to himself over the whole idea of using his circumstance like a new fitness machine, the little girl woke up, looked at him, and smiled. She didn't cry. Instead she reached out her little hand, and he then extended his own. She grabbed his and pulled it toward her. He touched her face, softly. She giggled and she squirmed. She wanted down. He walked over to a patch of grass in the park, carefully took off his jacket and laid it down with a small baby blanket he'd purchased. She crawled and crawled and then holding his leg stood up and looked at him. She smiled and laughed… "Mommy, mommy…"

She can talk. Whoa!

"Mommy," and she took a step.

Wait! Did she just take a step?

And another, and another, and she fell on her blanket landing right on her butt. She was just fine, a little cry, a little laughter, a little tear and a little smile.

Jon picked her up. "It's ok, that was amazing. You are amazing! Try again."

He sat down and bent his knees and she walked with a hand on his knee then along side him, knowing she was safe right next to him, by his face. She stopped, looked down, and plop. Only this was a different plop.

"Ewww. Good thing I have those diapers." Jon reached in

and glanced at the diapers, grabbed a wipe, and thought to himself like many of my great accomplishments, *I'm best when I just dive in and access the situation as I go.*

"Well here I go, diving into the stinkiest pool of challenge I'll ever know!" He laughed as he changed her and she laughed with him.

It was as if he could hear her saying, "It's ok. We're going to be ok."

And he believed it, so she believed it.

It was time to go home. Jon walked out of the park and called a taxi, handed him cash and said take me home. Giving the man his address, he sat in the back with fewer thoughts and less anxiety, at least for now.

As he approached his apartment, carrying the baby up the stairs his phone rang. *Really*, he thought. He dropped his keys as he went to open the door and reach for the phone at the same time. Words came to mind, but none he dared utter with the child in his arms. He grabbed the phone only to miss the call just barely seeing that it was a number he didn't recognize.

Great! All this, for a missed telemarketing call!

He went inside, laid the baby on his couch and took the bag off. *Where is she going to sleep? The couch isn't good. The bed isn't good. Oh no, this is not good at all. Baby needs a place to sleep.*

Just then, she began to cry. *She's dry, so she must be hungry.*

He'd learned from his friends with kids, these were the two primary reasons most babies cried. So he grabbed some milk and baby food. He passed her the milk first.

Then, he heard his phone notification go off. *Voicemail? I guess I should check it.*

"Hi Jon, it's me." *Wait, it's her!* "I know you probably won't be able to answer this as you're trying to get into your house right now with your hands quite full." *She is watching me. I knew it. But how, where? Why would she continue to do so?* "Jon, I just want you to know, I had to do this. I know I can trust you. I've seen you. I know your heart. Regardless of some of your actions, I know your potential and I believe in seeing the best in people. I've seen your best, and it is at its best very good. I will check in from time to time for as long as I can, if I am able. Meanwhile, take care of my little girl. She's yours now. It's not as hard as you might think. You just have to love her and the rest will come naturally.

I know you know how to love, because you love yourself, quite well. If you share an ounce of that passion and love with Charity, you'll both be more than fine. I've noticed that somehow, in some way, she already loves you."

Blast that accent; it just made her that much more, more… ahhh!

"And charity…? What charity? Wait… Charity?! The little girl, he'd forgotten. Her name, is… Charity."

He dropped down in the chair next to the couch where she laid drinking her milk. He looked over and saw a giant round pillow he had for a dog he'd never bought. At first, he felt disgusted with the thought but he couldn't imagine where else he would trust her to sleep. His bed was huge, but he didn't want her just laying on it with a fear she could roll off.

He got a spoon out and helped her with the baby food and then gave her back her bottle. Then he arranged the bed with the big round pillow on one side of the bed, and then surrounding every side except the one he slept on, with smaller decorative and extra pillows. He made a fort to protect her, just in case she some how rolled over the exterior fluff of the dog pillow.

"Ah, the innovation of a 35 year old bachelor. Well none the less, that should work."

He decided it might be good to wash the baby up after the long day. After all, New York City cabs weren't exactly germ free. She had just about finished her bottle and was looking a bit sleepy. *A warm bath would probably take care of the rest,* he thought. So he put a small amount of water in the tub and grabbed soap from the baby bag. He laid out clothes and lotion and he became a dad.

Somehow, the thoughts of stocks, sports and 'the game' had all gone away.

After he bathed her, and got her ready for bed. He laid her down and began to talk to her. She was close to falling asleep, but she began to cry.

He checked her diaper. It was clean.

He ran his fingers across her forehead. "It's going to be ok. Sleep well my little princess."

He began talking to her softly again and as she appeared to drift off, he began to walk back to the other room. She again began to cry. He'd heard the phrases let them cry it out and let them cry through it. *Is this what they mean?*

Just in case he took her the bottle. It only had a very small amount in it but it was worth a try. She only pushed it away and then, she opened her eyes fully and gazed at him, longing for his touch again.

He leaned over and kissed her on the nose. Then he sat next to her and watched her as she drifted off, to a place where only children dream. He was about to fall asleep along with her, when he heard his phone ring from the other room. The familiar ringtone filled the room & he unconsciously sang along.

The best things in life are free
But you can give them to the birds and bees
I need money (that's what I want)
That's what I want (that's what I want)

Your love gives me such a thrill
But your love don't pay my bills
I need money (that's what I want)
That's what I want (that's what I want)

Money don't get everything, it's true
But what it don't get, I can't use

I need money

Jon answered the phone after seeing Ruth's name blinking on the screen, "Hello, Ruth, I'm so glad you called."

Chapter 6 – Moving Forward

"J, what is going on? You sounded so nervous, so anxious. Is everything ok?"

"Had you asked me that a few hours ago Ruth, I'd have responded with a whole different response. But yes, I think everything is going to be fine."

"J, you work in one of the most volatile industries I know of in a city where there is more change in a day than most cities see in a year. Nothing flusters you... nothing. What got to you today? What could possibly have you call me like that then sound so at ease now?"

Jon takes the deepest of breaths. "Ruth, I haven't told anyone. I'm telling you because I know you'll be honest, I know I can trust you and I believe... I hope... you'll respect what I am doing.

Ruth, I have a baby." Jon begins and then goes on to explain the entire story.

Shortly in, she stops him. "J, are you sure?"

"Yes, more sure than of anything I've ever done, of any choice I've ever made. It's not just what I want, it's what I know it's all been leading too, my life, my move here, who I was, who I--"

She cut him off once more, "'who you were' J?"

"Yes, Ruth, I know it hasn't been that long but it has been many months since we've talked. The experiences of these past months have been shifting me, preparing me, and now I am beginning to understand. It wasn't just for me to be better; it was so I could be what she needed."

"J, I've known you for a while now. This is far, far from the guy I've always known. Tell you what--" she said with a flare in her voice, "--why don't I bring over a 6 pack of Brooklyn Lager, you light up that fireplace of yours, and we can talk about it until time for breakfast."

A little taken back he didn't respond.

She pressed him. "You know, all night Jon. Jonathan, I want to stay for pancakes."

Jon smiled, "Ruth, I don't know if you're serious or not but I'll pass, I think I called the wrong person."

Just before he said goodbye, stunned and realizing he was serious she hurried to speak, "Jonathan! Wait. You, you have changed. Ok, I'm on my way. Brew a pot of coffee. Be there in 5."

**

She pulled up, grabbed a bag from the back, and heads up the steps of his brownstone and knocked at the door.

"Ruth thanks for coming."

"Sure J. Sorry about earlier, I needed to know I could come alone, I needed to know..."

"It's ok, I understand, I can't blame you. It's why I chose to start with you. Thanks."

"Start with me?" Ruth responded under her breath

Jonathan continued with the story of how he had fallen for this woman unlike any other. He explained how she captivated more than what was in his pants, but how his heart and his mind were no longer his own it seemed. From there, how he began to choose to be something different, longing for new things and to be someone new. He went on to explain what the woman had said to him and how he tried to connect the dots and understand why.

"--But I've realized, it's not about me understanding. It's about the choice I have. And I choose her... and I choose a better me."

"Wow!" Ruth sat back on the couch. "I can't believe it J. That's really, really amazing." She pushed herself up, went to the kitchen for another cup and then seeing it was coming upon morning, looked over her shoulders at him. "How about those pancakes? Making plans as big as this on an empty stomach seems like a bad idea."

They exchanged smiles and nods and she got started. Grabbing his tablet he began to make notes, "I'm thinking I start with a list of 'owe me's'."

"Ohmees?"

"No, owe me's. People who 'owe me one,' you know? Especially those in high places: judges, doctors, lawyers and politicians, especially politicians."

"J, you're talking blackmail."

"Um, no, no, I'm talking owe me. I made them money or did them a favor and this is only, folks who have always, always offered me to do favor in return. Each one, who said something along the lines of: 'If I can ever do anything for you' or 'I owe you one, call me for anything'. I hold nothing over them and would never do such a thing."

"Wow, J, who are you? I mean I like you. I like you, a lot like this. You're real. More than that, you're passionate and you're genuine.

Ok, in that case, get started on that list. More coffee?"

"Yeah, I'll take another cup, thanks."

The two of them sat down to their pancakes and took a few moments to take a break from the serious talk.

"One thing I've learned as a cop over the years J, you gotta take little breaks from yourself, your thoughts on solving the crime. You just have to take yourself back out of it all. That's what we're going to do over breakfast. Plus, when did *she* eat last?"

"Who? Oh…" Jonathan chuckled under his breath, shook his head and responded, "pretty late, last night."

"Well, I'm betting she'll be up soon. Let's chat. Ask me something, anything that doesn't have to do with the situation at hand."

"Ruth."

"Yes?"

"No. Ruth. Your name where did you get it? I've known you for years but feel I really have never taken the time to know you. I've never taken the time to really, listen."

"Um, okay, I feel like asking why you ask, but I'll save my questions for after I give you the answer. It's a family name. My family is of Spanish heritage and I grew up Catholic."

"Ohhh boy," he responded.

"What?"

"Sorry. It's just I always feel everyone who I meet of Catholic raising has a story, a 'but' story you might say that follows."

"A 'but' story?"

"You know, 'I was raised Catholic, but... but then this happened or but I never really knew or believed or but something.' I'm guessing you have a 'but' coming?"

"Um, no, actually, I don't."

"Oh."

Stunned he tilted his head sideways, raised his eyebrows and embraced Ruth intently with his eyes, with curiosity.

"--So, I grew up Catholic and coming from a Catholic and family strong in the faith. My parents wanted to name me after a woman of the Bible. They chose Ruth. 'Ruth,' was known for her loyalty to her Mother-in-law and actually her loyalty in general. I also think of her, as one without a lot of shame and that she was resourceful.

It stuck. Not just the name, but I took great pride in the fact that I was carrying forward the name of a great woman, of great history, a woman of honor. I even memorized one of the famous scriptures about her."

"Really?"

"Yes, really, does that surprise you?"

"Well, no. Well, maybe a little. I just don't think I've ever met anyone with such history in his or her name. Or, maybe they just didn't care."

"Many have history to their name. There is almost always a reason to a name, a purpose. Even if it's buried in the unconscious of the ones who came before you, it's there."

"What is it?"

"What is the meaning of your name?" She responded surprised by the question and unsure of how to answer.

"No," he chuckled, "what is the scripture?"

"Oh... **But Ruth said Do not press me to leave you and to stop going with you, for wherever you go, I shall go, wherever you live, I shall live. Your people will be my people, and your God will be my God. Where you die, I shall die and there I shall be buried. Let Yahweh bring unnamable ills on**

---

me and worse ills, too, if anything but death should part me from you!"

"Wow. I mean, Wow," he pressed his hands to his face, he laughed then looked her straight in the face.

She sounded stubborn and faithful even when she had nothing of her own to believe in.

"You're right. I'm okay with that," she smiled then continued, "other than that, my parents had lived in Westchester and started a family, moved to the city later and then moved again just before I was born. I grew up in Jersey City, just a stones throw from the Statue of Liberty. I went to Rutgers because it was what I could afford and well, it isn't a bad school. I did an internship with the NYPD. I watched and learned and although I saw all that is bad or that I wished could be different, I knew… I knew it's where I belonged. And, well, you know the rest."

"Wow, that's amazing..." they were interrupted by the baby's crying as she woke up.

"Ah, here we are. Do you want me to help?" Ruth asked.

"No, honestly, I'm good. I'll be right back. Could you get her milk from the fridge? It's already in a bottle, middle shelf to the left."

"It's, what? Um, yeah, sure." Ruth responded completely in awe and amazed still taken back by this new Jonathan.

"Hey baby girl, it's okay, I'm here," Jonathan picked up the little girl, and as he turned, Ruth was inches away from his face. "Whoa…"

"Oh sorry," she chuckled, "Um, here's the milk." Ruth said with a smile, and began to hand him the bottle but placed it in the baby's hands all at the same time. She looked at the baby, then up at Jonathan and watched as he just gazed into the baby's eyes.

"There we go," he said to her. "Let's see where we go from here."

"Well, I have the day off. I'd really like to stay and help."

"Ruth, you don't have to."

"I want to. I really do, for her, and, for you."

"Thanks, that sounds great."

"So, what now?"

"I think you may need to start calling in some of those

favors. Who's on your list?"

"Well, let me ask you this first, what's my first step?"

"What do you want to do? Help her find a family?"

"No. I can't explain it, but... Ruth, I am her family."

"Okay, *Dad*." Ruth spoke with truth and love. She said it to see his reaction. The way someone uses 'wife' to a new husband, to catch the fright in his face when he is confronted with the truth of the commitment he has just made or acknowledge his comfort when he knows he's just chosen to love someone he knows he can choose to love every day of his life.

Jonathan didn't reply at all. Jonathan noticed some drool; he nonchalantly took the baby's bib, and cleaned it around her lips. He then helped her continue to drink her milk.

"Oh, oh are you okay there. Wait, I remember this. I saw it in a movie." he put her on his shoulder and placed a towel there and began to pat her back slightly.

She burped. A little milk projected onto the towel, and a little more hit the side of his neck, while he simply laughed, "Yep, Dad" he said.

"Okay, well dad, first, I gotta say, you're sure passing all the tests. You know if I saw any reason to argue I would. The only reason I have is, this isn't going to be easy, but I don't think that argument will be enough. If you're going to keep her you're going to have to bypass some steps. If I'm going to help, I'm going to need to ask you some questions. Do you think the mom will help you?"

"I don't even know how to get a hold of the mom. I just know she wanted me to have her. There must be a reason."

"Okay. Could she be family? A long lost cousin, maybe?"

"I don't think so. I'm the last person I think anyone who really knows me would ever choose to be the dad of their child."

They laughed and as they stopped, Ruth said, "Well, before today, I would have said the same thing. Maybe she knew something others don't. Something even you don't know about yourself, at least not yet?"

After a short moment of silence and a glance at one another they continued. "Okay, usually when a baby is found, we have to turn it over to the Department of Family and Children Services.

Then we'd check to see if the child has any family that has the means both financially and physically along with the mental health and overall capability to raise the child."

"What if there are no relatives?"

"Then the child is placed into foster care," the words sinking in, "Foster care! That's it. Jonathan, you let me go with you. We turn her in, she goes in and if there is no family then you can go through the process to try and adopt her out of the foster care program."

"I don't know Ruth."

"What?"

"I just, well, what if they find someone, someone else. I mean wouldn't the mother have given her to them? It's clear she wanted her to go to me? I can't risk losing her. This wasn't a last minute choice by her mother. Her mom pre-meditated this decision. She clearly knew me, watched me, and found a way to make absolutely sure that she was placed into my care."

"Jonathan, she left her in a cab!"

"No! She left her in my taxi! She knew! This is not a coincidence."

They were speaking intensely, yet watching their tone and volume. The baby had fallen back asleep in Jonathan's arms. A tear ran down Jonathan's face as he went to lay her in bed. Under his breath, "she left her to me, I don't know why, I don't know how but she did."

"She did what J?"

"She knew."

"Knew what?"

"She knew it was her I couldn't get out of my head, it was her who was causing me to see life different it wasn't this exquisite long legged, mysterious woman. It was her! This little girl, whose eyes looked up at me lost in mine. I got lost in her soul, her young soul. New to this world, I don't have all the answers but this I know. I need to raise this child to find them. Keep going. Tell me more about the steps."

"Okay, if there was no family, the child goes into foster care with a licensed foster parent. Then the child would be up for adoption of course. Whoever found the child could try to adopt the child, but it's a lengthy process requiring substantial legal fees and special training courses."

"Okay. Let me think this through. Well, we know money isn't an issue. I've always made sure to be prepared and do for myself as much as I would for any client. Practice what I preach you might say."

"What about personal references?"

"That's actually not a problem either," he glanced to the table at his notepad.

"Right, your owe me's."

"And, I know other people who would give me a reference."

"This isn't about your work. This is the responsibility of a life J. Who, that doesn't owe you one, would say you would make a good dad."

"I've volunteered a time or two. I've helped a person or two here and there."

"What did they do for you?"

"What?"

"I'm just curious, was it just out of a response to do something good or was there an expectation."

"You're right. You are. You've only seen that side of me and I get it. But Ruth, you have to know for all you know about me, you have to know that I'm not always looking out for only my own interests in every single moment, in every little way. I wouldn't push an old lady out of the way to make the train or catch a cab."

"I'm sorry J, it's just--" He cut her off before she could continue.

"--No really, I get it, but you're here and you're helping me and I know it's because you see it but also because you saw it when we first met. You knew some day this moment would come. That's why you've always been there."

Ruth sighed and dropped her head nodding it slightly.

"Okay so you have references, but how do we get around the family issue, social services and what if a report has been filed from someone who knows the mom? What if the police come searching for her? What then J?"

"Okay, so it looks like we need help to, A: avoid a search or have a way to intercept and shut down any search that may come up. B: help from social services so that we skip the process of putting her into foster care and help me adopt her."

"Sheesh J, how? I mean you can bribe or you can cheat but it's going to take more than just knowing a person here or there. You have to BE family to go through social services."

"Or…"

"Or what?"

"Or you said that if the police found her and she didn't have family she'd go to a licensed foster parent. What if I was a licensed foster parent? What if we could be sure no family showed up according to the report? What if from there, I adopted her? Then we work within the system, at least to some degree and I never have to let her go. That could work."

Shaking her head, she looked up. Searching once again for an argument to make that could change his mind. "There's only one problem J."

"Talk to me."

"The process of becoming a licensed foster parent doesn't happen overnight. It takes a while, at best a few months. You have to attend trainings, pass a background check, and ensure your home meets safety guidelines which I'm sure would not be an issue. Also, agencies look to place children in the neighborhood where they come from, whenever possible."

"Well, I did often see her in the area."

"Yes, but we already established she was seeking you out, this may have been the only reason she was around, still I think that is the smallest of obstacles ahead."

"Okay, I have an idea," he responded and reached for the notepad full of notes and names.

"All right, what do you have in mind? And who do you have on that list?"

Chapter 7 – The Gift of a Father

"Alright, so let's start with the first possibility, she goes to family." Jon said, waiting for Ruth's reaction.

"But you've already said you aren't open to even exploring if there is family."

"Yes, but what if somehow, I am family. What if I was able to actually get records saying I was an uncle by marriage or something?"

"How?"

"I guess we'd have to get her details, then we'd have to get details on her family then--"

"Wait, Jon, --" she said concerned, "--I don't know who or how many folks you know, or think you know, but that's a whole lot of people you're going to have to get involved in this. If there is anything I know about those who've broken the law and got away with it, they keep it simple. We should make sure that first of all, there is no conflict of interest."

"Tell me more." His palms gave away his anxiety.

"Well, when two crime lords are going for the same thing, there's always trouble. If this little girl does have someone come for her, it may not be something you can hide her from no matter how hard you try. So as part of our plan, there has to be an element of truth."

"Ok. So after family there's our second option, foster parenting." He said this more to bring himself back to reality than to show Ruth he was paying attention.

"Correct."

"So, what if I..." he paused trying not to scream, "what if I become a foster parent!"

"Um, we went over that. It takes weeks, months and then you still have to be able to somehow get her too," she said as if explaining to a child the rules of the classroom.

"Well, what if I was already certified?"

"Are you?" she looked startled by the statement.

"I know someone. They can make that happen. Of course, I'd do the studying. I'd be ready for every question. Access is easy. Learning is easy. If he can come through, that part is done."

"If what you say is true, and you can make that happen, that could actually work, J. Then we could turn her in, work with one person on the scenario of family and then move to you being the foster parent. Do you know anyone with the Administration for Child Services also?"

"I think so. That is, if they're still there. It's been a little while."

"Ok, so those are the two key areas. What about Doctors? Do you know any pediatricians you can trust?"

"Not a problem. I have a list of doctors on a whole separate page, but one or two stand out."

"Ok, make your calls. I'll watch the baby. You have some favors to cash out. Let's see if you can actually make this whole foster parent thing a reality."

**

Jonathan started calling all those he knew who might be able to help and sure enough he reached the first of them, a politician who used to work in social services and has pull beyond compare.

"Joey! Joey, how are you?" he said a little too excited.

"Jonathan, is that really you?"

"It sure is."

"What's going on? My portfolio seems to be doing fine. We haven't chatted in a while? My accountant is taking care of you isn't he? Do I need to get Jones on the phone? I'll get him on the phone right now!" The man bellows in a boisterous typical New York accent with all the attitude one my expect from a man who started pushing papers and made his way to helping make some of the biggest changes known in the nation's largest city.

"No, no, fact is I just called to ask a favor."

"Oh?"

"Yes."

"Oh… excuse me a moment, Jon." In the background Jon could hear him say, "Holly, could you excuse me and hold any further calls. Also, please lock my door on your way out. This is important and it could, it could take a moment."

Joey would remind you of Big Daddy Warbucks, big, brash, rich, and better looking in his own mind, than he really was in the mirror. It didn't matter, his money and clout more than made up for it. He wasn't really that old but he was old-school, riding in Bentleys, wearing suits that look like he walked out of Macy's in the 1940's, complete with two tone wing tips and a fedora. He was adamant that he'd have only one butler and one maid who lived in the brownstone with him. He took good care of his employees. He took good care, for that matter, of anyone who took good care of him.

**

He sat in his pin striped suit behind his shiny oak desk. Holly walked away. He couldn't help but watch as every curve moved like the waves of water on the ocean as she stepped one foot in front of the other, in 4 inch heels, a long, very business appropriate but still tight skirt and a satin top. Her auburn hair shifted side to side and she turned throwing it over a shoulder as she looked back. "Call me when you need me," and closed the door.

He shook his head, took a deep breath with a half grin.

"Ok Jon, I know I owe you one, just be honest, is it going to be a big one? I've not forgotten you, so ask of anything but shoot straight with me kid, shoot straight and let's talk what you need. What's the final result you're trying to get?"

"Well, I need to be a certified foster parent Joe."

"Ok, so that's easy. All the information is online. Hell, I'll even have my assistant Holly help you. She can draw up the paperwork. We can probably help speed things along if you need be, maybe 60 days or less?"

"Joey, I need it sooner than that. I mean I need it real soon. Not in 60 days, not in 6 days. I need it yesterday or even further back. Someone I know has left me..." he hesitated.

"And?"

"Someone I know has left me with a responsibility."

"What kind of responsibility?"

"The responsibility of a child Joey. And, it's one that I welcome, that I want. I know that the only one who is supposed to raise her, is me."

"Wow. Ok, meet me here tomorrow. 1pm. I'll have the paperwork ready. I'll also have a stack of material for you."

"I know. I have some studying to do."

"That's right. I'll help you but you gotta make sure you're prepared for any question, any time."

"I will be Joe."

"Oh, one other thing. When it comes time to turn her in, 'cause I think I know your plan here. Ask for Sam Rosenthal. Tell Sam, you spoke to me. That I personally helped you, and you need the help of someone with this situation and I sent you specifically to him. No one else can do what Sam can do. I know. I'm the one that made sure Sam was in charge when I left."

"Ok, will do. See you at 1pm tomorrow. And thanks. Thank you Joe."

"It's the least I can do for the man who ensured me and my family would always be taken care of, even after I pursued a place in office so much that I lost my family," he said, while glancing over at a picture of a simple yet beautiful woman and 3 kids ranging from early 20's to late and mid teens. It's a genuine look, one that comes out when even the hardest of men realize what they've lost from a bad decision in life. He continued, "at least I know they'll want for nothing, thanks to you Jon."

"Joe, you know…" Jon stopped, realizing he was the last man on earth that should be giving another man advice on how to re-build relationships. After a short period of silence Joe responded. "Yes Jon, you were going to say?"

Jonathan realized he had the respect of the man on the other end of the line and if he was making changes then anyone could.

"Joey, I was just going to say, it's never too late. Not for you, not for me, not for any of us. Not until we're gone."

Joe glanced back at the photo. "Right you are my boy. Right you are. I'll see you tomorrow"

"1pm sharp!" Jon said in agreement.

"Ha!" Joey exclaimed with a bellowing chuckle, "I know you. 1pm sharp means 12:45! See you then my friend."

Joe picked up the phone again. He found the number whose picture next to it matched that of the woman in the photo from before. Just then, his secretary re-entered with a light knock as she unlocked and opened his door.

"Sir, did you still need my services this evening?"

The clock marked 5:30 on his desk. She tossed her hair and he couldn't help but notice one, no two, additional buttons had been undone on her blouse. He put the phone down, glanced back at the photo, then again at her, nearly hypnotized by the lighting off her matching red hair and shoes and all that fell between them.

With a slight shake of his own head, he responded, "No Holly, I have something important to take care of."

"Ok, I have a bottle of wine waiting, and I don't want to be late. Good night."

She turned, and as she walked out. Joe raised his phone and made the call, he knew, he wished he'd made long ago.

**

Jon and Ruth were staging everything out. "Ok so, we have the key points in place," Jon said to Ruth.

"Still, I think it'd be a good idea if you have a steady go to pediatrician. Someone you trust to help you along the way, *with anything*."

"I'll make a call. There's a Doctor I met a long time ago. He's the only Doctor who doesn't owe me because of what I did for him."

"I don't understand?"

"He always said he was there for me, because of what I did

for someone else, someone dear to him, though I had no idea at the time. He should be heading into his shift. Wow, I haven't seen him in ages in action and he's working in a hospital now or I think he still is. He was for the last few years. I think he's my best place to start."

"Ok then, make the call J."

**

The phone rang in the chest pocket of Mike's white doctor's jacket. He reads the name on the screen and quickly picks up. "Hello, this is Mike? Jon, is that you?"

"Yeah Doc, it's me."

"How are you? How have you been? It's been a while!"

"I'm good Doc. Life is good. You?"

"I'm pretty good. Living the life of a full time surgeon now losing my life to save others, no sleep but doing what I can to rest here and there."

"How's your dad Doc? I've been thinking about him."

"Oh J, I'm sorry. He passed a few weeks ago. I didn't think to reach out to you."

"I'm sorry Doc," the sincerity of his pain could be heard in his voice.

"It's alright Jon. Thanks to you it was by natural causes, not by his doing or as a result of the bottle or hunger on the street. You know, one of the things that night taught me was that it's good to have your life shaken up every now and then. It's good to have another life come into yours and make you face your demons."

"It sure is Doc. I wish I would have known. I would have come to the funeral."

"It was simple Jon. We had a simple service. He was cremated. I keep him on the fire mantle, in a vase, just like they do it in the movies. So tell me, to what reason do I get the pleasure of getting your call? No bad news I hope? Remember, no more risky investments for me? I'm in a good place and I'm sticking conservative from here out."

"No Mike, this isn't a business call. I need a favor."

"Ah, I knew this day would come."

"It's just... I'm not sure who else I could call."

"Jon, you know tons of Doctors. Most of whom I know you know and I know you handle nearly every penny they've got!"

"It's not business Mike. This call is personal. I needed to know someone who knows me."

They both could feel the sudden change in the tone of the call.

"What is it Jon? What can I do? Anything. Just ask."

"I need a good Pediatrician."

"Huh?"

"For whom? I didn't know you had much family that would concern you with help with their kids."

"It's not for someone else in my family."

"Jon, I'm confused."

"Mike, let's keep this simple. I'm adopting. Or at least I'm hoping to."

"Jon! That's amazing! But Jon, I'm no pediatrician or even doing family practice any longer. I'm a full time surgeon now."

"Ok, so who can I call that no matter what I tell them no matter how crazy, no matter how ridiculous they can handle it?"

"Oh, Jon! What are you getting into?"

"Mike, I need this. It's the last piece of my puzzle right now. I need help and I need to know it'll be confidential no matter what happens or who decides to come calling."

Mike took a deep breath looked around at the nurses near by. He shook his head thinking about how much he took on to help others. "Ok, Jon, you've called me, let me call someone. You do what you need to do, and when the time comes, call me. I'll have your pediatrician. If you ever think it's needed I'll even go with you to ensure the visits are secure from any outside influence and to hold 'em accountable."

"Thanks Mike. I don't think that'll be necessary but it's good to know you'd do that."

"You're welcome. I do have one restriction."

"What's that?"

"No more year or two in between phone calls? Emails and rare subway bump intos aren't enough for friends like us."

"You bet, Mike. I promise you."

Jon turned his head and looked over his shoulder. "Ruth, we're all set."

"Ok then, just one question. What was that about? What did you do for that man? Did it have to do with his Dad?"

"It's a long story."

"Well, we have plenty of time."

"Ok. A long time ago, I was walking in the West Village near Hudson and Jane. I saw an old man slip in the road, I thought this cab was going to hit him so I grabbed him and dragged him to the sidewalk. The man reeked of alcohol and was bruised and beaten. A sign hung around his neck that simply said 'HUNGRY.' It meant so much at that moment. I basically picked him up, got him into a cab and took him to the nearest hospital. I didn't stay though. I couldn't."

"Why?"

"I don't know, the fear maybe?"

"Fear? Of what? That they'd think you did it to him?"

"No, the fear of change that somehow that one 'good deed' would mean I'd have to change, become something different than who I was. I just saw this part of me I hadn't seen in a long time. A part of me I thought was gone and it scared me."
Ruth slowly shook her head side to side. "Wow. So that old man? What happened to him?"

"Turns out that that old man, was Doc's--Mike's Dad. He'd left years ago and evidently tried to come back to New York but had too much pride to re-enter Mike's life without something, anything. He was also afraid. Afraid Mike would assume he only came back to take from him his money, his success, when all he really wanted was to say he was sorry for leaving."

"So how did your friend figure out it was you?"

"We had coffee the next day and I told him what I did. Turns out he was in the ER that night. He was there when they admitted his dad. They saved him and the rest as they say, is history."

There was a long period of silence as they realized what had happened, what is happening, and what was about to happen.

"We should get a little rest, she's fallen back asleep and we have actions to take tomorrow."

**

Morning came, and with it the cries of Charity. Ruth and Jon woke up on each end of the couch.
"Alright, I'm going to shower, change and take her."
"Whoa, Ruth..."
"J, the sooner we move the better."
"You're right. Okay."
Ruth headed to the bathroom and Jonathan started to change the baby's clothes. "And don't change her clothes!" Ruth said.
"Why?"
"We need her to look like I just found her."
"How can we make sure it doesn't get to the media? How can we make sure someone doesn't come for her?"
"J, you know we can't be sure of anything. Sometimes you just gotta have faith."
Jon shook his head, and took the new stuff away from the baby. He laid her back in the carrier he found her in. "Hmm, faith..."
A little later, Ruth came out, ready to go. "J, everything's going to be fine. Get cleaned up. Go see your guy. Stop by immediately after, 3pm work?"
"Sure, why 3pm?"
"The timing should be good, by then she should be processed into the system and given to Child Services. You come in, asking me about lunch, asking me what happened to the little girl, etc. If your guy is who he says he is, we can set up a meeting right away. Let's just hope all goes as planned."
"Of course! Ruth, I hadn't even thought about that, how to take those steps exactly."

"Well, that is why you called me."

"Okay, I'll see you then."

Ruth took the child and headed out. She placed the little girl in the back of her vehicle and looked back up at Jonathan who was looking out over the stoop with hope and fear all at the same time. He was calmed quickly, seeing Ruth smile at him, his heart beat quieted and he headed in.

Jon got ready to go to work. Ready to make a deal unlike any other deal he had ever made.

Before he traded, he had to sell, and from time to time he still had to sell his clients. He would dress the part and be sure he was prepared for anything. He had copies of any paperwork that might be needed: Passport, birth certificate, recent financial records and insurance documents.

**

Meanwhile, Ruth pulled up to the precinct and it was nearly noon. She got the child out of the back and walked up and inside. Everyone's head slowly turned as they saw her with the child carrier walking to her desk. She placed her in a chair next to her and looked around.

"She just showed up on someone's stoop. I was in the area and a friend called me when he found her outside getting his paper this morning. Crazy, how people will just abandon a child."

I'd like to thank the Academy and all those who helped me get here, she mocked in her head.

Everyone shook their head and just then. Something she couldn't have ever expected with such perfect timing. The perfect distraction came through the doors.

"We got them!" a voice called from the door.

Everyone turned, as another detective and two street cops manhandled two men in their mid-twenties who were being brought into the precinct, fought them with every step. Each already had their hands cuffed behind them. They sat them down and slapped a second cuff from one hand to the bench that was bolted on the floor. One of the female cops recognized them right away. "You're them aren't you!"

Snide and nasty unshaven rough faces, they grinned as one of them looked up.

"We are and you could've been so lucky to have been one of those who got to enjoy us."

"Oh, but I am going to be able to enjoy you."

"Yeah baby…" One of them replied and leaned his head toward her mid section, as she stepped near enough for them to get close as she slows a step walking by. Quick, with a left hook she turned and slapped him then the other one went to kick her.

She wrapped his leg and did a move of self-defense and a loud crack could be heard. Nearly breaking it she left him with his foot dangling along with a slightly fractured ankle.

"Well, I certainly have to admit, I enjoyed that. See, until now you've only attacked defenseless women. I am far from such a woman."

The one who had initiated the response still not knowing when to keep quiet spoke up again, "we like a challenge."

The one in pain looked over at him. "Shut up! You never know when to shut up."

Suddenly a typical NYPD Captain looked over and interrupted the drama that had come about. "Let's get these guys into the system and get them in front of a judge and get them put away. Oh, and they say they have friends, let's get Jones, Morris, Kwan, Griffin, Manzo and Hannigan out in the field. We need at least three of you on rotation working with them and keeping an eye on them as well as getting some beat cops watching over those already attacked who provided the descriptions.
And Garcia! Garcia, looks like you have your hands full, we'll take care of this, you take care of…"
He nodded toward the carrier. "That!"

"Yes sir."

Wow, perfect, she said as she looked back down at her computer and continued.

She wanted to call Jon, badly. But she knew she couldn't let her emotions be cause for abrupt and potentially bad decisions.

As the chaos around her continued that was normal for an everyday New York precinct, she picked up the phone and called the contact that the man Jon had spoken to said to call, when the time was right to turn the child in.

"Hi, I need to reach Sam Rosenthal please." She took a deep breath knowing that now that she had done the paper report and entered the information in the computer that this was the best next step.

"Hello, this is Sam Rosenthal."

"Hello, um, Mr. Rosenthal, this is Detective Ruth Garcia of the NYPD. I'm calling because we found a child."

"A child? And you're calling me directly instead of one of my case workers or instead of bringing her in because... why?"

**

Sam Rosenthal was intense. His care for the children of New York went deep. He could never quite explain why, but growing up in Westchester just outside the city, he always knew he had it better than so many of the kids in the city. He had a yard and got to still come in for the weekends. He was able to enjoy Central Park and an occasional Broadway show then go back to his comfortable home with good parents and a good school.

He got to have the best of both worlds. However, each time his family drove in he'd pass Co-op city and wonder what it'd be like to live there, as a kid. Sometimes when his parents took him out to Coney Island or to the Bronx Zoo or the Brooklyn Botanical Gardens he'd see the rougher areas of the outer boroughs and he'd imagine himself, playing in fire hydrant water in the summer, playing in the streets and ducking in before it got dark and the lights came on. He'd heard that's when the worst of the worst came out to hide in the corners of the bad neighborhoods.

He couldn't tell you why his mind imagined himself alongside these children, but it did. He loved them as if he was one of them from before he was ever able to help them.

**

"Well, a friend said maybe I should call you directly." She nearly whispered.

"What's your friend's name, Detective?"

"Joey."

About five to ten seconds of silence passed before Sam spoke again, "why of course! Of course, Ms. Garcia, I'm glad you reached out. I'll have an attendant here ready to meet with you. Come on over and bring your report. Have you already entered the details?"

"Yes, but I need to turn the paper report into…"

He cut her off. "--You've done your part. I'll take care of the rest."

Trusting people was never exactly Ruth's strength. She'd been hurt too many times and had to really take her walls down to tell if it was her emotions and her baggage that was in the way or if this person was really a threat.

She took a moment and thought about what she knew. What she'd learned about how to hear under the tones of one's speech when they delivered their words in a conversation and she responded.

"Yes, that's perfect Mr. Rosenthal. Should I ask who I will be speaking to when I arrive?"

"Ask for Jeannie. She is my Head Case Manager and supervises any cases that I have a vested interest in. I'll work directly with her. I'm looking at your report on the internal system. I want to make sure this little girl you found is well taken care of. I never like hearing about an abandoned baby, helpless, and open to so many risks. Thank you for handling Ms. Garcia."

Ruth prepared everything and looked down. The timing was good. By now Jonathan had surely made it to visit with the man who was arranging the details for him to be a foster parent.

She picked up the phone again. This needed to be public so that there would be validity.

Up walked a fellow officer she'd known for sometime. "Hey Ruth, would you like some coffee? Whoa, a baby?"

"Yes and yes. Hold on one second, I need to make a call."
She hoped he'd wait around long enough to hear her make the call.

"Hi, J, It's Ruth. Yeah, remember that report of a child you called in?

Yeah, it was nice catching up with you too. I just wanted to let you know that she's going to be fine. I'm about to take her to child services. I spoke to the top person and she will definitely be placed in the best of care.

I just wanted to thank you again for calling it in. You know some people, just see things in this city and never do anything about them.

Alright then, have a great day Jon."

She hung up the phone and smiled, "Thanks Charles, I had to get that out of the way. An old friend thought he saw a child carrier on his block when he got back home from his jog this morning. When he called it in I happened to be nearby and ended up going to pick it up. I didn't even know but it was nice catching up and now here she is."

"Wow. So, coffee?"

"Actually you know what Charles, I better get this little lady over to CS. I already spoke with them and they're expecting me."
"Of course, well have a good one. I have a triple shot cappuccino with my name on it waiting for me."

**

Jon and Joey sat in Joey's office, talking.

"Jon, your paperwork is complete. Everything is in the computer and dated back 3 months. I just heard from Sam and your detective friend is on her way with the baby. We need to get the paper documents scanned in now so sign 'em quickly. I'll put them in myself. I'm one of the only persons who can backdate items to show differently than the date scanned."

Jonathan quickly went through everything signing each one. His heart, which he expected would be beating much more rapidly, seemed calm and at a typical pace. No sweaty palms or nervousness.

Just diligence, like the signing of a contract on the best deal he'd ever made.

Once completed, Joey grabbed the papers, reviewed them and scanned them in. After making sure the date on the E-scans matched the date on the papers. He had a file already back dated and a way to re-create the 'original date' so that everything matched up.

"There. We're all set. Here's your study material. Don't let me down. You have everything you need. I'll send people to check you myself if I think I need to Jon. This is much bigger than you, ya know. Are you absolutely convinced about what you are doing?"

"Yeah, I couldn't be more confident and yet I have no idea why I am."

"Good enough. If anyone asked, we had lunch. Hope you don't mind, I ate both portions."

They both glanced over towards the trash where a to-go bag with empty containers sat inside. They shared grins and shook hands.

**

Ruth and Jon nearly bumped into each other as he was walking down the hallway of Child Services trying to find her.

"What are you doing here?" There was a crowd around and they used this to validate their lie.

"I couldn't help it. I had to see her."

"Jon, I don't know if this is a good idea."

"I know Ruth, but you know me.

I wouldn't do it but something in me says I'm supposed to see her."

"Ok Jon, I'll take you to the person attending to her but you have to promise me, whatever you do, you consider it, consider it well. This isn't about you."

Ruth talked with passion, care, love and seriousness. Not anger and not yelling just terse and strong. Jon nodded his head as they headed down the hall and up the elevator.

They didn't speak. They've put on their show. The people saw it, the cameras saw it and it seemed satisfying to the common eye. Ruth walked through a door. Immediately the receptionist recognized her and glanced over toward an office where the child was in her carrier, which sat in a chair to the side of the desk.

Ruth walked over. Jonathan right behind her and she leaned in, tapping a light knock on the door

"Jeannie? Um, hi, sorry to interrupt you in the process of your work."

"Oh, it's fine Detective. I just had assumed you were gone and was going through the usual motions and... excuse me, is he with you?"

Jonathan stood closely behind but had gazed just over Ruth's shoulder and was found by the quick eye of the case manager.

"Yes, yes he is. This is Jonathan Harris. He's the gentleman that called in the child."

"Oh, well good to meet you Mr. Harris. I think I know why you're here."

"You do?"

"Yes. Often those who find a missing child feel the need to follow up on them. Or in some cases they feel the need to avoid them at all cost in the future.

Detective Garcia says you're old friends. She told me the story of how you two met. I do say I love small town stories in this big city of ours. Would you like to see her?"

"Yes, if that'd be alright?"

"I have a good sense about these things. For some reason, I think it's the only right thing to do."

Jonathan stepped forward slowly. He clearly needed it to appear as if he'd really never seen the child before. He actually didn't have to try very hard. In this setting, in these concrete off white walls with bad florescent lighting, standard wall posted paintings, and information posters as were so typical in a government building of this type, it was in fact as if he was seeing her for the very first time all over again.

Now his heart did begin to race, however, not out of nervousness, but just out of joy and an interest in caring for this child.

"I'm sorry, Miss but I have to ask. What will happen to her?"

"Well, most likely she'll go into the foster care system. So far we can't seem to find anything almost at all about her. A little information, here and there, but certainly no family to speak of it appears. Seems we have a mother's name but not a lot of details tracking her birth records back, etc. Who knows, sadly many children are had in all kinds of situations in this city, trying to be hid, sometimes even bought and sold before they are even brought into this world. We don't even focus on that as much as we do the now. If she's healthy and nothing else is needed then we, well we place her up for adoption if no family member comes knocking."

"Well, Ruth, I don't even think you know this, but I'm actually a licensed foster parent. I've really been a little overwhelmed with work, but things are in such a good place, I don't need to work as much. And I was thinking of hiring a proper nanny to assist with any children I took in. Miss?"

"Jeannie Holden." The woman quickly replied.

"Miss Holden, do you think maybe I could care for her?"

"Do you have any experience with babies? Toddlers even?"

Jonathan spoke about his 'lady friends,' and helping with their children as needed. Some were neighbors and some were more acquaintances and then Ruth stepped in. "Miss Holden, if I may?"

"Why, of course."

"I've known Jon for a while now and he's really, you might say, grown up, since he's been in New York. I've watched him and I can say without a doubt whether it's an adult or a child, you can trust him to care for a life."

"Well, with a recommendation like that from a well respected member of the NYPD I think we can work it out. I have a pediatrician coming by tomorrow to look her over. Meanwhile, she'll stay in an on-site nursery we have. Mr. Harris, how about you come by around 3 O'clock tomorrow afternoon? By then, if all is looking well, we can do a short interview process that's required and hopefully move forward."

"That'd be fantastic, thank you."

"My pleasure, now if you'll excuse me this day is passing by quickly and this added little task is going to make it a bit more cramped to wrap things up before 5."

"Of course, thanks again."

They don't even share a smile. Knowing they have to consider how every interaction they have could be reviewed later if ever to come under suspicion of fraud or possibly even something worse.

The next day, Ruth was back to her usual business. She and Jon hadn't spoken to one another and he was headed back to Child Services with nothing but hope.

Jonathan called ahead from the back of a taxi. "Hello, Miss Holden, it's Jonathan Harris. Why yes, I am on my way. Bad news? Good news?"

There were a wide variety of emotional tones he picked up in her voice.

"Ok, I'll be there shortly."

A few minutes later he arrived and hurried to the office where he'd met the woman on his last visit with Ruth.

"Mr. Harris, please have a seat. We have a few things to discuss. It turns out the child you called in as being left on your block has lost her mother."

"I'm sorry. I don't follow you." He said, feeling the floor almost shaking under him.

"She passed away."

"What? When? How?" More than the floor almost shaking under him now it felt like an earthquake had hit.

"Take a breath Mr. Harris. Would you like something to drink, perhaps a bottle of water. Please help yourself." She nodded toward a small mini-fridge near him, and he reached in and grabbed a bottle, took a drink and she continued.

"It turns out she knew this might happen. She had no family and didn't know the father of the child. If there was more to it we'd have to conduct a deeper investigation but she was a nurse at a hospital here in New York. I'm not at liberty to share more at this time. We spoke to her boss and co-workers, and therefore, also her primary physician and in fact she had some intense heart issues that developed some time ago. They couldn't believe what she'd done with Charity, but it turns out like many of us when we get near the end of the line, we see no hope and so we do things we never otherwise might do. Clearly, she had something in mind because she had a will that was found on her, it said that she wanted the child to be adopted by the first well fit father figure available. Well, we believe you are that man Mr. Harris."

"Wow," Jonathan dropped his head in his hands, bewildered by this turn of events. He knew he'd just seen the woman a few days before. She had called him after he gotten home with the baby. *How?*

"Wait, you mentioned she worked with charity a lot. Were there any specific organizations that she worked with?"

"No, no Mr. Harris. Charity is the name of the little girl you are taking home today. As I said, typically there would be more to this but all the information we really need came through today. The pediatrician stopped by and gave her a clean bill of health. There's only one more step here really."

Just then, there was a knock at the door and a man stepped in. "Are you Jonathan Harris?"

"Um, yes." Jonathan held his composure like he'd just made the most horrible trading decision for a multi-billion dollar client and was about to be confronted.

"Jonathan, I'm Sam Rosenthal. I just got off the phone with my old boss, Joey Falcon. Turns out you're a pretty up and up guy. He told me how you helped him. I told him we'd need a pretty strong recommendation to release the child to you but after what has transpired this morning and what he's told me, I think we can do a little better than just let you take this child into foster care."

"You do? I mean, what can I do?"

"You can promise me, this child will grow up to change lives because you sir, will have changed hers."

"That Mr. Rosenthal, I can promise you. I will do everything I can to make that happen."

"Well, from what I've heard you're not one to fail on your word or anything you put your mind too. I've brought the paperwork. Come with me. Oh, and Jeannie, if you would, please prepare everything Mr. Harris will need or could possibly use to take this little girl."

"Charity," Jonathan interrupted.

"I'm sorry?"

"Her name, Charity is her name."

"Well then, Jeannie. Please prepare everything for Charity to go home with her new dad."

Chapter 8 – Home

The sun shone brightly the next morning. The rays blasted through the bay window off of Jon's bedroom, as if God himself had stepped in to sit down with Jonathan for his morning cup of coffee. The trees out front had just started to bloom. New life was the theme of the day. Maybe it had been that way yesterday or the day before but today was a day he'd never forget. Today was the day.

Today is the day I became a dad. Over the years to come, I'll become a father.

He sat on the edge of his bed, with his eyes squinting, taken back by the brightness of the light coming into his apartment. He stood and slid across the floor, in a sort of, electric slide dance kind of way. Shirt off, striped pajama pants on, he skipped right past his slippers and headed for the cup of coffee, already made and waiting. All thanks to a timed Italian espresso maker that prepared the perfect cup for him each morning.

Wait, wait, I was up 3 times last night, how in the world am I even this awake! In his daydream, it hit him he is a dad.

I have a little girl who hasn't made a peep since I woke up.

It seemed like a mix of dream and reality. *When I was checking on her throughout the night making sure she was fed or not wet when she cried out.*

Jon darted back into his room.

Sure enough, that 5am wake-up must have been the last one. Here it was, 7am and she was sleeping like a... well, like a baby. She looked so at peace. It's as if she knew she was home.

In the midst of the morning peace, the ringing of Jon's phone startled him. He ran over to his end table and grabbed it looking at its screen debating on whether to answer.

It's Ruth. I have to let her know everything is ok.

"How's it going J? First night alone with your little girl go alright?"

"Yes! Thank you for checking in. We're fine.

So unreal, I have a lot of work ahead of me."

"You sure do, and that's why I'll be there tomorrow at 7am."

"Excuse me?"

"It's my day off and you my friend have to get back to work at some point."

"True. Thanks Ruth. Maybe you can help me interview nannies."

"I'd be happy to."

"Listen Jon, are you going to go? Are you going to take her?"

"I don't know Ruth. I just don't know if it's a good idea. I feel like I should, but is it smart?"

"Well, I already checked. Service is this Thursday, 2pm. They will be doing a viewing that morning from 9am-12pm as well. Maybe you can slip in and out if you feel the need to pay your respects."

"Thanks Ruth. I think it's best if we stayed back. Maybe, well, maybe you could visit. See if anything is said that might be useful for me to know?"

"I'll try. Maybe I can make it part of my ongoing follow-up. Do you know anyone else who might be able to go?"

"Yeah, yeah I think I do."

**

Billy Jones was a city bike messenger. Jon had used him for years. He was one of the only persons who still called him, BJ or Billy. Everyone else knew him as William Jones. He didn't do a lot of messenger work except for the most important packages of VIPs and they paid well. As a young man, Billy had moved to New York City with a number of aspirations, acting, partying, and whipping through the taxis at high speed down Broadway and up Madison Avenue.

One of those dreams did come true and turned out to be pretty lucrative, mostly because Billy developed a reputation of trust beyond measure. He always put his client's package first, always.

He took risks at times, short cuts and some crazy moves but

all while considering the package he was carrying. The importance of it, the sender, and the recipient were always number one.

Billy, like always was cruising through the city on his single speed bike. His headset announced there was an incoming call.

"Hello. William Jones, Transporter."

"BJ! You're on the bike aren't ya?"

"Jon! Jon Harris old friend how are you? You know me too well."

"Well I've known you for a long time and I know the bike will always be in your blood."

"I'm actually just pulling up to my car. I just went for a spin along Riverside."

Billy stopped next to his Maserati Quattroporte, fully equipped with a roof rack for his bike. He popped his trunk, and threw his gear in the back. "Hold on Jon."

Billy touched a small black square with the slightest red tint to it underneath the right side rear area of where the fender curves up. A small green LED light flashed, and he closed the trunk. Inside the lower half of the trunk was a multifaceted custom designed vault; water tight and fire proof. "Ok, Jon, go ahead, what can I do for you?"

"Well, I have a job for you."

"Oh?"

"Yes, I need you to attend a funeral. How would you like the details?"

"Same as always. I'll be back here at 7am tomorrow for a short ride. I'll be back at my car at 8. You know the rules. Will that work for you?"

"It'll work fine."

**

Looks like Ruth was right, I will need her help tomorrow.

Jon searched his phone for her name and shot her a text.

Can you be here at 6am tomorrow?

Ruth reached for her ringing phone. *I knew he wanted to get back to work.*

**

Jon went about his day, taking care of Charity, tending to her every need. From changing diapers, to making sure her formula was ready, and feeding her. He read her stories and sang her songs. While she slept he had classical music playing and read up on being a foster parent, as well as all sorts of information he'd been given on the adoption process and working through the paperwork still required to finalize that step.

She was his in theory but there were still some additional work that needed to be done. In addition whenever he could, he followed up on his client's portfolios and made sure those he'd put in charge of them hadn't caused any to crumble.

Everything was fine, though there had been the usual fluctuation in the market. He'd picked the right guys for the job and his clients were fine.

When the opportunity came, and Charity had fallen asleep just before Midnight, he decided it'd be a good time to get some rest as well. He suspected based on the prior night of her sleeping in 3 hour increments generally, that she'd wake up around 3 and 6, which would work out well.

The next day came all too quickly, with the sound of a baby crying and a door bell ringing and the most annoying snooze alarm one could imagine all at the same time.

Jonathan jumped out of bed so completely startled; he nearly lost his pajama pants.

"I'm coming, I'm coming. It's all right baby girl, I'll be right back." She continued to cry. He saw through the door that it was Ruth.

"Come in, come in."

Ruth glanced toward the kitchen, the coffee was still hot, she could see steam rising. "I see you hit the snooze button. Let me guess, 2 no 3 times?"

"Hush, everything's so loud."

"Ah, new dad baby hangover. A little different than the kind you're used to."

"What?"

"Well, I'm guessing it felt like you had just gotten back to sleep about the time you were supposed to wake up. Then, I woke you up and she woke up a little sooner than expected, and…" Ruth reached for Charity who was now in Jonathan's arms. She let her lay against her chest.

"A child knows when she's in the arms of a woman. The comfort of her father is in his strength. She knows she is protected with you, but the comfort of a woman is of a nurturing nature. Let's just admit it J, you ain't got what I got, and you don't want to either." Ruth turned her eyes downward, clearly referring to her breasts.

"I see that!" he smiled, "I gotta get ready. Thanks for helping Ruth."

"No problem, however, I am going to grab that first cup, and have another ready for you when you get out."

Jon continues to get ready and Ruth laid Charity back in her crib. "J, so tell me, where are you headed first? The office?"

"No, actually I have some business with a client on the Upper West Side first. Also, I sent over the paperwork last night to my lawyer for him to review. Since he felt everything looked in order he encouraged me to sign and deliver myself since it'd make it more personal.

Then, I'll check in this afternoon and set up some things so I can work mostly from home these next few weeks."

"Oh good, I was worried you didn't have a full day planned."

Not catching her sarcasm he replies quickly, "Nope, I'm good, thanks for the coffee."

Jonathan grabbed the to-go mug she had prepared for him, and headed out the door.

**

6:30 AM

He ran out and wondered if an uptown train was the best move. It was early but traffic was already developing.

"Taxi!"

He caught one quick and jumped in. He had taken some time the day before to prepare the information for Billy both on a flash drive and printed out a copy separately in his brief case for his own reference.

"Riverside drive, I need to be there before 7:15 at 93rd St."
The taxi shot off.

"I can take West Side to 96th? I'm hearing 10th Avenue is a mess, and I don't think you want me taking Hudson all the way with the lights and passing by Port Authority," The driver spoke in a thick Brooklyn accent.

"Do it," Jonathan replied. "If I need to I can walk the three blocks down to 93rd if you get stuck at that exit…Wait. You, you look familiar." Then he realized. This wasn't a typical taxi. He saw some slight variations. This was one of the mock taxi's the Police used in the city as decoys and as a way to move about undercover.

"Ruth," he said shaking his head. He knew it was strange to catch a taxi on his street so easy. Stranger, was a cab driver that was so helpful!

"Thanks for the help," Jonathan said. "Thank you very much."

As they pulled up and the clock ticked 7:14, he knew he had a little time to give. The key with Billy was to neither arrive when he was leaving or returning to his car. You needed to hit the unique window in between.

Jonathan spotted Billy's one of a kind sports sedan and walked up to it as if he owned it, after all he could and he looked the part of just such a man who would own one. He touched his thumb to the emblem center to the back of the vehicle. He held it for 3 seconds and it slid to the right. Recessed inside about 2 inches deep were 3 USB slots. He slid the flash drive into the bottom slot and then stepped back and as he was about to walk around the vehicle the emblem slid back over and locked.

He brought out a thin envelope and slid it just behind the license plate where only those closest to Mr. William Jones would know there was in fact an automatic sensor for a mail type slot that dropped the items into a secure part of the vault built into the rear of his car.

Jonathan then took a short walk a block away, got inside his Original European Mini, that he'd had a friend park there for him and headed to his next stop.

"Jeannie," he says as he walked in, "Good to see you."

"Where's the baby?"

"Actually, Ruth is with her."

"Ruth?"

"I'm sorry, you remember, Detective Garcia."

"Is there a problem?"

"No, not at all. She's… well, she's really the only woman I know."

"I find that hard to believe, Mr. Harris, you're a wealthy good-looking man."

"She's the only, good woman I know Miss Holden."

"Ah, fair enough."

"Jonathan, good to see you again," Sam Rosenthal said as he walked in. "I was just having lunch with an old friend. I think you know Joe."

"Joey, good to see you."

"You as well Jonathan."

"Well, I brought you everything you needed." Jon said to Jeannie

"Let's talk a moment."

Joey shut the door and the three began to quiz him with a barrage of questions.

He missed none of them.

"Guys, and my apologies," he turned to Jeannie, "to each of you I must give you my upmost admiration for the work you do. However, I am not only more than knowledgeable, not only am I more than capable, I am and have reviewed everything out of my sheer choice. I hope to be able to love this child with everything I have for all that she deserves as she grows up and becomes who she was made to be and knows me as her father for her entire life."

"Well, it seems so," Jeannie said with a smile.

"Thank you, all of you." Jonathan stepped out.

**

Jeannie turned towards the other two staring at him as he left the office.

"What? We had to make sure. Still seems a bit strange that this man comes up out of nowhere for this child. I'm sorry I questioned either of you. It won't happen again."

Joey quietly spoke to Sam as they walked out of the office, "Sam, I assume you'll handle this. And, let's make this adoption happen ASAP. We can use the funding. Maybe we offer him something special; like a wing in a building with his name on it? Or better yet offer it in her honor in exchange of course for a healthy contribution he might be interested in making to our non profit supporting agencies."

"He said anything he gave had to be anonymous and it had to go to helping orphaned children. He wanted to no recognition."

"All the better."

**

One last stop, Jonathan thought to himself.

He headed for his office. When he arrived he made his rounds, gathered some things and talked with IT on how to make the transition to working from home easier. He held a quick meeting and explained the new role he'd be taking and set up a time to return in one week to review the plans ahead. He pretty much had everything on autopilot these days. It was time he began to let his hard work pay off for him as much as it had for everyone else.

Then, after a few hours of making his presence known, he headed home. He took a taxi, leaving his car in its primary lot near his office, which he preferred over locations near his West Village apartment.

He had the driver drop him off a few blocks away, he ran inside a nearby market for some groceries.

Though admittedly he had to stop and think about what he wanted more than what he figured Charity needed. He wasn't used to eating in or cooking too much. Aside from the occasional breakfast food the women in his life had made him over the years: eggs, pancakes, coffee and wine. Those were generally all he kept consistently.

Such a new life ahead, he was realizing. He stepped slowly down the aisles. There was a near permanent grin on his face as he took in this new adventure in life. It's not that he had never been grocery shopping however, it was the first time he'd done so as a dad. Everything here on out would be new. Even if he'd done it before, he knew it would now be as if he was doing it for the very first time.

Afterward, Jon was on to the next stop, the bodega next door for some flowers, and as he was walking he came upon an old fashioned hand made toy store. He knew he couldn't get her something every time.

Yeah, I'm going in, he thought.

He picked up a simple toy carriage that looked similar to something Cinderella would have ridden in to the ball. The horses even had little wheels in the bottom of their hooves that you could barely see. It was small and simple and he figured any toy that rolled was a good toy.

He looked down noticing he had quite a handful of items, and laughed as he envisioned himself pushing one of those 'granny carts' around the city. *That's not happening!*

"Hey, Good day?" Ruth expressed as she heard Jon walk in.

"Yes, very good. Everything is in place and everything I need is right here." He tapped the side of his leather messenger bag. "And these are for you," he handed her the flowers and dropped the bags of groceries. Taking his bag and hanging it over a hook on his coat rack by the door, he immediately took the folder from inside, opened up a safe that was hidden inside an end table by the couch and locked it up.

"Why, thank you. But Jon, you have to know--"

He cut her off, "--Ruth, it's a simple thank you."

He put one hand lightly on her arm. "Have you had lunch?" he looked toward the groceries.

"No? I can cook us up something."

"How about we team up, I'm guessing she's asleep?"

"Yes, she was great, good eater, good pooper. Pretty much you have a perfect child."

They both laughed a little and immediately got to work in the kitchen on a quick and easy salad for lunch.

They had light conversation, and towards the end, Ruth, looked up. "J, Are you going to be ok? Is there anything more I can do?"

"Ruth, thanks, I'm going to be just fine."

Just then Charity began to do the light cry of a waking child. They both started to get up, and quickly Jon looked over, "enjoy your salad, I've got it."

**

About a year and a half after the adoption had gone by, he finally stopped into the hospital where his Doctor friend worked. They ate and he talked about the beauty of the child. They discussed the strange way that he came about adopting the girl. How her mom, Eileena, clearly must have had some difficult struggles in order to come to a place where she left her daughter the way she did. He left out some of the more confidential details he'd learned through the Police investigation.

Later he began to build real relationships with some of the women who were more than just a one night single serving from the past. He also joined a group of New York City dads who would have special events gathering together, supporting one another to be the best for their kids. It was clear this was one of the best decisions he'd ever made.

Over the years to come Charity and her dad really got to know one another. She learned to talk more; she started walking, then running, then riding a tricycle, then a bicycle. They'd go out of the city for weekend trips to the beach or to the mountains camping. She started school and was now in the 2nd Grade.

Jonathan sat at a ballet class watching Charity as she prepared for a recital the dance company was going to be doing for a special fundraiser and had planned to bring some of their best 5-7 year olds to perform. He began to reflect on the past 5-6 years.

Everything was as amazing as it could be. Jonathan's business continued to thrive and at this point he'd brought a few of his best people to his own firm. He now worked directly with mostly only the VIP clients he'd come to know the best and that knew him as well. Each visit to the doctor his friend had recommended went well as she grew steadily following in that 25-40 percentile of height and weight. Again and again after each visit the Doctor would always say the same thing. "She has a really strong heart."

And he'd always think, *She has to. To love me.*

Chapter 9 – Life Interrupted

Every now and then, life gets interrupted. Every now and then, even those who appear to have it all together get hit by an unimaginable force we could never plan for. A force that causes pain but also causes growth, a force that makes you search deep inside and find out how deep you can really go and reveals who you really are and what you are really capable of.

Shortly after Charity's 7th birthday, that force hit me. Our life was suddenly and brutally interrupted.

Getting up, it was like any other day. The sun rays struck through the bay windows and I was putting two scoops of sugar into my coffee, with still not a step on the floor from my wonderful daughter, whom I had already told to get up twice.

I yelled toward her room. "Charity, time to get up and around for school!"

I used that 'I'm serious and strong but not angry' voice of a dad. Still no response, "Ms. Garcia is going to pick you up today. I know how you love getting to ride in her new undercover car. Maybe she'll let you turn on the rear window light."

Hoping to entice her a little, still there was no response. I knew letting her stay up to finish watching that movie last night was a bad idea.

I take a sip of my coffee. And, as I exit the kitchen I slip past the dining table, and walk down the hall. Not a squeak. I step in and she's out, completely. I reach down and wake her.

"Charity, it's time to get up honey, you're going to be late. I have a 9am meeting as well."

I throw in a bit of humor, "so if you're late, then I'm late and next thing you know the moon is late. Then what? The sun get's tired and we're all thrown off."

Her eyes open slowly and she smiles. "Oh dad."

"C'mon, you're only 2 weeks away from spring break! A week off and I have a week planned like no other."

"I know, I know but you haven't told me anything about it

so how can I look forward to... ow!" Suddenly Charity leans forward and pulls her right arm to her stomach in pain. She uses her left arm to brace herself. She shakes her head, as it seems to go away. "Wow, must have been the pizza from last night."

Then she cringes a bit again, hand to her chest. "Dad, I don't feel so good."

"What is it, a little gas? A little too much junk food from our fun daddy-daughter date night last night?"

"Yeah, I'm sure that's all it is."

**

The pain subsided and they laugh. She got up, got dressed, and went through the usual motions. While brushing her teeth she noticed a little blood on the toothbrush.

Jon walked in as she was cleaning it. "Um, what's that?"

Embarrassed, she said, "I think my teeth may be bleeding a little, I think I have a couple getting loose in the back."

As soon he looked at her, she responded, "I DON'T WANNA GO TO THE DENTIST!"

Jon chuckled and said, "Look, let's start using mouthwash, flossing every night and brushing twice a day. Do that for one week and we'll talk about it."

She just stared up at him, as if to hope somehow he would just say, "or not" and forget about the whole thing.

Parent and child begin a stare down. Charity gives in, "OK!" She exclaimed and rolled her eyes.

"Don't forget I'm taking you over to Hudson Park to ride your new bike along the river after school today. I'll meet you and Ruth over there at 4:30 after the market closes."

Ruth had stayed active in Charity's life since Jon adopted her. They never developed any kind of relationship beyond friends and she had become like an aunt to Charity. Her family had really become their family. Charity had even learned to speak some Spanish from her time with her and her nanny who was one of Ruth's younger cousins.

At the school she smiled, hugged him and headed in the

door with a teacher as he headed off to work. Jon really only had to go to specific meetings with key clients nowadays. He was also working mostly with businesses rather than only affluent persons for personal investing. He helped better prepare business owners and their advisors on full future investment planning based on trends for the long term success of a business so they could have a strong cushion and back up plan in the light of recent economic ups and downs.

"So, you're thinking of bringing your fast food chicken chain to New York huh Bill?"

His old friend he'd helped long ago wanted to cash in on a promise to give him that fast food chain he'd discussed.

"Well, after you and I talked that one time, and the way you got my finances turned around in such a short time. All while getting you a little girl adopted and starting a new life along the way…"

"Bill, I really wouldn't begin to know what to do with these places. It's great that you've turned to giving more and being more active for positive change in your life but I'm not sure brining this chain to New York is such a good idea. I've done some research and it might take a while for it to really succeed, that is after the initial excitement of it being in the city starts to wear off. I'd get your research team on it a little longer before you make that call. I think one or two folks have tried to franchise here before with them and it didn't fare so well."

"Ah, son you've gotten cautious as a dad."

"Nope, not cautious just a mix of trusting my gut and my senses with my knowledge, that's what I've always done."

"All right Jon, well I still owe ya', big time. So, you let me know what I can do."

"I will Bill. Are you catching a game this time around?"

"Yeah, I was going to actually see if you wanted to bring that little girl and sit in my private box."

"That'd be great Bill. The game is at seven so I'll see you there about six thirty?"

"That's it. See you then."

The two shook hands and Jon went about his day. A mix of time on the computer, making and taking a few calls, and time spent meeting with each of his representatives that do so much of the work he used to do.

Watching the clock nearly the entire time, 4 pm and the closing of the market couldn't come soon enough. He had it on line and on the flat screen on the wall.

As the clock ticked 3 pm, the bell rang at Charity's school, kids ran about and Ruth arrived to pick her up. Charity walked up and gave her a hug. As she took a deep breath, Ruth noticed something.

"Honey, you ok?"

"Yeah, just a little tired."

"Long day? I know they work you guys harder than when I was your age."

Charity took another deep breath.

"You want to go straight home and take a little nap before we go to the park?"

"No, I think the water and sun just might be what I need. I think some fresh air could help my lungs. I haven't felt like I could really get a good breath in all day. You ever feel like you just can't breathe Ms. Garcia?"

"Every time I have to go back to Jersey," she shook her head and they both laughed as they walked to the car. Ruth glanced at her watch. "You know we have a little time, let's hit that lemonade stand you love so much before we meet up with your dad."

"Yay!"

**

Four in the afternoon and the market finally closed. As the bell rang, Jon had his computer ready to shut down.

Finally!

As he left, he thanked everyone for their hard work, praised them, and invited them to a special event just as a thank you.

"I'm renting out the roof top bar at a nice little spot near my place. You'll all be getting a direct invite for two weeks from this Friday. I hope you can all make it! Food and Drinks on me."

A cheer came from around the room.

Jon arrived to the park in a taxi after picking up Charity's new bike from a shop near by and met up with the girls around 13th Street.

"Hey guys, how's it going?"

"My bike, my bike! Oh dad, it's awesome!"

It was light blue with flowers that then sort of flowed into a mix of darker and lighter blues like a flame going down the frame. A matching helmet hung from the handle bars and on the top tube of the frame it said 'Charity's Chariot.'

It was a special gift he'd promised her for when she kicked off the training wheels of her old one. She threw her leg over it, pulled herself onto the seat, and then grabbed the helmet. She stopped.

Taking in a deep breath, she started to cry a few slow tears.

"Peanut, what's the matter?"

"Nothing, nothing at all, I mean maybe it's just the excitement of the bike. Maybe, it's that I've had a bit of a hard time breathing today. I don't know but I just feel so lucky to have you dad. I know you tell me how much mom loved me and that she chose you for me, but how in the world could she have known?"

"I don't know, I don't know a lot of things."

"Oh dad, you know everything!"

"No, no I don't. I'm still learning. We never stop learning. And, one thing I've learned is to just accept when things go our way and help others whenever we can with the gifts we've been given."

They each looked at one another and nodded. Ruth even had a tear fall and then jumped in. "Ok you two, let's see this girl ride!"

They stand at the edge of the trail near Pier 59 where people are walking, talking, sitting and taking pictures. It was a fairly quiet scene and plenty of room for a little girl to try out her new bike.

As she rode off Ruth and Jon turned and looked toward each other. They've known one another for a long time now. Suddenly though after all these years, for no apparent reason, they connected in a way they hadn't before. Shyly they looked down at each other's hands.

He reached out first. She tilted her head, afraid and unsure. Then he reached over and extended his fingers toward hers just touching them slightly. Almost without option she responded and they began walking, hand in hand.

Just then, Charity came shooting by. "Come on! I want to try out riding on the trail with everyone!"

It wasn't too busy, and so they ran after her. She cautiously pulled out and headed north along the river. Soon, Jon and Ruth had to jog to keep close. Charity realized how far ahead she was getting and slowed down, turning her head, she looked back to see where they were.

Sheesh she thought, *this is the best I've felt all day and they can't even keep up.* Just then, a pain hit her chest; she gasped for air and tried to sit but lost her balance.

**

She was at the trail crossing at Pier 62 when she passed out and slid down. The bike went just slightly into the street where it crossed the trail. A car screeched to a halt just before hitting the bike.

Many gathered around her and in seconds Ruth and Jon were there. Jon picked her up.

"Jon, she could be hurt, we should wait."

"Wait for what, who?"

"Sir." Two police officers arrived quickly. They had been directing traffic on West Side highway. "An ambulance is on the way."

"Dad, I'm ok. I think I just bruised my knee."

"Thank you gentlemen, I have a pediatrician on call who I can take her to."

"Jon, you go ahead, I'll get the bike and take care of it." Ruth flashed her badge to the cops and they agreed. Ruth walked over, picked up the bike, and spoke to the driver of the vehicle.

**

Jon calls a taxi over and they get in.

"I think you need some rest."

"Dad, really, I'm ok."

"Really? Ok, then please tell me what happened back to there?"

"I, I…" Charity hung her head and took a deep breath, "I don't know. I was just riding along. I slowed down to wait for you guys and suddenly it was as if everything around me stopped except me. You know how when you're doing something on a computer and it freezes but you keep going a little before you realize it's frozen? That's, well, that's how I felt back there. Everything froze but me and I just fell off my bike."

"I think you passed out sweetie? You mentioned having a hard-time breathing and getting air. Maybe we should get you to the doctor."

"Dad, I think you're right. I just need to rest. I'm sure of it."

"Well, I'm going to call him and at least let him know what's going on."

"Ok."

Jon reached for his phone. Dr. Jenkins' number was on speed dial.

"Doctor Jenkins, it's Jonathan Harris."

"Jonathan, so good to hear from you."

Doc Jenkins, as many had come to know him was a young-grandpa type. You know nearing 60 now, but acting 30, and people thought he wasn't a day past 45. He took good care of himself and loved it when folks would upon seeing him say, 'What's up doc?' He didn't wear a typical white coat. No, good ole Doc Jenkins would wear a white coat with a polka-dot bow tie or one that looked like a tuxedo. He was genuine and he loved his work. He was also the best.

He had to have been for anyone to really take him serious. He said that he didn't always walk around showing off his sense of humor. However, he told the story, that once he had gained the respect of his teachers and peers he quickly began to show off his lighter more fun and relatable side.

"Jonny! Talk to me! How is that little firecracker princess of yours?"

"Well, that's why I'm calling. She's been having difficulty breathing and seems to have had a little episode while riding her bike down Hudson River Park today. I think she may have passed out."

"Oh Jonny, you really are the typical dad. Allergies! Allergies are awful this time of year and this year especially! Make sure she drinks more water and start giving her an extra dose of Grapefruit Juice and honey twice a day and let me know if she gets the sniffles, starts coughing or wheezing over the next few days. Meanwhile, why not call Lyla and set up an appointment for early next week, just so we have a set time to take a look. She's turning seven, right? We haven't had to see her in about a year if I remember correctly. Whenever we've talked business, you've always said she's fit as a fiddle."

"Yes, yes Doc. She's always been a very healthy little girl. That's part of why such a case has me concerned."

"Well, we're all different, she's still young and it's good we take look at each case individually and not shew it like a fly over head just assuming it's nothing to worry about."

"Thanks Doc. I appreciate it. It's always good talking with you." About that time they pulled up to their home hopped out and went in.

"Charity, why don't you take a nice warm shower, I'm sure the steam will help clear your system. I'll rub a little mentholated rub on your back and chest and--"

She cut him off, "Dad, a shower does sound nice, but really, I'm just a little tired. Can I just rest? Maybe we can just pop some popcorn, watch a silly movie? You can even do all your goofy voices trying to pretend to be the characters."

"Yeah, sure, I'll make us some sandwiches but as always, (together they comment) 'we'll make the popcorn together'."

Charity laughed and headed off to her room and then the shower.

As Jonathan began to reflect on the day it hit him,

"Her birthday!" he said aloud but quietly altogether as to not exclaim it, as part of what had just hit him.

She always got a little depressed and sad around her birthday. Why hadn't he thought about it? Usually she asked him to tell her stories about her mom. She typically didn't know if they were true or not. She figured even an imaginary idea of a mom was better than never having had one at all. But this year she hadn't brought her up at all.

Maybe she wanted to visit the coffee shop where he had seen her, or take a walk by St. Vincent's where she worked before it closed down. She loved daffodils. She loved them and he always thought her mom must have too, because that definitely didn't come from his side of the family. He picked up the phone and ordered daffodils to be delivered first thing tomorrow by a private florist he worked with which usually only handled large events.

"Eva, We Shower you with Flowers!" The woman answered the phone in a thick Ukrainian-type accent.

"Eva, it's Jonathan Harris."

Eva was a thick, tall beautifully aged woman yet sharp in bone structure and in speech. While he introduced himself he could hear her shouting directions and commands to those in the shop. "Yeah, Mr. Harris," she continued directing those around her.

"I need daffodils."

"I'll have a truck full at the address you provide any time after next Friday."

"I need daffodils, tomorrow. Just a couple small bunches for my daughter. It's her birthday."

"Oh, Mr. Harris, you know I can't say no to that little girl. Ah, she takes my breath away. I have a wedding on Saturday and they have daffodils. I can pull a few from my order and have someone drop them off tomorrow, early afternoon."

"Thank you Eva."

"You know I expect a referral."

"Always, Eva. Big company event coming up, we'll do flowers for it. Go ahead and call the office, let them know you spoke with me."

"Will do Mr. Harris, thank you."

"Thank you Eva."

Eva hung up amid her shouting and screaming orders to workers.

Well, that's a start, he thought. *What could I do to surprise her? I know. Mike! Doctor Mike! It was about time to catch up with him again.*

Mike had also worked at St. Vincent's. And though he said he never knew a woman named Eileena with a French accent, but he did know the hospital. Maybe he could at least share something new with Charity. Give her a feel of what it was like to be there when it was open. What is was to walk the halls and treat patients there.

Immediately, he picked up the phone.

"Dad, what are you doing? You didn't put Mayonnaise on my sandwich did you?"

"No of course not, actually, I have to admit, I haven't even started them."

"Dad!"

"I'm on it, just jump in some PJs and come pick a movie."

Jon sat his phone down, and realized that making that call was going to have to wait. Instead, he had some sandwiches to make.

It's not long after that that Charity falls asleep, with popcorn in her hand. Jonathan picks her up and the 3 pieces fall from her hand to the floor. He carries her into bed thinking how having her in his arms produced the same incredible feeling now that it did 6 years ago when she was so much smaller. He smiled, laid her down, covered her with her favorite blanket, put her favorite stuffed unicorn next to her, and says a little prayer.

"Goodnight sweetheart, goodnight."

The next morning Jonathan awoke surprised Charity hadn't already crawled into bed with him. He figured he would take advantage and give Mike a call. He reached for his phone and saw a missed call from Ruth as well.

Well, first things first… "Hey Mike, how are you? It's Jonathan."

"Yeah, I've been busy but things are good."

"Listen, you know it's my daughter's birthday and we know so little about her mom but I know you worked at St. Vincent's and thought… No, no I know you can't get us in probably… Wait, you can?"

"Sure Jonathan, I actually have been talking to some other Doctors about reopening it as New York Doctors' Hospital, been meaning to reach out to you for some advice on the whole deal. Why don't I see if I can have them open it around four o'clock. You bring your girl and meet us there."

"Wow, Mike, okay. Thanks! Also, I'm little worried about her."

"I'll bring my bag. Did you talk with Doc Jenkins?"

"Of course, we have an appointment early next week, it's just…"

"Don't say another word Jon, I'll see you both at 4 o'clock and I'll check the basics to see if there's anything I notice right away."

"Thanks Mike, I appreciate it. We'll see you then."

He turned his head to the door and listened for any signs of life. *Nope, quiet as can be.*

The phone rang, Ruth's name blinking on the screen.

"Good morning."

"Good morning J, I wanted to follow up. How are things?"

"They're good. She's been sleeping for a while though. I'm a little worried."

"Well, have you checked in on her in the night? How about this morning?"

"No Ruth, I actually just woke up. I'm about to."

"Alright well, I'm out on the streets. Call me if you need anything. Otherwise we'll catch up later then?"

"Actually Ruth…would you… would you be interested in joining me for a little surprise for Charity?"

"What do you have in mind?"

"I'm going to be able to give her a tour of St. Vincent's."

"Do you think that's a good idea Jon?"

"She's always wanted to know more about her mom. It's one of the only things I ever found out about her. One of the only things I know is that she worked there at least for some short period of time. Everyone there seemed to know so little about her, really like nothing at all."

"Well, sure, a woman might be good to have around to help read her emotionally too. What time?"

"4pm."

"I'll see you there."

Jonathan hung up the phone and walked into Charity's room. She wasn't there. His heart jumped a beat and he darted out to the living room where the kitchen sat just off to the side, he saw across to the dining table where a full breakfast was set.

He shook his head baffled. *Pancakes, fruit, juice and coffee, the works!* Then as he was walking through the space his eyes veer toward the couch where Charity laid asleep. She awoke as he went to pour a cup of coffee.

"Daddy! Surprise!"

"Baby girl, it's your birthday not mine."

"Well, for my birthday I wanted to make my daddy breakfast!"

"Ok well, then Happy Birthday to you!"

He reached out his arms and embraced her in a hug, gave a light kiss to the cheek and forehead before she slid into a chair on his left and they eat.

"So I have a surprise for you as well."

"Oh?"

"Yep, how would you like to go visit where your mom worked."

"The Hospital?"

"Yes."

"Wow, really? How? Is it open again?"

"No, no. I spoke with my friend Doctor Mike, and he said that he could show it to us. He and some fellow doctors might be opening it to use for their own practice. Maybe even as a new hospital."

"That's amazing dad. Are you sure?"

"Why, yes. It's something you've always wanted right?"

"Well yes, of course. I just… I just want you to know, no matter what I learn about her, it'll never change anything about us."

"Ah, honey, I know that. You'll always be my little girl and I'll always be your dad."

Jonathan and Charity sat and enjoyed their breakfast and laughed and even tear up a little as he told stories, from both the past seven years and a little about himself when he was her age as well. He noticed a few times that she stopped to catch her breath but trying not to show any worry, he said nothing. She did the same; she just wanted to enjoy her birthday like any seven-year-old kid would.

Most kids might want a party or a special event with other kids. Charity just wanted her dad. They had a special relationship. She knew she'd see her friends plenty but these moments with her dad meant the world. Even at age seven she understood, in a way, he was the reason she was there, able to celebrate life at all.

Later that afternoon the two of them walked over to what used to be St. Vincent's hospital. About a block away, Charity looked up and stopped. Jonathan got about 5 steps ahead of her before he stopped himself and turned around.

"You ok Peanut?"

"Yeah, or, well, I think so, just a little nervous."

"I understand."

He took a step back toward her and reached out his hand. It reminded him of when she first started walking. She'd get up and get going with her hands on the coffee table, or a chair and he'd look at her with that look in his eye that only a father can give.

One that says, 'it's ok, you can do it, and I'm here whether you fall, whether you make it to me, whether I reach out and catch you before you hit your knees, I am here.'

She took two big steps nearly jumped skipping toward him and her hand landed in his. "Let's do this!"

As they approached, they saw Mike outside the doors along Hudson Ave. "Jonathan! Charity! Oh my how you've grown! And Charity you've sprouted a little as well."

"Funny Mike," Jonathan replied.

"Charity, how are you doing? Your dad says you had quite a spell on your bike yesterday?"

"Dad!"

"Sorry! I had to tell him."

"Oh dad, I'm fine," just then she took a deep breath.

"Just fine, huh?" Both men responded simultaneously.

"C'mon on in, let's take a look around and then I'll take a few minutes to take a listen." Mike flashed his stethoscope from under his light summer jacket. "Ok?"

"Yeah, ok." Charity agreed.

Mike reached over, opened the door, and motioned to Charity. "Would you like to go first?"

"Really? Um, ok yeah. Then she looked toward her dad. Well, you always say it's all about taking the first step. Here we go."

Stepping in she envisioned all the usual chaos of a hospital that might operate in the city. She'd been in others like New York Presbyterian and Bellevue but she was stepping sort of back in time.

She saw in the hallways patients waiting in the chairs and families crying as they left rooms. Doctors and nurses discussing concerns with clip boards in hand. Then, at a station that appeared to be the kind where the nurses would work out of she saw her. It was as if she just appeared and knew that she was there.

She saw her look up, and look straight at her, the look of someone who hadn't seen her in a long time. She recognized her but couldn't quite make her out, as if her vision was blurred. She tilted her head, leaned forward from behind the station counter and then smiled a little, and then a little more. She came from behind to walk toward her, a strong woman with such a mix of looks French, Italian and Spanish and in good shape.

"Beautiful, my mother is just beautiful." When Charity spoke it was as if she was between the living and the dead. She was in that moment between two worlds. Had her dad responded, she'd not heard him. At that moment she was captive to a different place.

Her mother was walking toward her, trying to hold back tears but doing an awful job. They slowly began to fall on the cheeks of each of them.

As she got closer and closer Charity tried to move but it was as if something held her there, as if she couldn't move no matter how much she willed herself to try.

Closer and closer she came. Charity analyzed her like one would in a dream with someone they knew they might not ever see again. Trying to capture every detail and hold on to every piece of her that she could with her mind while she was there.

Just then she saw her mother slowly raise her hand toward her. Then before she could even slide her fingers lightly across her forehead, out of nowhere came doctors and nurses rushing a child by on a gurney.

"We've got to get her to the O.R. right away, Eileena come with us!" And as they rushed by, just like that the dream had ended. In a flash, she, those who had just come by, and the whole scene vanished and she was back.

As she stood there with her dad's hand on her shoulder. She just held the picture in her head. Her mom's smile, as she began to approach her was what she wanted to hold onto so badly.

"Charity, how ya doin? You sort of zoned out on us there for a second, you feeling ok?"

"Yeah, yeah, it's not physical. It was just... it was just as if I was here, back in time, when she was here, watching."

"And?"

"And, well, it sounds crazy."

"No, nothing's crazy when it comes to things like this. Whatever you experienced, whatever you felt or saw is yours."

"Ah dad."

Just then she turned wrapping her arms around him and falling into tears. He kneeled down to hold her. She pulled back and wiped the tears from her right side. His gentle, yet strong hand wiped those from the left check.

"Dad, I saw her. She was right there. And, she saw me. She saw me! She knew it was me, I know it! I... know it."

"Wow, amazing. That's really amazing."

"It was... it was like I got to live inside one of her moments, her thoughts, a part of one of her memories."

"Now, that's your memory Peanut. It's yours to keep and carry on."

"Thanks for bringing me dad."

"Thank the Doctor also."

"Thank you sir."

"You're welcome. Now, how about you let me take a listen to your lungs and heart? I'm sure you can give me some good deep breaths, especially now."

"Yes sir, I definitely can."

"Alrighty," Mike pulled his stethoscope out and began to listen. "Breathe in, breathe out. In and Out, ok, thanks. Now, I'm going to take your pulse, though I get that it might be a little faster than normal."

The doctor pulled his watch out from his sleeve and listened, counting along. "Hmm, ok, let me take a listen to it now." He placed it on her chest over her heart more directly to listen.

"Just relax as best you can, alright Charity?"

"Yes sir."

"Ok, that's good."

"Alright, I'd still like you to see Doctor Jenkins this week. Sounds like you might have something just making it a little hard for your heart and lungs to really do their job in there. Might be nothing, could even be an allergy but let's be sure ok."

"Yes sir, thank you sir."

"Alright Mike, thanks so much… for everything."

"You're welcome Jon. And Jon, could we meet up later for a drink? I'd really like to talk with you about um, this hospital and my idea."

"Oh, Mike you know that's not my area of expertise."

"Jon, I think you really need to know about what I have in mind. It may be closer to you and what you know than you realize."

"Well, sure, I think I can. Ok you know the little pub up the street at Hudson and Jane?"

"Sure, great burgers."

"How about we meet there, you let me know when works best. I don't want to interfere with your day with your daughter."

"Ok will do."

The rest of the day was a fun time.
Father and daughter walking along the river, hanging out at the Children's Art Museum with a few close friends and then taking a little boat ride out on the Hudson, and around the Statue of Liberty into the open waters and back.

While they were out on the water, Jonathan got a call from Ruth.

"Sorry I couldn't make it, not even in time for the boat outing. How's she enjoying it?"

"No problem. I assumed something came up with work. She's loving it! She's pretending to be a pirate queen."

He looked over and she pretended to draw a sword while wearing a tiara and in her birthday dress, she let's out a good 'Arrr.' He smiled.

"Well, that's great Jon. How was the trip to the hospital?"

"It was good, interesting as well. We'll have to talk more later about it. Actually I know you've had a long day and partially unplanned but would you be able to come hang out a couple hours tonight at my place with Charity, maybe even after bed time? I think she's going to be pretty exhausted and ready to crash quickly when we get home."

"Sure, why, anything particular come up?"

"Well it's Doc Mike, he said he wanted to talk to me about this venture he's considering, you know about teaming up with some other doctors and buying the hospital but I get the feeling there's more to it than that."

"Ok, so eight o'clock?"

"Yeah, that'd be great. Thanks Ruth."

"Charity, Ruth is coming over for a bit tonight after we get home, I need to go out for a quick meeting but it'll be after bed time. Maybe you can give her a piece of your cake."

"Ok dad, I'll share my booty." Laughing they continued to enjoy the day.

**

Later that night, Mike and Jonathan sat at the little tavern with drinks.

"So Mike, What's going on? Why do I get the feeling this is about more than just you and your business venture?"

"Jonathan," Mike shook his head and dropped it. Slowly he raised it back up looking at Jon. "Jonathan, what I'm about to tell you hasn't been spoken about in, well about 6 years."

Jonathan's phone rang. "Mike, hold that thought. Ruth, everything ok? Jonathan I think you better get over here. And, bring your doctor friend."

"On our way."

Without questions, Jonathan dropped a $50 bill on the table and motioned to Mike, "That was Ruth, I think something's wrong with Charity. She said you should come."

The two headed out quickly, and skipped the cab. Only 7 blocks away they walked quickly, trying to remain calm and rushing as well.

In the door, they saw Ruth sitting with Charity on her shoulder. She laid her down and called the men to the kitchen.

"I don't know what happened. She woke up and yelled she was in pain and I couldn't tell if she was dreaming or if it was real. She held her chest and was having trouble breathing and I sat with her, relaxed her, and carried her in here to sit with her. About five minutes ago, she fell back asleep. She seems fine now."

Mike took her pulse, pulled out his bag and began listening as he'd done earlier in the day. After a couple minutes, Jonathan spoke up. "Doc, what do you think?"

"I think it's her heart. It's hard to tell."

"Does she have an irregular sound to her heart beat?"

"It's more than that. It is as if it takes longer to beat that normal. Instead of a consistent thump, thump, thump or even an irregular one, it's as if you get thump thump and then the third one takes a little longer to complete the pumping of blood a sort of drawn out Thummmp. Like every few times it's having to work extra hard.

Jonathan, we may want to get this checked right away. Just to be safe. I know it's late, but why don't you come with me and we'll take her and do a quick chest x-ray and EKG just to see if we can get an idea of how it looks in there and what's actually happening before we draw any conclusions."

"If you think it's that serious."

"We never really know for sure until we know, that's exactly why I'd rather take a look now than wait."

"Alright Doc."

Jonathan, picked up Charity. Ruth put together a quick bag of essentials just in case they were needed, extra clothes, handy wipes and some snacks and juice. They made their way outside and down the steps and jumped into Ruth's squad car. She sped off and arrived shortly there after to Mike's clinic across town.

It was a small shared clinic he had opened with two other doctors that wasn't so small any more. It'd become a well respected specialty space for those with heart conditions, tumors, and other issues of the sort. His partners were a neurologist and a General Practitioner who had strong diagnosis skills.

"Come on in," he said and motioned them through as he opened the door, turning to shut off the alarm.

Turning on the lights, he walked them back and asked that Jonathan lay her on a table in one of the rooms. He moved a few things and put everything in place and then went to work.

The longer time went by the more worried and helpless Jonathan felt. However, he didn't interrupt or ask questions. He let Mike do his work and stood by where he was asked and waited. He remembered the baseball game and Bill's private box. Quickly he sent him a text that he was not going to be able to make it.

As they stood there waiting, Jonathan and Ruth were silent not even sure what kind of conversation to have. He knew her, she was probably praying under her breath quietly and hopeful, trusting for the best. That was her way of staying strong and yet being soft and sensitive to all that was going on around her. She didn't cry much but she did hurt, she hurt and felt the pain for others a great deal. She never became desensitized in all those years on the force.

Then Jonathan turned and looked at her. It was different than before. It was a look of fear and trembling. It was an eye holding back a tear and glistening in the light as it looked upon her. It was in that moment that he realized, he did have the love of a woman, and she had loved him for a very long time.

In one of those moments that stand still and last for ever all the same, he thought to himself. *How have I been so blind? How could I not have seen it? I know that she doesn't feel anything, but does what you feel alone dictate who you will love? And how do I really know, we've never really talked about it since well, since years ago when she made it clear that she wouldn't be one of the many women in my life. But that's when I was that guy. But now I'm not that guy. I have to... what? What do I say? Hey Ruth, we're pretty great together, got no one else, we obviously care about each other so wanna give it a go? Seriously!*

At this point the voice in his head was starting to give him a headache and he shook his head as if to sort of rattle out the little guy inside his mind talking.

Ruth responded. "You ok?"

He paused, swallowed back the lump in his throat of anxiety and fear to speak what he was thinking and feeling. "Ruth, I know I've said thank you plenty of times."

"J, you know..."

"Ruth, I have to say it."

"J, no really, it's ok."

"Ruth, please. I just want to say how thankful I am for you, for you today, for you yesterday, and for what I know will be you tomorrow."

Jonathan started to open his mouth and speak further and realized there was nothing else to say. After a few moments of silence, Ruth smiled and turned towards the window to the room where Mike was running tests. She extended her left hand to Jonathan and their fingers touched and intertwined, again.

A tear slowly ran down Jonathan's cheek though he dare not show it, so he just grinned. His heart was the one that skipped a beat. His anxiety was replaced with butterflies. Mixed with his concern he now felt hope creeping in and watched, waiting to see if his little girl was going to be ok.

A few minutes later, Mike shut a few things off, he picked up Charity, and carried her out and over to a more typical hospital type bed and covered her with a blanket.

"Let her rest. Let's talk. I think I know what's happening,

though I, I can't believe it. Jonathan, I need to know everything about this little girl."

"Well, you know I don't know much. I just adopted her. I decided one day I wanted to change and do something better than just be a selfish money focused womanizing…"

Mike cut him off, in a strong but quiet tone under his breath rising into a crescendo to make it clear he wanted an answer, a clear answer.

"Jonathan, where did you find her?"

"Mike, Doc, what are you talking about? I had spoken to a friend of a friend who mentioned she was a recent abandonment and that she needed a home ok. What else do you want to know?"

"Then I want to know where they found her."

Ruth stepped, in. "Doctor, I appreciate your concern and I'm sure there is a reason. However, without more clarification and some comfort in where this is going, I'm not sure this conversation needs to continue."

"Detective, I'd strongly suggest that if you don't want to get in the middle of a much bigger situation you kindly let me ask the questions. Help me with the answers, or we can push back and forth and walk away waiting to watch until that little girl in there dies."

Chapter 10 – Answers

"Mike, please just tell me what's going on."

"Jonathan, a long time ago I did a surgery to help a close friend, who was also a co-worker, have a baby. Just over seven years ago while she was still pregnant we did a fetal heart surgery. Something that had never been done using an experimental method at that point only authorized by the government to 3 of the Top Surgeons in the country for testing. Only thing is we were only allowed to test it on persons over the age of 75 with a signed release by them and their three closest family members. This little girl seems to have the same symptoms or strangely close to a similar problem to what we saw then in those trials. Now I'd have to get more info but I have reason to believe, and I can't believe I'm saying this and it seems nearly impossible, but this, might just be the child I operated on then."

"Don't you have records?"

"No, it was a small crew of persons who all agreed to never speak about it. Our government pulled the procedure, and the substance we used, only two months later. We never spoke about it. The young lady whom I had helped that had been such a good friend had agreed that it would be best that we cut off communication and not discuss anything about what was done ever again as soon as the baby was born. I left the room as soon as it was over. I never knew the child's name or what happened to the mother after she had the baby. It was just part of our agreement. If she needed me, she'd call. If not, I trusted all had gone well. Now this."

Ruth looked up, "Looks like we're all in this then... The 3 of us are tied to this little girl. J, I think you better tell the Doctor the rest of the story."

Slowly Jonathan began to explain how he'd met Eileena. He mentioned how while she captivated him when he laid eyes on this little baby girl with her, he felt suddenly connected to something bigger than himself, unlike anything before.

Sure part of him chocked it up to just another opportunity with another woman but this wasn't about Eileena and he had realized that soon after meeting the two of them. He was drawn to this little girl through her mom but this was not about hooking up. This was about something else. Before he had time to realize what that something was the little girl was in a taxi next to him like magic. Eileena seemed to know his every move and where he was and even who he was, better than himself. He went on to explain how he and Ruth decided to turn her in as a child left on a stoop and only release details that would determine her outcome and protection. While he didn't give names, he mentioned how he arranged things so that he could adopt her if no one else claimed to be family. And how he has cared for her ever since. Mike, at least to some degree, knew the story from there.

Mike shook his head looked up and says, "Maria, Maria, Maria."

Ruth and Jonathan look at each other bewildered then toward Mike, together they questioned, "Who's Maria?"

"You said her name was Eileena. But you always said it with that French accent. She wasn't actually French and she didn't have the accent, when I knew her at least. I'm guessing she pulled it out to throw you off, to keep everyone thrown off. Maria Elena Mendoza. Her family was from the Basque country, her mother was more Spanish and her husband more French in origin but after meeting, their families moved to the Basque country to take over farmland left to each of them by other family members. Soon after, they sold it and came to the states. At a young age, Maria's father ran off. Most believe it was with a young woman he'd insisted come with them to care for Maria when they moved, as she happened to disappear around the same time. The good thing in all this was their home and the land they lived on was all paid for and Maria's mother had a significant amount of savings from the sale of the land that had come from her side of the family. Each of her parents had kept a certain amount separate. She sold the large home in the country and purchased a smaller yet comparable one with a much smaller piece of land and invested that income so that she could focus her time on raising Maria.

At a young age however, Maria's home caught fire and her mother didn't survive."

Ruth jumped in.

"Wait was this in Westchester by any chance?"

"Why yes, on the outer edge."

"My mom used to work as a police officer in that area. I, I, think I've heard this story. Did, did you ever hear if Maria lost a Bible in that fire?"

"You know about that? How would you know?"

"My mom was very fond of her, in her short time as an officer. That story is part of what always made me consider joining the NYPD later in life. She quit so she could focus on my siblings. Especially since my dad wanted to move to the city and was afraid it wasn't a good idea for a mom to be a New York City cop at the same time. She said she'd never forget the look on the face of this young girl, Maria, and how hard it was to see her in that moment, lose everything she knew. I must have heard her tell that story a hundred times!"

"Wow, that's crazy. Well, it seems our world continues to shrink around her."

Michael continued. "Well, Yes. Maria was adopted with a new last name, Smith, but after she got older, she began using her birth name again. When I went to the funeral I didn't think much about the name showing Elena Smith because I knew her story. There weren't many of us there just me, and a few of her closest co-workers. A couple strangers whom we assumed knew her outside of work but no one really spoke. We just paid our individual respects and let them bury her that day. There weren't a lot of questions and the casket remained closed. Originally there was going to be a viewing but we were told for undisclosed reasons that the casket was kept closed out of respect. Again, no one really asked, we just said a prayer or spoke some final words her way and trusted the best outcome had happened for her daughter. I would have never guessed this."

Ruth engaged quickly. "So, can you tell us more about the surgery?"

"I can but I haven't spoken about it since. Please understand, this whole conversation must remain confidential or we all risk not only our lives, but also hers, and potentially the lives of others being dragged back into this mess."

"Oh Doctor, we understood that when we made our decision so that I could adopt her years ago. This doesn't change anything."

"Oh, but Jonathan, it does. You see…"

Michael explained Charity's condition from when she was still in the womb, the surgery that was performed, and why they believed the result of the seeping radioactive fluid likely killed Maria.

"Now, I think what's happening is it's like a battery dying. The fluid jumpstarted her heart and helped it so it could run for a long time, now her heart is giving out but not her whole heart just the small part that was struggling to grow before. It also appears it's sort of like a balloon running out of air, slowly shrinking or that that it was tearing apart and not holding together completely but not bad enough yet to be fatal.

This would explain the difficulty in breathing and her passing out."

"So, what do we do? Can we do the procedure again?"

"I wish it were that simple. First of all, as far as I know, all quantities of that medicine were destroyed for safety purposes.

Second, the materials that made it up came from 3 different countries and I'm not even sure the providers still exist. One of those being, an Aloe farm outside Chernobyl where they learned the radioactive effects on the plant had increased healing capabilities.

Another, being a special bean that grows in the rain forest of Africa called a Cincaberry. When ground and introduced with the aloe and a similar fluid to what we now use to fight cancer it would sort of graft onto whatever area was immediately around it like a mix of glue, radiation and the strongest version of a healing cream you can imagine that could be safe to use inside the human body. The last of those, we might be able to recreate. Heck we might even be able to use a lighter dose of the same thing we use on some of my heart cancer patients but the other two. Well that's another story.

Not to mention, if you do go looking for either of those. It's going to raise a whole lot of questions.

Questions you better be ready to answer with something other than a sick little seven year old girl. Otherwise, it'll get traced back and we'll all be in a lot of trouble. You want to know part of why St. Vincent's really got shut down? The government nearly got found out about the testing they'd allowed. The other two hospitals where this was happening got shut down too. They covered their tracks nicely. No one really caught on because all the folks were older so live or die no one thought much of it. But if word got out about what we did it'd raise a whole new subject of research and she'd be at the center of it. She'd turn into nothing more than a lab rat for some of those white coats from Washington."

Now, it was Jonathan who had to take the deep breath. "Ok, how long do you think we have? I need to rest but I know I need to get moving."

"Jonathan, I've given you all the answers I have for now. Two minutes, two hours, two days…" He continued after shaking his head.

"Two months, even two years could be possible I guess, but I think two months is the best guess I'd have before we see irreversible damage."

"Ok. Ruth, I think it's time we all went our own ways."

"Excuse me?"

"Ruth, I just don't want you…"

"J!" She took a deep breath and relaxed her tone. "Jonathan," she places her hands on his. "Doctor Phillips has trusted us. You have to trust me. I'm in this. Let's not kid ourselves. We are all in this. Whether we like it or not, we just have to be smart. Right now, only the three of us know anything. We all have too much invested to make a mistake. Doctor, thank you, we will be in touch and you'll know if we need to speak to you about this further. I'm sure at some point we will."

"Jonathan, you had the right idea when you said rest. I think we could all use some."

They all did just that. Ruth took Jonathan and Charity home. Michael jumped in a taxi and Ruth herself went home to get some rest.

The next day, Jonathan was awakened by the sweetest sound he'd ever heard.

His daughter's voice, "Daddy." She said rubbing her sleepy eyes, standing there in her princess nightgown. "Daddy, I had a bad dream."

"You did?"

He pulled her into bed to lay with him, rose up and put his arm around her and started stroking her hair.

"Yeah, I dreamed we were in the dessert and I was being pulled to the sky and you were running after me but you couldn't get me. You ran and ran daddy. But you couldn't help me and I floated away." Charity began to cry, and through her tears she said choking, "Daddy, don't let me go, never let me go."

Jonathan pulled her close. "It's okay, it's just a dream."

"But, it felt so real."

"It's okay."

He ran his fingers through her hair and lifted her hair. He knew right then wherever this journey ahead led him he'd have a companion the entire time. He had to take her with him along the way.

He wanted to tell her. He wanted to share all that he had learned. He wanted to hit the road for radioactive plants and crazy wild berries from tiny villages and whatever else he had to do and help her. But, he knew right now this little girl just needed her dad to hold her, then make her breakfast, and spend some quality time so she knew that it was all going to be all right.

"Daddy, am I going to be okay?" She took a bite of her cereal.

"Yes, why do you ask?"

"I don't feel okay. I know you took me to that Doctor's office late last night."

"Oh well, yes."

"I know Miss Ruth was scared for me last night, but that was when I was having that dream I think. Am I going to be okay?"

Right then Jonathan knew there wouldn't be any waiting period. Instead it was time now to tell her the truth. "Charity, let's get dressed and go for a little walk to the park."

Charity could always trust him for the truth and he never wanted to lose that trust.

Along their walk he began to explain what the doctor had said and even gave her a glimpse into her past. He told her while it wouldn't be easy they did believe they could get her what she needed to be healthy and live a long and happy life.

"Charity, I need you to be in this with me. I know it's a lot to ask. You're so young, just a little girl."

"Dad, I'm not that little, I'm seven, remember!"

"Of course, you're just... always going to be little to me."

"Aw dad.

"Peanut, I need you to make sure you tell me when you feel anything. For the next several weeks we are on a mission, we'll call it an adventure. We're going to probably go lots of places and see lots of things and get to meet a lot of new and different kind of people along the way."

"We're going on a trip?"

"Yes. Yes, we're going on lots of trips."

"Is Miss Ruth coming?"

"Huh, what?" Taken back a little startled by the question

She asked shyly, "Well, is Miss Ruth coming?"

"I honestly don't know. Maybe we can invite her for lunch on her break and ask her if she'd like to join us. I mean did you want her to come with us?"

"Yes. But, I meant is she coming on our trips?"

"You really love her don't you sweetie."

"Aw dad, it's you that loves her. I may be seven but I know what my daddy needs. You need her to come with us."

"Wow, so you're the smart one huh?"

"Oh, Miss Ruth says, all boys are the same. None of them want to say what their heart really feels so they just act silly around girls."

"Oh that's what she says huh?"

"Yep, and that's exactly what you do around her."

"I do nothing of the sort."

"Okay, dad."

"Wait, wait, that's what I do?"

They both laughed and Jonathan pulled out his phone and sent a text to Ruth about having lunch. She responded shortly after accepting the invitation.

Jonathan and Charity finished their walk. While he explained that Ruth probably would not join them on their adventure, he did continue to go on about the situation and prepare her for both the best and worse case scenarios. He also explained some of the amazing things he learned about her history and how he hoped to help her learn about where she came from along the way.

She, always caring about her dad more than herself just continued to remind him that while that all sounded amazing and that she was ready to go on this adventure, that she had all she needed when he held her.

All Jonathan continued to think about to himself was, *I was given this amazing gift, a gift that I can never let go.*

The two walked over to a little French spot near the park and met up with Ruth. From there forward they didn't talk about the sickness, Charity's history, or much else in public, they just talked about traveling and finding treasure.

Ruth mentioned she had a lot of vacation time she could use and was excited that she might be able to help in finding such treasure.

After a little discussion they decide they would make the arrangements to try and get started the next day. The question was, as one would expect with any adventure, the first question was nearly always the same. Where do we begin?

"We begin with sleep, off to bed."

"Okay…"

"I have a few things to put into place sweetie, sleep well."

Ruth followed, "Goodnight Charity."

Jonathan walked out.

Thinking back to when they held hands he spoke up, "So earlier?"

"You know I'm with you on this, I was, from the moment I agreed to help six years ago."

She paused and then continued,

"Jonathan, let's just focus on helping her."

"Yes, let's." He replied with an emphasis on 'let's.'

"I'm going on home to get some sleep. Do you need anything? I want to put some things in order and prepare to take off whenever you need me."

"No, no I'm good. Let's catch up tomorrow to go over my next steps."

"All right. Good night." She kissed him on the cheek, and picking up on his anxiety over all that was happening, "Everything is going to be alright J."

Jonathan closed the door, sat down at the table and opened his laptop. He began going to work scheduling clients with other representatives and emailing those who worked for him about taking on new roles and having a short meeting the next day at 4:15pm.

As soon as the bell rang he would have a feel for things and be able to go over how the next several weeks were going to operate.

Jim. Jim can take on the primary leadership role and I'll still be available in some way via email and mobile.

He also put things in place to get the promised party for his team in place. He might not be there, but he would try to at least video-conference in and say a little word or two. It was late. He'd call his nanny to keep an eye on things while he's away, pick up the mail and so on.

As he thought about things he realized a list would be a good idea. He sat down and began checking off all the things he needed to gather. He broke out the good luggage and realizing they needed to be able to travel light picked the smaller pieces. Opening up the safe he pulled out their ID's, Birth Certificates, Adoption Papers and Passports.

Reaching into the luggage he found his international travel packs to keep important documents under his clothes. He found his locks and reset the combinations. As he moved a few things around in the closet he looked up and noticed a small black locking case. He paused for a moment to consider if he should get it. A moment later, he decided to move on and pull out a notepad.

He began listing every possible item he could conceive of needing. Then he began to cut items one by one that he knew he could get by without. Having no idea at all what may come, he wanted to take both everything and nothing. Hoping for the best, planning for the worst was a tricky thing to do.

Research, he needed to get started on where he was going to find these things. He began online. Looking up everywhere he could, first for the 'Cincaberry.' Doctor Phillips had mentioned the rainforests and sure enough this strange berry had been found in various locations but there was such little information on it. It turned out many of the rare berries around the world had never been given English names.

This isn't going to be easy.

Jonathan dozed off as he searched through information on the rainforests and rare berries of the world. He found that the last public recorded transaction involving the berry was in Tanzania.

He decided to go his own route and hire a friend he knew in Johannesburg, South Africa to join them. He was a translator with capabilities in over 20 countries, and 10 languages, plus various dialects of African villages.

Tumelo had helped him before and they'd worked together on many global financial related projects where he needed translation assistance. Reaching over into a drawer he pulled out a phone, different than the one he generally used. He pulled up an app for private transmission and sent a quick text.

Flying in 9am Tuesday I need your services indefinitely 24/7. Double your usual daily rate until travel is completed. Will need travel to Tanzania Rainforest. Searching...

He stopped and thought. *Should I tell him now what I'm looking for? On one hand it could be good, get us a jump, on the other hand... Whoa!*

He nearly dropped the phone and in an effort to catch it and keep it from hitting the floor he hit send.

Sigh, it'll be fine.

Opening up a second browser page to a travel site, he clicked around. Glancing over to the clock he realized, he too needed to get some rest. Shaking his head he realized he was still missing some paperwork he'd been waiting on.

I guess I'll finish up. I'm sure he'll come through for me before morning.

Chapter 11 – The Search for a Cure Begins

As the sun rose, Jonathan woke up to his alarm and hit snooze. A second later he heard the same song. He went to hit snooze and realized it was actually his phone ringing.

It's Ruth. This early?

"Good morning," Jonathan answered in a tired voice.

"What's your plan?"

"We were going to fly into Johannesburg in twenty-four hours, then take a boat to Tanzania where we'll see if we can meet up with someone who knows the rain forest. I have a translator waiting to meet us in Richards Bay and travel with us as much as we need him."

"Whoa, Johannesburg? Tanzania? J, are you sure? Do you have your shots? What about paperwork for you to go?"

"Well, I was sure until I realized that it could add as much as two days to our trip. I started thinking, that that'll give me time to discuss in further detail what is happening with the translator. Two days is also a lot of lost time. Instead we're flying directly into Tanzania."

"I repeat, J, are you sure about this? I mean you're trekking around the globe to a part of the world, I'd never even considered traveling to about until you spoke of it being a possible location of this rare berry just now. Which we also knew nothing of until the last forty-eight hours!"

"Ruth, I'm not sure of anything, how can we be sure of anything. Even Doctor…"

He paused and realized he had to start being more careful of what he said over phone lines and in public. He didn't want to raise any attention to what they were doing. He needed to discipline his way of expressing, and verbalizing what was happening. *May as well start now*, he said to himself.

"Even the Doc isn't sure and he should know more than anyone!"

"Jon, I just want you to be careful. It's like when you're running out of gas and you get off the highway thinking you'll just find a gas station and after driving all over you just end up getting back on the highway only with less gas than you had before and that means less time to find a gas station. Don't waste her fuel on a goose chase, that's all I'm saying."

"I know Ruth, but I have to start somewhere."

"I'll come watch her, I'll be there tonight since your flight leaves so early in the…"

"Ruth, hold on."

A notification had just come through. A couple of clicks on the phone and his printer began to print. *Perfect!*

"Watch her? She is going with me. If anything is going to happen, I need her with me. I can't do anything for her if she's here. Everything we need is in my hand… just in time."

"J, I think…" Suddenly she stopped. "I think you're right."

They were both a little shocked by her agreement with him, each taking a deep breath.

"Call me." She said.

"I will."

"And be careful."

"I will."

"Bring her home."

"I will."

"Listen, we have to be smart and careful."

"I'm leaving you a gift. It'll be in the elephant."

"J…"

"Ruth, I really need to get things ready. We'll talk tomorrow when I land."

"Okay."

A shadow from the hallway fell into the room. "Dad?"

"Hey Peanut."

"Who was that? Was it Miss Ruth?"

"Yes hon."

"Is everything alright? It's early."

"Yes, sweetie everything's fine. Are you still tired, wanna sleep a little more or are you ready to get up and around."

"I'm good, I slept well actually."

"That's great to hear."

"Dad, should I be scared?"

Unsure of how to answer, afraid to give her too much false hope and yet not wanting to discourage he responded. "Are you?"

"No. I'm not. That's why I ask. Shouldn't I be?"

Realizing this was not about giving her the answers but helping her to find them he asked her another question. "Why do you believe you're not scared?"

"I just think, if I was supposed to die, then why this? Why all of this? I just think if it was supposed to happen. I would have never ended up with you. It's just... I have a sense of comfort I can't explain. A sense of knowing, deep inside, that no matter how hard it gets, no matter how crazy things may seem along the way, we're going to look back afterward and be able to enjoy the story because, well, because it's all going to work out in the end."

"Well then Peanut, I think that's exactly what we should go with. Let's not second guess our intuition. It's you and me kid."

A chuckle and a hug, a kiss and a smile ensue. "Let's get dressed, get something to eat, and talk about what's next."

Over breakfast they discussed what was needed and what he had learned in his research, and the part of the plan he had put together.

He let her help with packing her bag. He knew it'd be important to let her be involved in any small area possible. It's one way he could strengthen her for the journey both prior to, and along the way. It was getting close to lunchtime when he turned to her.

"Let's get some lunch and then let's go shopping!"

"Shopping?"

"Well, we need a couple things. We're going on an adventure. I want you to have a couple of things that could come in real handy."

"Like what?"

"I'm thinking some water proof hiking shoes, a good compact first-aid kit. I did some research and found a sporting goods store that has some amazing breathable pants that can pretty much but break the tooth off a snake if it tries to bite you. Also, some really, really good bug repellant lotion since spray can be a nuisance to travel with.

And, I don't want to take my big camera but I'm thinking we document this whole thing. I want to get a new one that's really good but also easy to carry anywhere along with a waterproof case and can work off regular batteries that we can also recharge. I'm going to buy a small fast charger that has all international plugs built in."

"Wow, that sounds awesome dad!"

"First things first, we gotta' eat, where too?"

She picked one of their favorite spots, a little diner around the corner. They followed with a hot chocolate and coffee at the very spot where he first remembered seeing her as a baby. As he always did for her when they went, he recounted the story as best he could remember it.

"--And that's when I knew there was something special about you, I just didn't know exactly what that meant yet."

They headed up the road to the specialty outdoor store to pick up the items they discussed.

"Look at me, look at me dad!"

Jonathan turned his head and saw Charity wearing a safari hat and jacket. He couldn't believe it, a pink supply jacket made to carry everything imaginable.

"Dad! Look the sleeves roll up and tie to be short sleeves. There's a rain proof pouch that folds out to protect items you don't want to get wet. How cool is this thing?"

"Done."

"What?" she looked confused.

"Done, let's get it."

"Seriously? Dad. Just 'cause I'm sick?"

"No way, are you kidding? It's pretty cool and I actually think you should have something you like and that will also be good for the trip, it's a no brainer."

"Yay!"

After a long day, he tucked her into bed, reminded her they had to be up early and went over what was ahead.

Tomorrow they would be in another country, and in less than 2 days they would likely be standing in the rainforests of Africa looking for a berry he couldn't even read about on the internet.

**

Jonathan's alarm blasted in his room all too early. It felt like minutes of actual sleep. *Ugh...* Then it hit him. *Today it begins.*

He leaned and looked to his left out the window where the sun was just beginning to shine in the darkness. He thought of all those times where he used to have a woman at his side, when he'd be getting up to rush out or escape the bed at this time of the morning. Now he had one girl and only one girl on his mind, the only one he'd cared for or even shared his bed with over the last six years, usually when she had a bad dream or just needed to know he was there... his daughter.

I'm going to save her.

Looking up, he continued.

You're not taking her, not now, not ever, not as long as I'm around.

Jonathan shook his head... as if trying to shake something off.

Who am I talking to? I don't even believe there's anyone out there to talk with like that.

A slap to the face and he turned and sat on the edge of the bed, slid into his slippers, stood, threw on his robe and walked into Charity's bedroom.

"Charity, honey. It's time to get up."

"Okay daddy." Her tired voice said from under the covers.

"Okay?"

"Yep." She rose from under her covers.

"Well, wow, that was easy considering the work it is to wake you up for school."

"Dad, school isn't an adventure. I mean, I like school but this is going to be amazing and best of all I get to do it with you. You get to be my personal explorer leader.

We're like Diego and Dora for real!"

They laughed and hugged.

"I'll make us a quick breakfast. I've laid your clothes out over there."

She could see her outfit by the desk, complete with her new pink explorer jacket. She smiled bigger than she had ever smiled and then her dad looked back, they exchanged smiles before he headed to the kitchen.

"Hello? Yes, fifteen minutes should be fine. Thanks Steve."

Steve's on his way with a car to pick us up. This is it. We're on our way.

"Where are we going first again, daddy?"

"Well, we're flying into Tanzania. We'll fly into a port town called 'Dar es Salaam.' We're meeting a friend who's traveling up from a small town off the Eastern coast of South Africa, about fifteen hundred miles south of there."

"I thought South Africa was a continent? And fifteen hundred miles sure seems like a long ways to come meet us."

"No sweetie that's South America. South Africa is a country in Africa. Africa is a continent. That's the continent we'll be on as we get started. We're flying into Tanzania, which is only separated from South Africa by one other country, Mozambique."

"Cool. Can you show me?"

"Sure, take a look here."

Charity and he meet at the globe he had next to the fireplace. He pointed out their travel plans and she saw a place she recognized.

"Madagascar!"

"Yep, it's right there."

"Wow."

"I tell you what, I saved a lot of information last night and printed out a few things. I can show you more on the way there."

"Cool."

"What about after that daddy? What about after we land?"

"We'll go over it again on the plane sweetie, Steve should be here soon and I want to review everything and be sure we're ready."

"Okay," she said sort of drooping but also understanding.

Pulling bags to the door, grabbing a smaller pack that Charity had promised she could carry along with a new safari proof bag, or so the salesman said.

Camera, check, water purifying tablets, check, charging adaptors, check, pen and paper, check and phones, check

"All right, I think we have everything. I also packed your bag with some snacks and brought a couple of water purifying water bottles so we can grab and go just about anywhere."

"Wow, dad, you really did think of everything! How? I mean, we only found out what was happening like two days ago. How did you think of all this so fast?"

"Oh Charity, I've always been an adventurer at heart. I've read so many books, watched so many movies, and more important, I've watched and read several documentaries on real life explorers."

"What's a docrumentrary?"

"No honey, its documentary. It's a movie made based on a true story and often shows the actual events of someone doing something, in these cases, mountain climbers and safari leaders and more."

"Do you think they'll ever do a docrumetra... I mean doc-u-men-tary about us?"

"Well, I'm hoping no one ever finds out, but you never know. You never know..." He repeated with his voice quieting as he finished it nearly under his breath.

His phone rang loudly, "Hey Steve. Yeah we're ready, we'll be right out.

"Let's go."

"Okay dad."

Just before Charity's feet touched the last of the stairs on the stoop he said, "Wait. Charity, wait inside while I load up the car."

"Why daddy?"

"Just wait."

"Okay daddy."

He stopped her while she starts to walk back in the door. "It hit me Peanut, I have to be careful, and I'm so glad you responded the way you did coming right back."

"Dad, I get it, I know what's going on. I've seen the movies."

"Good."

He looked down at her with a questioned look on his face, "Wait, what movies?"

"Jon, we better get going if you're going to make you're flight." Steve called from the car.

"All right." He responded.

He turned to Charity touched her arm and said, "Grab your backpack."

Jon placed his bag over his shoulder and they headed out the door.

"Steve thanks for the early ride."

"No problem. So where did you say you're going again?"

"Oh we're…" Charity began to reply excitedly.

Jonathan quickly cut her off. "We, um, are going wherever the next plane out takes us."

"Oh Jon, you're a wild and free spirit. Wish I could do such things."

"Well, maybe you can Steve. Where would you go if you could go anywhere?"

"I don't know, California?"

"I said, ANYWHERE Steve…"

"Alright, alright, Egypt or maybe Greece…"

"How about both?"

"Well yes, I've had that dream before."

"And, who would you take?"

"Oh, I don't really have anyone in my life but you know, I think I'd find someone and just go in some crazy way. You know if it's a dream, why not live wild and meet someone in the airport and then just take them along for the ride of their life."

"That sounds like a good idea Steve."

"Yeah, just an idea… that's all it'll likely ever be."

"Well, you keep dreaming okay Steve. Never stop dreaming and dreaming big."

"Sure Mr. Harris, you bet. Looks like she was still tired."

Steve noticed in the rear-view mirror that Charity had fallen asleep on her dad's arm.

"Yeah, she woke up excited but it was a pretty short night's sleep and her excitement kept her up though I think she was just laying in bed imagining quietly 'cause I didn't hear a peep out of her after tucking her in."

"Ah to be a dad," Steve responded.

"Yes, to be a dad. You ever think about having kids?"

"Oh, I told you I don't have a woman in my life."

"Well, look at me."

"I don't know how you do it. For that matter, how you did it? I don't know Jon. I just don't know if I could ever pull it off, I can barely take care of myself."

"I repeat, look at me!"

They both laughed and Jon finally said, "Seriously, I'll tell you something Steve, they help you take care of yourself better and they help you keep dreaming, dreaming big dreams."

"All right, which gate is it?"

"I'm thinking international? Let's see what flights are going out this time of the morning."

"Looks like the British Airways gate is starting to get busy. You could always start with London, or maybe Manchester, you know, everyone goes to London, but Manchester... then venture into the old Queen's country."

"Yes, yes, I like where you're going Steve, not the popular start but maybe somewhere a little different. You know I believe they also fly out to Edinburgh daily."

"Scotland sir?"

"Yes, Scotland!"

"I'm sure she'll love the castles of Europe."

"Yes, I'm sure she'd love to see them. Charity, sweetheart it's time to wake up, we're at the airport." The two got out and said their goodbyes. "Thanks again Steve."

Steve waved and pulled away. Jonathan already knew they were three terminals away from the one they needed to be at. Standing there, each with a bag on them and two at their side, he walked up to a car dropping off a couple of pilots.

"Excuse me, we need to get to Terminal 4."

"Well, what do you expect, me to just give you a ride?" the driver lashed out the window.

"Yes," Jon said showing a twenty dollar bill to the driver, "I do."

"Get in," he said without hesitation.

He threw the two bags in, and then picked up Charity and crawled into the back.

They pulled up and they quickly jumped out. He handed the driver another twenty and said, "my name is James McHenry remember it, remember it well."

"Yes sir, Mr. McHenry. Thanks." Before he could nearly finish the statement Charity and Jonathan were headed inside and approached a fairly quiet counter.

"Where are you flying today?"

"Dar es Salaam, Tanzania."

"Oh? You're a bit early but we can definitely check you in. What takes you there, business or pleasure?"

"Pleasure, I'm taking my daughter on an adventure."

Jonathan glanced down, a sort of motion toward Charity for the agent to look her way as well.

"Well, this should be quite the start. Going on safari while you're in Africa I hope."

"Yes, definitely, I have friends whose family is from there, and they plan to show us everything after we see the rainforest! I've heard the water is gorgeous as well."

"Yes. Yes it is, Mr., Um Harris, Mr. Harris and little Ms. Harris. I hope you have a wonderful time."

She handed them their boarding passes and the two headed for security which was just starting to get a bit busy for this time of day it seemed. *None the less, it is early. We'll be fine,* Jonathan thought to himself.

As they were walking through, a family was pulled aside who were clearly returning home but had purchased a one-way ticket.

Jonathan thought to himself, *This is exactly why I bought round trip never wanting any questions, especially when traveling international. Buy a one week round trip and no one thinks it's more than just a regular vacation. I mean c'mon they're a family of five clearly headed home.*

"Next!" A stern voice called.

They stepped up.

"Passports and boarding passes." The large man said almost automatically without looking at them.

He handed the items for each of them to the security agent.

"Thank you." He looked over at them. "What takes you and I'm guessing your little girl across the ocean?"

"Well, honestly sir, I had the time to take her on an adventure and she can't get enough of Diego and his safaris."

"Enough said." He stamped their papers quickly and smiled,

"I have 4 grand kids. I think they'd spend their life in a zoo if they could. Course they're all boys so you know they're pretty much half monkeys anyhow."

"Next!" he said after a breath in the same automatic voice. The man motioned to the next person in line, not interested in more small talk; just making his comments for himself and that was fine with Jonathan who was content to keep moving.

They placed their bags on the belt and moved forward. After gathering their things and getting themselves back together on the other side he looked at Charity and said, "So, what do you say, let's hit the newsstand, get some water, maybe a snack to take along and see if they have the latest National Geographic? I read last night the latest edition focuses on each of the world's rainforests. Great, and you're going to tell me why the rainforest is so important again right? I think I dosed off a little last time."

"Oh, dosed off huh?"

"Well, I know it's a forest and it rains a lot… I'm right so far aren't I?"

"Yes, yes you're right so far."

"Oh boy. We're having school time on the plane."

"Ah dad…"

"What do you want to drink?"

"Orange Juice!"

"Of course, I know how you love your orange juice. I'm getting us a couple of extra waters for when we get there. What else?"

"Can we get the wavy chips? I really like the wavy chips in

the can."

"Of course, that's fine. They'll serve food on the plane though, so not too many snacks. Let's grab a candy bar to split and maybe some gum for later."

"Perfect!"

"We are now opening the gate for those on Flight 243 now boarding for Dar es Salaam, Tanzania. We'd like to first welcome anyone needing special assistance and then we'll begin boarding anyone flying with children or those in first class." A static voice called from the speakers.

"Well, those last two apply to us." He said smiling at Charity.

"First class?" Charity reacted in excitement and surprise

Jonathan thought about how after 6 years of not wasting money on one night stands, emptying one bottle after the next, big tips to bartenders to cover his good times and so forth, it's amazing how much he was able to save up. He was always better at advising others before than following his own advice he'd realized. Well, now he could reap the benefits of listening to the wisdom he'd given his clients.

"Yep, first class!"

"Woo hoo, woo hoo!" she hopped around in circles.

"And she's doing the happy dance… come on let's go get our seats"

"We'd now like to welcome all passengers flying with young children as well as all of our First Class passengers and Diamond travelers."

"Good morning and good morning to you young lady. Travel the world often?"

"Nope, this is the first stamp in my passport ever!" she said holding tight to her passport.

"Well, your dad clearly has the best in class for you today. You are in seat 1A with a great view from that window and you'll be at the front for the movie as well."

"Movie?"

"Yes we have a large screen at the front."

"Going to the movies while I'm on a plane? Crazy!"

"Yes, looks like you are living it up. And, I assume you're dad?"

The agent takes Jonathan's boarding pass and raised her eyebrows in a way to welcome him with her eyes as much as her voice.

"Yes. My daughter and I are taking a trip. Just, the two of us."

"Well, let me give you a couple things you might enjoy along the way. Here is one of our airline pins." She bent down and reached for Charity's jacket flap.

"Oh, not on the jacket, please." Charity said as she quickly unzipped it just slightly, "but please on my shirt. Thank you!"

Afterward the agent handed her a little plastic gift bag with crayons and an airline game pack. Then as she came up she smiled at Jonathan. "We are here to serve you... first class."

He glanced back with a 'thanks for the offer' smile but with his body language saying 'no thanks,' as he took the boarding pass receipts she handed back to him and they continued onto the plane.

"Dad, you know you don't have to do that."

"Don't have to do what?"

"I saw how she looked at you... I told you I watch the movies."

"Oh I wouldn't even begin to know."

"Okay dad... whatever..." she laughed lightly. "Silly, boys are just silly," she continued

"What, wait, where... oh boy..."

They placed their larger bags in the overhead bin and their secondary bags in a small storage area just in front of them along the partition wall. Then before he forgot Jonathan sent a quick text to his office to authorize a very special gift and bonus to be provided to his driver, Steve, to help him keep dreaming big dreams. Then they both laid their heads back as the plane went out onto the runway.

"Sir, would you like something?"

"Huh?" Half daydreaming, Jonathan was slightly startled by the attendant.

"Would you or your daughter like anything?"

"Yes, one coffee and two orange juices please."

"Mm, orange juice..." Charity said with her eyes still closed

"Always love your orange juice."

Her eyes slowly open, "I sure do. Where are we?"

"Well, we are in the air now. They just reached what they call cruising altitude where it's safe for them to allow the attendants to serve us."

"Can we use the bathroom?"

"Sure, why?"

"I really need to use the bathroom."

"It's just around this corner here. Do you want me to go with you?"

"Dad, if I'm about go around the world with you searching for treasure in the jungle. I'd better be okay using the bathroom on an airplane by myself."

"Of course, well if you need anything there is a button you can push to call an attendant in there."

"Alright dad, I think I've got this. I am seven."

A few moments later she returned. "Everything good?" he asked a bit too worried.

"Yep, those bathrooms are tiny!"

"Yes," he finally caught his breath.

"They remind me of the ones in those little restaurants in the city."

"Yes, I guess they do."

"Except these are cleaner."

"Well that's good."

"Not if you need to use the bathroom at one of those restaurants."

They laughed, "Dad, can we look at the magazines and stuff now?"

"Sure! Let me get them out of my bag." He pulled out various papers and the National Geographic they had picked up from the newsstand.

"Here we go." Jonathan said while turning on his tablet and

plugging it into the armrest. "I want to keep this charged when I can. I almost didn't bring it but thought it might be a good idea.

All right, let's start here. This is a map of where we'll be flying in. Then, we'll be meeting my friend who will be traveling up from here, Richards Bay." He said pointing to the map.

"Richards Bay is a small port town on the northeastern side of South Africa. It'll have taken him a couple of days to get there but he said he was leaving shortly after I called so he should be able to meet us at the airport. From there, I'm not sure exactly but in some form or another we'll be traveling into the Eastern Arc Rainforest of Tanzania. We're looking for the Cincaberry. Which from what I understand might be related to a berry found in the rainforest of India that really has no English name but look! I found it on this website for rare herbs and berries around the world. I couldn't find anything else about it. But if it's right, it makes sense.

See here, where it says this rare Indian berry found in the rainforest secretes a white sticky substance almost like a fruit based glue itself. The doc mentioned something similar with the Cinca so I'm thinking that must be part of what holds everything together where as the Aloe helps expand and heel it. Also, the Cinca is supposed to have anti-oxidants with the sort of qualities that bond and strengthen both red and white blood cells aiding in quick rejuvenation.

Due to the qualities of it, it sounds like it would help your oxygen intake and transmission of oxygen throughout your body, muscles and yes, organs like your heart, which could ease the workload of you heart as well while it heals and strengthens. Some of those things I just mentioned will also be huge in offsetting a negative reaction from the radiation."

"Did my hair just blow? Because, wow, that went way over my head! But I think I get it, it's good for me, helps me get better by helping me breathe better and heal faster."

"Well, yeah, you could say it that way." They smiled and he continued.

"The thing is, finding it. I have such few leads but Doc said this would be where he'd start if he was looking though he wouldn't say much more and said he couldn't give me any leads on who to talk to."

They continued to look over the magazines. They studied the rainforest and read about what made it special and the many animal and plant life that lived in the over 250,000 acres.

"Wait 250,000 acres!"

"Yes, that's why I called my friend. That's why we'll need a guide, someone who knows the forest."

"Wow."

"I couldn't have said it better. Just in case we have to hit the ground running, let's be ready."

The smell of food caught Jonathan's attention. He began packing their items back in his bag. "Let's eat and then try to rest."

"That's a big forest," Charity said under her breath, her head hitting the back of the seat as she began to stare out the window over the clouds. "What language do they speak there?"

"They speak many languages. They have many tribes. Although many speak a language called Swahili, and many also do speak English as well."

"Here you are sir."

"Thank you." Jonathan turned towards Charity. "Eat up. Soon those day dreams you're always having... well, let's just say we'll be living them."

"Okay dad, but I just realized something. There's going to be bugs aren't there!"

"Yes, sweetie there's going to be bugs."

"Ugh, I don't like bugs," she said as she took a bite of her food.

Chapter 12 – A New Land

"All right Charity, we're about to land."

"Wow, that went by quicker than I thought," she said in between yawns.

"Well, you watched the movie, fell asleep, woke up and said something about something and then fell back asleep."

"Dad, I should tell you something."

"What's that?"

"I didn't sleep at all last night. I tried but I just couldn't, I just laid in bed. I was dreaming all night but I never fell asleep."

"It's okay. I'm glad you were able to rest on the plane. Alright, seat up."

"Ladies and Gentleman this is your captain and we'll be making our decent for Dar es Salaam shortly. Please bring your seats to a full and upright position and stow all bags and loose items. In addition please replace your tables to the stowed and locked position. Thanks again for flying International."

"Amazing," Charity said as she looked down and saw the ground below. "I can't believe just this morning we were in New York."

"Here, it's actually tomorrow."

"Wow, how'd that happen? I thought we were flying for 13 hours or so."

"Well, from the time we took off, the length of the flight and the change of time zones we are just starting the next day."

"Oh, sure, yeah, that makes sense now. I was wondering how your friend was going to make it in time to meet us. He had a full day head start!"

"He sure did."

The plane descended and after the landing, the two grabbed their bags and walked out into the airport. They had checked a small bag with liquid items so they headed for baggage claim to retrieve it and meet the translator.

Walking, Jonathan saw him. A tallish, dark skinned, well built man in his early 30's. He stood in high-quality short top hiking shoes, a pair of khaki cargo shorts and button down light-weight shirt. Sunglasses hanging around his neck, he held a sign with simply, 'J. H.' on it. He also held a small bag in his hand. Seeing him, the man stepped in Jonathan and Charity's direction.

"Sir?"

"Yes."

"I believe this may be yours," he said while holding the bag up.

"Yes, it is."

Jonathan opened it, pulled out a much smaller bag. An American flag covered fanny pack. "I brought you a gift. I thought you'd like it."

"Fantastic, I'll put it on my dog when we go hiking." Jonathan responded sarcastically then followed with excitement, "Tumelo, it's good to see you!"

"And you my friend," he replied with a thick accent. It's a mix of his South African cultures and those that have rubbed off from his travels.

Tumelo Le Roux was of mixed race from a set of parents each of mixed race. It was what led him down the road of going from working hard on farms and laboring to his current work as a translator. He grew up learning four languages and continued to have a knack for them learning one after the other. One day while working on a rich mans home outside Johannesburg he helped clear up a dispute between two men who couldn't quite understand one another due to communications issues. The owner of the property picked up on the value of this and immediately hired him to assist with his business.

As his business grew, he needed someone to help him be the center man for all of his importing and exporting business that happened in Richards Bay. As Tumelo met more people and learned new languages he found there were others who also could see great value in his gift and were willing to pay a great deal for his assistance. His first freelance opportunities came from some of the lesser than appealing persons of the country both in politics and crime.

He didn't realize at the time the two were using him to

launder words the same way money is laundered which in the end was exactly the result. And so, when the opportunity to split and work with affluent and respected businessmen arose, he took it. The first of those businessmen was Jonathan Harris, who he met when one of his clients was trying to employ his financial services. Luckily for Tumelo, Jonathan saw right away what was happening and despite his greed Jonathan always knew who and who not to do business with.

He offered Tumelo a job and began helping him get the business of respected men similar to him from around the world while charging a small finders-fee but much like any good agent he made sure Tumelo always made more by knowing him than he would have otherwise.

One day he turned to Tumelo and spoke these words, "You have earned all that you have. You owe me nothing more. The service you have provided for these men and I will carry forward in many ways. Take your gifts and your money and your work and continue on."

Jonathan would still call upon Tumelo from time to time as needed but most of the standard languages such as Spanish and French and even a little Russian were not a problem for Jonathan and he employed some much cheaper translators for this work now.

Tumelo traveled a bit more under the radar than one might expect. He lived in Durban and held an apartment in Johannesburg and a flat near Cape Town. He loved his homeland and its people and knew it well. However, in his business it was good at times to not be known, making who he knew that much more important. He'd traveled from Durban to Richards Bay and hopped on a ship that had a short stop over for a small pick up in Beira.

**

The journey to Dar es Salaam took almost 48 hours. In his journey he stopped at one of the banks. "Yes, I'd like to make a deposit. May I have a deposit slip? It's for a friend."

The teller passed him the paper and he filled it out. He pulled out an envelope with cash and passed it back to her with the slip.

"Do you need a receipt?"

"Yes, thank you."

"Were you sure you wanted to deposit this entire amount into Mr…"

Quickly Tumelo cut off the teller, responding. "Yes. When a friend asks for help, you don't question them. If you have the means you help," he kept his tone simple, sincere and yet clearly wanting to move on.

"Yes sir. Good to have friends." She presented him with a receipt of deposit and he thanked her and immediately went to request access to a safety deposit box in the vault.

"Come this way Mr. Le Roux."

He walked in, pulled out a key, opened the box and pulled out another envelope and another and another. He placed the 3 of them into the box. He then opened a second deposit box placed the key inside for the first, closed each of them and exited the vault thanking the security guard for his assistance.

As he left he hailed a taxi and was taken immediately back to the port.

"Yes, I'm here assisting with the inspection of the Axis Chemical load up," he flashed a paper with a bill of lading and held up a plastic name tag badge and was sent through.

He approached a man walking toward him. "Jones, how are you?"

"Good, thank you. I made the call and your arrangements are in place. He'll be waiting to meet with you."

Jones heard his phone. "Just a moment T."

"Oh, well, that's convenient and well timed. I see all expenses have been taken care of and we are just finishing the load. Come with me. I'll show you aboard."

"I have a gift of thanks for the ride." Tumelo handed him a small box. He opened it.

Had a fly been on Jones' shoulder they would have seen that it was the very imprint of the key to the second safety deposit box. Thought it appeared that of a coin collector's box and had 3 coins setting in it under a light piece of cloth. The coins in order were, 5, 20, and 15 which when were placed one after the other made up the number on the safety deposit box itself.

"Ah, T, it's what I've always wanted. What a friend." He dropped it into his pocket and Tumelo grabbed his bag from the car and they headed toward a large ship in the slip.

"One moment, I promised a friend I'd make a large environmentally friendly donation to a good world cause." One of his assistants brought over a laptop.

"Here you are sir, just needs your authorization." He strikes a few keys and hits Enter.

"There. Now all is right in the world and everyone is taken care of I believe."

For Tumelo it could be difficult knowing so many languages. The workers of the port were from all over and spoke even some of the oldest languages of the country such as a dialect of Bantu where he picked up on a man speaking in the distance. It stood out because of its rarity to hear.

"Jones."
"Yes, T."
"How secure is your ship?"
"Top notch, you know I don't waste any…"
"Jones!"
"Um, yes?"
"How secure are we right now?"
"Well, as secure as we need to be."
Four men began to approach them immediately. Tumelo recognized the voice of one of them clearly as the voice he had heard earlier.

"This isn't good."
"Plan?"
"Walk for the car, but be ready to drop when I go to unlock it."

The men saw they were rushing to make a get away run toward the car. Tumelo and Jones stopped. Jones, with his keys in hand, touched the unlock button and the vehicle exploded into flames.

As they dropped they realized that two men on either side scurried back toward the containers.

"Sir, we got your signal." Immediately, four men rode up on motorcycles. Riding off and up a ramp directly onto the ship, Tumelo saw the anchor come up.

"Jones, does this have anything to do with…"

"This has nothing to do with you, but you may want to continue with caution. These guerillas are everywhere these days. Between them and the pirates on the high seas we're ready for about anything. I may make a deal with politicians and environmentalists and even my competition but these men; there is no making a deal with these kinds of men."

A container door being closed showed signs of a vintage vehicle while another one glowed with a shine that only the finest material could give when the sun hit it at that angle.

Tumelo spoke up, "when we get to Dar es Salaam, I think I'll make one of my more traditional exits."

"I understand."

Arriving into the Tanzanian port Tumelo rose out of the water near a small dock to the north. Pulling himself out a few people see him.

"Can you believe it, my 40th birthday and they just leave me out there? What a bunch of wankers."

A couple of men fishing on the dock laughed as he walked over to a small boat, got in and changed clothes pulled from a water proof pack on his back. A couple hours later, it was time to pick up a tourist friend that would be arriving from the United States very soon.

**

"So, Jonny," he said, "we're off on an adventure you say?"
"Yes."
"We're heading into the Eastern Arc?"
"Yes."
"Well let's get something to eat. We can chat about what it

is you want to do and the things you'd like to see. This way," he said, motioning them to the door. They stepped outside and into a car.

"I have a nice little spot and it's on the way. Not far from the conservancy headquarters. I think you'll like it."

"Sounds good."

"So, what again are you looking for?"

"I don't know how to explain it Tumelo. A friend said it might be referred to as a Cincaberry." Jonathan explained the many qualities of the berry, such as its size and what it looks like. As he finished they pulled up to a small almost shack type building.

"Here we are."

Tumelo jumped out and opened the door for Jonathan who then in turn helped Charity out as well.

"I've asked a friend to meet us here. He'll be taking us on a tour."

Jonathan, figuring cost would be involved, began to reach for his phone or possibly a checkbook from his bag.

"No worries friend, all inclusive, a deposit has already been made. I think you'll like this spot, it's a quiet space. A good place we can talk about this berry you are looking for."

As they walked in they saw a man in a typical green vest and safari hat sitting at a booth. He waved a simple short wave to Tumelo.

Think of Harrison Ford way past his exciting days and more into his grumpy older years. Clearly still capable of holding his own, once something great and still well respected no matter how annoying he'd become.

"This is Mr. Richardson. Mr. Richardson, this is my friend Jonny."

"Hello Jonny. And, who is this?"

"This, Mr. Richardson is my little girl, Charity."

"Well, have a seat. Order some food, some coffee or something."

Mr. Richardson was in his 60's but had clearly taken good

care of his appearance, barely looking a day past 40. He had that grumpy old man sort of short talk, as if he knew exactly what to do and what you should do and what everyone else should do and he wasn't about to hold back. He sort of scoffed with each breath. Yet, he had a sort of welcoming appeal as well that couldn't quite be explained. "Okay, so we've got some time, this place is slow as snails."

"Well, okay here we go." Again, Jonathan explained all that he knew, which felt like such a small amount. When he finished, the food arrived.

"Ah, right on time!" Tumelo responded.

"I told you this would be a perfect place to talk."

They ate and for a while it remained awkwardly silent. Jonathan was trying not to show his frustration with the old man not giving any feedback after what he'd shared. *If this man knows nothing why are we still sitting here,* he thought. Charity sensed it, looking over and just smiling. "Enjoy your food dad."

"Thanks hon."

The man suddenly spoke up, "ah the love of a child and a father. Nothing like it! I know of several things that have similar qualities to what you speak of. When do you want to go in?"

"Go in? To the forest?"

"There's a small tribe, The Kabila la Waganga."

Tumelo questioned him, "The tribe of healers?"

"Yes. They are men raised up to go among other tribes using only that which they are given from the earth to heal those who are ill. If anyone would know about this berry you are searching for it is the men of the tribe."

"Can we go now?"

"Tumelo, are they ready?"

Jonathan gave Tumelo a nod.

"Yes, they are ready."

"Good, I hate waiting. Let's finish up this food and get over to the headquarters so I can check-in that I have a specialty tour group I'm taking into the forest. But first, I gotta use the facilities. Excuse me."

When Mr. Richardson left the room Jonathan turned to Tumelo, "Where did you find this guy?"

"He's a local. Born here to an Australian father and an American mother, his parents were here as part of an effort to help save the rainforest. He spent a couple summers in his teens with his grandfather in Texas during his last years but interestingly; he knows this place better than the locals themselves."

"Well, he certainly seems to have an idea of where to begin with helping us. That's all I can really ask for."

"Alright, kiddos, you ready to go?" Mr. Richardson said while opening the door.

"Yes sir." Charity was quick to answer.

"Got your paperwork?"

"I have everything right here," Jonathan responded pulling out the papers he had gathered just the morning before. "We had to show everything when we arrived also."

"Well, alright then. Let's move."

Without haste they made their way for the Conservancy. Mr. Richardson was first to go in.

"James, I'm just checking-in before I take a special expedition into the forest."

"Richardson, you know you can't just waltz in here…" a man obviously younger than Mr. Richardson responded in a harsh tone.

"Excuse me. I sat in that chair before your daddy gave me the right to pretty much do whatever I wanted to. I protected this forest and these people. What have you done, other than wheel and deal with every country's scientists and energy companies to suck the life out of it and not all on the up and up? Am I right? Yeah, I'm right. You know I know that you can't say anything to me about nothin'. So, I'll be taking a few folks in to visit and see some frogs and some giant leaves and such and you don't need to worry about a thing. You know how I work. And just maybe, I can help you get that new outpost you wanted built on the other side of the Arc, for um, what you would call… research."

"Got money huh?"

"Ah, I knew I'd get your interest if I talked bounty. I still take care of the forest and its people first. One more thing, if we build that outpost, it'll have a small medical facility, I know someone who wants to set up shop and help out folks who otherwise don't get such help."

"But…" the young man said in a softer tone.

"I only said if. If, I get you what you want."

"If you can do that, then yeah sure, sounds good."

The men shook hands and Mr. Richardson signed a couple forms and handed them over.

"Standard procedure doesn't change." The man said in attempts to sound friendly.

"Yep."

"Cover your tracks out there, literally!"

Richardson turned to leave, tilted his hat, smiled widely with a quick, "I always do," as his back faced the young man.

"Alright everyone, we'll drive this fire road in but then we'll have to leave the jeep and continue on foot. Anything you don't have to carry and don't mind losing, I'd leave there." Mr. Richardson barked the memorized instructions.

"Why? Is it dangerous?" Jonathan asked with a hint of concern.

"Ha, Tumelo! I thought you said they were ready."

Tumelo cleared his throat, "Mr. Richardson likes to be a bit dramatic, he knows these woods so well he can talk to the trees and better than that, hear them speak back. We'll be fine."

In another language he muttered something and Mr. Richardson scoffed with his hand extended as they all hopped into the jeep and headed down the road.

Tumelo pointed out various things in the forest as they went. Special trees, plants, and animals but mostly mentioned the various small living things that grew and lived among them. Much, which were unseen, especially when going by in a Jeep.

"It's a short walk from here. Tumelo, help me secure the Jeep the best we can."

"Tumelo, you've been here before?" Jonathan asked.

"Jonny boy, you know me."

"Of course, why do I ask? You've been everywhere." He smiled at him.

"Tumelo and I go way back working with these tribes. This man was a born communicator. It started when he came through as a tourist. Now we take turns putting each other to work from time to time, eh Tumie."

"Tumie?" Jonathan said looking at him with a grin and chuckle

"Oh Man, don't let it leave the forest okay?"

"Yeah, and who would I tell, huh? Who?'

They laughed and carried on preparing the vehicle and putting on their bags with what they'd need the most and wouldn't want to be caught without. Tumelo quickly put on some long tights and everyone tried to cover their limbs best they could on the advice of their guide.

"Never know what you're going to come across out here or what you might see has come across you. In the Eastern Arc it's not the big things you're afraid of, it's the little things." Mr. Richardson led the way, machete in hand but he made every effort not to use it as they moved along the trail. He picked up a large stick waving it in front of him, to clear anything unseen and maybe move a few of the smaller poisonous critters from their path.

"The walk isn't too far, let's do our best to keep moving and not get caught up in the sights along the way. If this is as important as you say it is, the sooner we get to the camp the better."

"Alright," Jonathan said. He glanced down to Charity. She stared around in awe. *She's a city girl through and through.* Sure he'd traveled with her and had some weekend trips to the beach or mountains, a mere one to two hours outside of town but this was unlike anything she'd imagined in her wildest dreams.

**

It felt like seconds later when she came back startled by the sound of her dad's voice.

"Charity! Charity!"

"What? Huh?"

"Watch your step hon. You almost caught yourself on that root and fell right over on your nose."

With a giggle she responded. "Oh dad, thanks."

"Alright explorers, there's the camp just ahead." Mr. Richardson announced.

"Already?" Charity said.

"Well, young lady you were daydreaming for most of the walk. This place will do it to you. We often call it the *Nchi ya kutoroka* or Land of Escape. It swallows you in like quicksand for the mind. Natives said it originally was part of their defense against enemies. Hiding in places where those who came to inhabit would get lost in their search from the things they'd see. As their surroundings mesmerized them, they would easily be trapped or overtaken by the natives who stood so much closer by than any would know."

"This place is amazing. I mean I've heard stories, but it's really, really amazing."

"It sure is."

Tumelo moved forward and began speaking in various dialects of a few different languages.

A moment later, men stepped out from each side of the trail and a third from what seemed out of nowhere and began to walk toward them.

**

A normal conversation that not even Mr. Richardson completely understood.

I stood my daughter at my side. Oh, how far I had come from those small towns of Iowa. More than all those years in New York, as I stood here in this place in this moment confronting side by side with my daughter the very fear of death without fear or concern but throwing it all to the wind and saying, we will not fail, we will believe, we will choose life.

Oh, yes. How far have I come from where I once stood, where I once would lie night after night.

**

Tumelo and the man clearly had a talk that went something like this...

Native: Hello, how do you speak our language? You do not to appear to be one of our tribe.

Tumelo: I am not. I am a friend, helping a friend. Here

with a forest guide.

Tumelo motioned toward Mr. Richardson. He was clearly recognized by the man and each traded nods.

Native: If he is with you, we can assume you are to be trusted but that you are also here for a reason. He doesn't bring tourists to our home. He looked toward Jonathan and Charity.

Tumelo: It's true. The man is a friend who has helped me many times over, over the years. His daughter needs help.

Native: Come, drink with us, sit, share a meal and tell me more. I will invite our Chief Healer.

Tumelo: Thank you.

$**$

The two men, who appeared to be guards, disappeared behind the trees to each side as quickly as they had appeared.

Tumelo turned his head. Looking over his shoulder he gave the rest of the group an advancing wave.

"Dad, where'd they go?"

Jonathan shrugged his shoulders and then continued walking with her. They entered a moderate hand-built home from items in the forest.

As they sat down there was soup, some sort of meat, and vegetables. It was really not clear as to what any of the platter really contained and no one dared ask. They poured fresh juice from that which grew on the trees and bushes surrounding them.

In some ways it was as if we had just entered the land of OZ. I have to admit, a part of me fully expected a man in a green suit behind a curtain or maybe a sort of character like that of the Mad Hatter to suddenly appear and we were all about to follow a bunny down into the earth. But of course it wouldn't be a bunny at all, right down the rabbit hole. Where were we? Quickly Jonathan shook his head. His daughter looked up.

"Did the Land of Escape swallow you up there dad?"

"Yeah. Whew." He shook his head again, nodded, and leaned forward to say thank you. Tumelo translated their appreciation and gratitude to the two men sitting with them and those who had served them.

The lead man, (whose name was never spoken) motioned

and those serving left them. Tumelo said the man was not really their leader but more like a mid-level Politian who did speak for the people and was also a bit like him, a sort of a translator or chief communicator for the Tribe. We heard Tumelo refer to him, as *Akida*, which translated, to Officer. Akida turned to the other man, the Chief Healer, and spoke quietly.

As Akida spoke we saw this man of healing nod his head slowly. After a short conversation Akida spoke and Tumelo translated.

"He says he has seen this nut or berry as you call it. It is both, the gundi karanga. It begins similar to the look of a coffee cherry but as it ripens it hardens on the outside and softens on the inside. During a short phase of the ripening process the inner lining of the nut and outer part of the seed ooze through cracks in the outer shell. This ooze both forms a protective shell around it and once inside the nut fills those cracks like natural glue. It has many, many great uses and can be used for healing but often must be heated to an exact temperature for use.

He is amazed anyone outside of this part of the world is aware of such a use. Until now, he has only heard those of his tribe pass this down from generation to generation, healer to healer and to no one else."

"Tumelo, do they have it? Do they have the gundi karanga? Can we get it?"

The man continued.

"It is grown nearby on the cliffs and on trees that stand at height where the ocean blows them to the west. There it catches just the right amount of salt-water air and moisture during the midlevel rain months."

Then the man's head dropped, "there is none and won't be for some time. The season has recently passed."

"How long?" Jonathan's voice trembled.

"Too long," Tumelo said. "Maybe we find the other things we need and come back. Jonathan, I'm sorry. Maybe another forest, maybe another tribe…"

Tumelo asked them in their native tongue. He began to talk with them. To tell them further the story of Charity and her circumstance.

Then the older man's head perked up. He looked at Richardson and spoke.

"He is the key. He brought men here many years ago, 8 or 9 years ago sounds just about right. They took many things. We were promised they'd leave things as they saw them when we came and were advised not to interfere if we too did not want to be taken back and studied.

He knows. He knows who they were. Maybe if you find those men, you find a man who knows what they took. Maybe they took this glue nut and found a way to harvest it. If so, you may have a way much sooner to get what you need to save the little girl."

Jonathan turned to Richardson. "Talk!"

"I don't know..." Richardson's voice trembled as he stammered back a few steps.

Immediately the guards similar in look to those they encountered when they entered the camp appeared from the darkness into the light of the fire by them. This time four not two appeared.

"These guys are really like magic. How do they do that?" Richardson tried making the tense atmosphere a bit lighter.

"Talk!" Jonathan stepped closer to him.

"Okay. But I'm going to have to ask..."

"It's already done Richardson."

Tumelo jumped in. "It's already done but it can be undone very quickly."

"Okay. There was a man who brought his expedition here a long time ago. He didn't say much about what they wanted but let's just say a deal was made. Some might say that deal was made many years before that day. Nonetheless, we had no choice but to let him and his men come and collect and do as they please. We simply asked they not engage the natives. We asked no mater what that our ecosystems remained unharmed. They agreed."

"Who were they?"

"Scientists, researchers, those with big dreams of big money from that which many have tried to harvest elsewhere and use in ways... ways I'd rather not know about. Later I heard about him again, advances in stem cell research and uses of radiation in unimaginable methods but never again did he come calling to the

Eastern Arc. I assumed they had failed."

"I need a name, a lead, anything you got."

"Go. Go with Tumelo. Get some rest. Tomorrow we'll see what we can do."

Jonathan filled with frustration, worry, anxiety, and love is awoken from this trance when he feels the hand of his daughter, then her smile. Together they took a deep breath. The way he had taught her to do over the years when she didn't quite know how to react in situations that brought out every emotion inside her.

They said their goodbyes and thanked the tribesmen and promise to return if they must for what they needed. The tribesmen offer all that they can do to assist.

The men then ride quietly out of the forest with Charity who drifted off in her father's arms. The jeep arrived at a small home in Dar es Salaam.

Jonathan put on his bag and Tumelo grabbed the others. Carrying Charity, Jonathan followed Tumelo as they waved to Mr. Richardson who drove away slowly.

"It's not much, but it'll do. It's clean, there is food and drink and the beds are... well they are beds and again, they are clean."

Jonathan clearly tired, and worn from the long journey already logged gains Tumelo's empathy.

"He'll be back tomorrow. We will continue this journey until we have reached the destination you desire."

Chapter 13 – The Chase Begins

"Dad, you should have some breakfast."

"I can't. I can't begin to think about eating. Where is he? And where's Tumelo?"

The knock at the door made Jonathan race to the door before Charity could even react.

"Finally!" Jonathan pulled the door open.

"It's time to go."

"Tumelo, where's Richardson?"

"Gone."

"And the money?"

"Also, gone, but I think I know the next move. And, he left us the Jeep. Look what I found inside with the keys."

"What is it?"

"It's an expedition document. Richardson had said he kept them every time a true expedition came through."

"This is it?"

"I think he meant for us to find it. Look at the date."

"That's about nine and a half years ago."

"Exactly, I think this is the lead he promised."

The phone in Tumelo's pocket rang, interrupting Jonathan's train of thought. "That's strange," he said staring at the screen of his phone.

"What is it?"

"I just had a deposit into my account... actually two unexpected deposits, one for $29.90, and the other for $103.85."

"Were you expecting payment from someone?"

"Not for $133? Not without a few more zeros. And no, actually you're my only client at this time. I've cleared my calendar until we are finished, and I made that clear once I accepted this job."

"Do you know who it's from?"

"No idea and not sure I can find out."

"We need more than this!" Then looking over the paperwork a bit more Jonathan notices something. "Wait? I think I recognize something about these names here?"

"Really? What is it? Who are they?"

"Yes, yes! I know a few of these guys, Texas millionaires. Look, a few are politicians as well. Flipping Oil, Banking and Technology. Ha, often because of the stolen information they got through contacts I worked with."

"Okay, but why would they have come here?"

"Are you kidding? There are two reasons why Texans do audacious things. One: to one up the next guy, and two: to one up that guy's bank account."

"Wait, bank account... bank account. What were those deposit numbers?"

Jonathan began to scramble for his tablet. Clicking hard on its screen once it was in his hands. Tumelo read them off and he started trying to transfer them into account numbers going back through client records.

"It has to be here. This has got to be it."

Search after search and to no avail. *I was sure of it.*

Frustrated, Jonathan went to toss the tablet toward the couch when Charity stepped in and put her hand on it before his can extend.

"Dad, we'll figure it out. We will."

Jonathan dropped down and embraced Charity holding back tears of anger, frustration, and pain that he dared not show.

Tumelo cleared his throat politely trying to end the embrace, "Jonathan, let's get packed. Clearly what we need isn't here."

"But where do we go?"

"Well for one, do you think these guys are still in Texas?"

"Let me see that list again." His eyes scanned the papers, "Hmmm, no, I don't know, maybe. Wait, Ralph Mason. I don't know how I missed him before. I know Ralph. Ralph is Texas through and through. Has a box at all the major ballparks and one of the biggest pieces of land in the state and that's saying something when we're talking about Texas."

"Well it might be a start."

"I have a client in Dallas. Tumelo, he knows these guys I'm sure of it. Let's start there. We can at least try to get a meeting. A few of them are foreign investors. I'm sure I can bring you along."

"What about Charity?"

"Well, it's a long flight. Let's work on it."

Jonathan and Charity completed their packing. Tumelo turned to them moments later. "Next international flight to Dallas goes through Dubai, gets us in tomorrow night. We fly out in 5 hours. I say we eat and discuss where we'll be staying."

"Oh man, you too?"

"What? What me too?"

"Oh, peanut here has been trying to get me to eat all morning. Well, I give in okay. Let's do it, we got time. What do you have in mind?"

"Well I know a spot."

"I figured you did. Let's go."

Grabbing their bags they headed out the door, jumped in the jeep, and drove toward Dar es Salaam.

About halfway to the airport Tumelo pulled over.

"I gotta tell you Tumelo this doesn't look much different than the last place we went?"

They laugh and head in. "Good food and some good conversation with a plan does me good."

"This was a good idea."

"Told you dad!"

"Hey... yeah, you did."

"So where should we stay?"

"Under the radar, somewhere outside of town."

"No. My guy is in downtown and we should stay in that area or within a short distance thereof. If any of the guys on that list are still doing business they'll likely have big offices in or near downtown too I'm guessing or in North Dallas. Let's go with downtown to start. I'll make a call."

"Wait," Tumelo handed him a phone. "Just hit one and pound for travel arrangements. Remember, I don't just translate languages; I'm here to make sure we avoid any, well, any kind of misunderstanding by anyone."

"Well done my friend."

Jonathan made the call and shortly after they were on their way. On the plane they talked and they slept. Yet, they did not figure out anything new. They continued to look for clues. They continued to ask questions: Richardson, the rain forest, the arc, this list, and now these men who had found ways to make money and stay ahead of the game.

∗∗

Hours later they sat, awaiting the plane to take off from Dubai.

"Wait, Jonny, you said some of these men were always ahead of the curve when it came to business investments."

"Yeah, they jumped just ahead of each major fall of an industry and rode the coat tails of the next big thing to triple their money.

"And triple their power."

"Yeah, I guess."

"You mentioned politicians."

"Yeah?"

"Well, it was shortly after this expedition," he said pointing at the papers, "that we saw major changes in your country's health care system, changes to how drugs were promoted, how they were prescribed."

"What are you saying Tumelo? Are you saying--"

"Prescription drugs, medicine, insurance... that's big business my friend."

"Let's look at that list."

"All right, other than Ralph anyone here who you think would be going down that road? You know someone looking to be just ahead of the curve, someone with an interest in the affairs of such industry. After all, if you had a rare cure no matter how you intended to use it or the knowledge of it, I'm sure you'd have power and money in it too."

"Of course! Jerry Zhang, actually it's Gerald Zhang."

"Should I know him?"

"Zhanger Enterprises."

"Zhanger Enterprises? As in Zhanger Pharmaceuticals that developed the pills that helped regenerate specific areas in response to ailments? White blood cell regeneration, cartilage regeneration, and so on? They were part of a bio-genesis program sports doctors used to help athletes heal and return to play faster right?"

"Yes, yes and yes. You got it, that's the one. But, those were ongoing projects and solutions that still required repeated care though, not cures."

"Exactly, if you didn't continue to get maintenance visits and increased dosage over time you could actually get worse. Or in other cases, yes you were all better but it wasn't permanent, so if you got hurt again you knew right where to go so you could get back on the field, the court or whatever the case might be. Or at least that's how I've heard the stories go. You know me Tumelo."

"Yes. I know you know folks who might tell those stories. I know they might be close enough to the top to be legit and I know that's the one business you never worked with. Is that why?"

"Is that why I don't know more about some of these men, some of the richest men in the world? Yes and no. Yes, I always keep those types close enough to me so I can find out what I need when I need it. No, I didn't speak much to it or work within the realms of the information I received to influence my decisions. Let me make a call. I know someone who can get us real close to Mr. Zhang himself. Maybe we'll even have a meeting morning after tomorrow."

"The Texan?"

"The Texan." Jonathan said with what resembled a smile.

**

"Bill here! This better be important, you're interrupting an intimate moment."

"Bill."

"Jon? Is that you my boy?"

"Yes. I need a favor. You said you were having a moment. Should I call back?"

"First of all my intimate moment was a three way with a chicken and a pig." After a couple seconds of silence Bill spoke up again. "I'm having my eggs and bacon Jon!"

They both bellowed in laughter and for a moment the mood

was lightened. Then as they came down from the laughter Bill continued.

"Cashing in on that Dollar Menu? A chain of 'Jonny's Burgers' 'Big John's Diner', what's it gonna be?"

"None of that, I'll tell you what, you help me with this and let's just consider it a fair trade with less overhead and investment."

"Hmm, that usually means less return."

"Not this time, Bill. This is life giving. It's not money I'm interested in."

"What's happening Jon? What's happened? Are you in trouble, are you sick. Name it, I'll get the best Doctors, I'll send my jet, I'll--"

"--Bill, it's Charity. It's her heart. It's failing."

"I'll line up the best Cardiologist, Cardiothoracic, and Cardiovascular Surgeons in the world. Remember I'm an older man who lives on meat. I've got these folks on speed dial." Though he said it with a chuckle it was clear he was not joking and really did have such professionals on call.

"It's more complicated than that. I know what we need to do, but I need to get to someone to get what we need."

"You keep saying what, more than who? It's not a doctor you seek. What or what and who is it?"

"We need time Bill. To buy that time, we need a serum. That serum is made up in part of a very rare berry that can typically be only found in a part of the Tanzanian rain forest."

"So, let's go."

"Bill, I've already been. We can't get it, not for many, many months still. It only grows during certain times of the year."

"So what's your plan?"

"Gerald Zhang."

"Jerry? How's this connect to him?"

"Bill, really? Stop and think about it."

"Jon, you're really getting in deep here. This ain't the mob, it isn't simple and cut and dry, these kinds of men, they're part of a kind of syndicate. I don't think you want to involve yourself with them. Not to mention, if they're into something, I can guarantee you every worldwide government agency is waiting to pounce."

"They're after them?"

Yeah, they want their piece. Did you think phone taps were invented to catch people and put them away? Hell no, I remember when JFK was shot. Everyone thought it was about JFK and Oswald and Ruby. It wasn't about any of those guys. The race for immortality goes back before today's technology race, the oil boom or the space race. It goes back to the beginning of time.

The Kennedy family was some of the first to jump in the race for manipulated cell regeneration and healing formulas. That shot was intended for him but not in the head. Fact is, an employee who saw Oswald walk by with his suspiciously large bag walked up just before those shot were fired and tried to shake him. It rushed the shots.

Ruby didn't kill Oswald out of fear that he would reveal that it was an assassination attempt. You see Oswald didn't succeed. He failed! A shot meant for an arm or another area of the body hit him in a place that no type of drug or regeneration biogenetic manipulation could have revived him and saved him either, by offsetting the effect of the bullet or in post-impact surgery. They couldn't let Oswald live after such failure! Imagine if it had worked. The power of a man, a President to not only survive being shot and nearly killed but return stronger! It's been going on for generations Jon. Everybody loved Reagan didn't they? Imagine the power of an Army with that kind of knowledge behind it"

"Wow, Bill."

"Jon, are you really at all surprised? This has been the objective of Man since the beginning of time I tell ya. Jon, do you remember how the serpent tempted Adam and Eve? Did you ever read about how it all began?"

"No, Bill, I don't understand what this has to do with--"

"Jon, I respect you and I usually let you cut me off but this is my turn. Jon, he said they could be like God. That's how he got them to eat it."

"Eat what?"

"Eat the fruit of the tree."

"What tree? Bill, I've never been a religious man."

"Hell Jon, you don't have to be religious to know the story. The tree! The Tree of Good and Evil, the Tree of Knowledge, the tree that held all the secrets to what God knew! If we knew, it would be to our ruin so he gave them one command. ONE JON! Don't eat of that fruit, but we couldn't resist it. We couldn't resist knowing."

"I don't understand."

"They'll never stop… We will never stop seeking that knowledge. Man will never stop seeking how they can be equal with God. That starts with immortality. That starts with finding a way to beat death. You can't be equal with God until you've beaten death. It was the serpent's promise then and it's the lie of a promise that keeps being made to men of power today. Not by living eternity in heaven but by living eternally right here on Earth having all power, all control over one's life. Adam was the first man of power and he couldn't resist it either. Zhang and so many are no different except one thing. See, these guys are different because they think long term."

Jonathan shook his head and let Bill continue with his rant.

"This has been going on for generations like I said. It didn't start with Zhang and it likely won't end with him, cause even if he's figured it out or if he and the men he's collaborated with have, you see, then it's survival of the fittest. It goes from having eternal life to killing off anyone who has such capability so that only one can be in ultimate control of such power.

This is the vampire syndrome at its highest level. Take from those who can easily be forgotten to heal and prolong the life of those at the top of the food chain. Yes, you know what I speak of don't you. All those vampire movies and TV shows sure became real popular as we gave our children more vaccinations and came up with a name for every little thing that seem to simply show human imperfections."

"Bill, that… that explains so much."

"Doesn't it? When someone's a patient you just get a Doctor to prescribe this or that and introduce it to their body and bam! There's your test subject."

"Bill. I just want to find out if he's growing any of these berries, if he is still seeking a way to rejuvenate cells with it. If he's growing them somewhere, I'll do anything for just a few of them."

"Be careful Jon. Never say you'll do anything. Be smart. Start with letting me probe a little into the matter. Be standing by.

We'll have a way to call you in, if in fact he reveals anything. Be at my office day after tomorrow, in the morning. I'll have a courier bring you security badges tonight for your friends, just in case. I'm guessing you still have yours." He didn't wait for Jonathan's answer. "Do you have anyone who can help with Charity? I don't know if you want her here with you, but I know you want her close, I know you are taking it on personally to insure her safety."

"By morning I will. I'll see you then. Thank you Bill."

"Jon, one more thing. What is it called?"

"What?"

"The berry Jon, what is it called?"

"The Cincaberry, or some refer to it as gundi karanga. It oozes a substance that meshes with our bodies' tissue and even the materials such as the heart or veins wherever it is placed with the proper combination and radiation and it attaches and seals while the other parts of the serum help it repair and re-grow and strengthen, healing whatever it is introduced to. But it wasn't permanent seven years ago and it may not be able to be made permanent but we need it to try or at the least to buy more time for a longer term fix. I have the people who know."

"I'm listening."

"I, I think that's enough. I think also they are calling for our flight to board. I'll see you day after tomorrow."

Jon got up and met back up with Tumelo and Charity, they headed for the plane.

**

A man sat in the Dubai airport on his cell phone. "I just overheard a man talking about Zhang. Yes and he mentioned the Cincaberry. I'm not sure what it means but we may want to keep an eye on Mr. Zhang and heighten security these next few days until we see if anything else surfaces."

"Where are you?" the voice on the other side of the line echoed in his ear.

"I'm in Dubai."

"Where is he going?"

"I don't know. I was stepping away when I over heard Zhang's name and didn't think much of it, but when I sat back down he was hanging up and rushing off. A lot of people talk about a lot of things you know."

"If you see him, if you find out where he is headed. Let us know. Zhang has a meeting in St. Louis tomorrow. Do you see any US Flights there? "

Just before he glanced toward the screen the departures refreshed. Dallas dropped off as it had just finished the last call for boarding and the door had closed.

The man responded, "I only see one to L.A. and it probably connects to various US Cities. I'll try to get on it."

"No, you're right, there's always talk of big corporations and those at the top. You stay in Dubai. Let's wait and see if anything unfolds. It is good that you called."

**

On the plane, Jonathan, Charity, and Tumelo sat together as the plane took off.

"Sixteen hours and we better be prepared. Who knows where our journey takes us next."

"What is next then?" Tumelo asked Jonathan without making any eye contact as if speaking to the chair in front of him.

"Well, Bill was right about one thing. I need someone to help me watch Charity."

"You know you can trust me, don't you?" Tumelo looked at Jonathan as to question a concern that he did not in fact trust him.

"Friend, I do, but I need you at my side. You have many gifts but I need someone who would protect her with their life. Protect it as I would, someone whose job has been to protect packages of all kinds from the hands of all kinds, a messenger."

**

"Woo hoo!" William's chest jumped as his lungs tried their best to inhale, " this 'Old man' has still got it better than all these kids"

Bicycle by The Who rang from his phone in between breaths. "Yeah this is the messenger. Speak to me!"

"William, it's Jon. Don't stop riding. Head straight for the seven train and head out to La Guardia. I'm sure you know you can ride over from Junction Boulevard. Catch the next flight to DFW. You'll have a room at the Hyatt Downtown the first night at least. We'll be arriving in exactly sixteen hours. When you get there buy anything you need. Use cash, oh, and text me a number."

"Jon…"

"William, one more thing. Clear your calendar."

"Jon… I need to know one thing."

He screeched to a halt on a quiet Upper West side block, "What kind of package is it?"

"Charity."

"Strange. Usually my services aren't needed for non-profits."

"No William. It's Charity."

"I'm not who you need."

"Then bring who I need. Then, that is the messenger service I am in need of."

"No problem, I'll just make a stop in Flushing before I catch that flight. I know an excellent nanny."

He looked over, Tumelo nodded his head, and then he looked toward Charity, who had fallen asleep. He would tell her when she woke up. Right now, he figured this was the best time to rest. Can't do much else from thirty thousand feet in the air, he thought.

He turned toward Tumelo. "Each time we have to travel like this… this, this is going to be the hardest part."

"Rest Jon, this is the time for rest and you must let that be enough."

**

William was on the seven train as the doors opened, stopping at the Mets-Willets Point station.

"Man I haven't been to Flushing in a while. Well, Mets games and the US Open aside, I've forgotten how much it has to offer."

Looking out over Flushing Meadows Park he remembered when he lived in the area for a short time after first deciding to be a bike messenger. The park was his training ground for much of his bike skills and he grinned as he recalled a memory of his skills for meeting the ladies as well.

**

"Hi, my name's William. I was about to head into the game. You two wouldn't want to join me would you?"

Two young foreign girls sat on a bench looking up at him giggling.

"Baseball? The Mets? Yes? No?" Then he opened his messenger bag and pulled out three tickets.

One of them spoke to the other in a language he had heard but couldn't place. "I think he is serious," she said to the other.

"Well, I thought you ladies looked like you might enjoy an afternoon of baseball, hot dogs and cracker jacks." He opened his bag again about to put them back in. Inside there was a glimpse of his last tip as well as a baseball glove with a signature on it.

"Wait, yes. We'd like that, very much."

**

So, maybe it wasn't so much skill but a little bit of luck and a few dollars in my pocket, he thought, but that is where I met Shu-Ling.

He later would learn Shu meant Pure and Virtuous, and exactly how true that was of her. She lived to care for others and therefore she cared for herself first by keeping her body and mind in discipline always.

"Whoa, drifting off is bad," he threw his bike wheel into the closing door's way as the train was at it's final stop and already headed back. "Can't let that happen."

The doors re-opened and he shoved out. "Okay Shu-Ling,

where can I find you?"

He began riding the roads looking around for anything familiar. Remembering her uncle owned a restaurant nearby and preferring not to call her first, he decided he would stop in.

Locking up his bike someone approached him from behind.

"Excuse me, the owners of the restaurant really prefer that no bikes be left here." It was a familiar voice. The voice of a woman yet the voice of a youth still.

He turned to look up at her.

"William!"

"Shuli!"

"Oh, when will you stop calling me that?"

"Possibly never. I need you."

"Oh? I've heard that before."

"You know my rules Shuli, so let me rephrase that, I know a man who needs you."

"William…"

"It's his daughter."

"I'm listening."

"I've known him a long time. He's calling in every favor he has, every connection he has. It's all about her and I can only assume all the worst. I know him well, Shuli. I also know he has no one, knows no one like you. Someone who can provide the services you can provide. I fear you may be exactly what he needs."

"Why do you fear that I am what he needs? If it is, then it tells me what he's involved in. It tells me how important whatever is going on is. I do not fear for you Shuli, I fear for him, for his daughter if he does not have you."

"Can he be trusted?"

"Funny you ask as that's all he would ask about you. Of course, yes, like no man I know."

"What's the plan?"

"Dallas, tomorrow, we leave now and catch the next flight."

"I need to make arrangements."

"How much time do you need?"

"Let me get you a bowl of noodles, by the time you are done, I'll be ready." She began to walk away and he grabbed her hand. She turned quickly looking back.

"Shuli, whatever you need, if you can't bring, we can get it there."

"You know what I need. You know what it can cost."

"Shuli, whatever you need, if you can't bring it, we'll get it."

"Let me make some arrangements. You may want to make some as well." She pulled out a phone and handed it to him. "I'm sure you'll want a car. You always want a car."

Shaking his head he picked up the phone. "Mack, I need a vehicle arranged. No not New York. No not Boston or DC. Dallas. Waiting at DFW airport tomorrow mid-day would be good, earlier could be better. Dual capabilities, big and small. Payment can begin as soon as it's in place feel free to draw daily until it's returned. Yes, the usual insurance. Thanks."

Shuli, grabbed the phone from his hands, "It's Ling. I need a contact with my usual kit ready for me in Dallas. Yes, Texas. Tomorrow, message me the coordinates. You have my secure text line." She looked over at the fax machine at the restaurant. An older gentleman at the register nodded. "And, I'm going to be gone for a little while. I think I may be catching a connecting flight within 48 hours so let's just see if we can get a replacement for a few of my kids okay? Most of them are with their families on vacations right now but it's always good to have a few other cats lined up."

She walked up some stairs and into a room with a single light, a single window, a bed, and a chest of drawers. In the corner what many might think a coat rack was actually a wooden dummy often used in martial arts training. She grabbed a bag, threw a variety of items that seemed completely unrelated along with a couple changes of underwear and outfits that could be crushed into a small bag and placed it over her shoulder. "Let's go."

William took a sip of the broth from his noodles pulling one more noodle into his mouth.

She was already headed out the door. He grabbed his messenger bag and chased after her.

"Wait up!" He ran out just behind her and looked toward his bike.

"Leave it. I'll make sure it's taken care of."

Suddenly a car pulled up. "Get in."

"Don't you need to tell the driver..."

"He already knows."

The driver looked over his shoulder and William realized it was the same older man that had been standing at the register.

"Make sure his bike is brought in and kept safe until we return. And watch the fax machine. You know in case you need to send me any messages that might come across."

"Fax machine? Really?"

She gave a tilt of the head and looked over at him as they sped along the road to the airport. "So where are we staying?"

"Downtown at the Hyatt, I have a room waiting."

"Do I have a room waiting?"

"You can, or at least I hope you can." He grabbed his phone making the call, "Yes this is Mr. William Jones I have a reservation. Can I add an adjoining room? Can I add a room anywhere? I can upgrade to one of your suites for added space?" He looked her way. She sighed then nodded. "Okay, yes, please. We'll be on our flight shortly and there in about five hours. Oh, he has the only other suite of this kind, well yes that is perfect. Thank you."

The two arrived and rushed through the airport protocol and shortly after they sat down and settled in on the plane as it took off.

Shuli turned to William. "So, what do you know?"

"Not much. I transported a small package for him recently. I know he has a daughter he adopted about seven years ago as I remember. He loves her. He used to be quite the antithesis of any sort of dad figure more than you could imagine but then he just sort of became this new man when she entered his life. From the moment he saw her, well as he described it, it was a sort of re-birth. Everything he was, was there but in the past and he just decided he wanted to take a new path and see where a new journey might take him."

"Hmm, people don't change Will."

"Usually I'd agree, but I saw it with my own eyes. Money, women, cars, clubs and nothing but good times and well now the only girl in his life is his little girl and the only club he belongs to is

NYC Dads. He still loves a nice car but he sold all but two. His favorite collectable and the one he actually uses regularly. He helps others make money and so he has plenty but it doesn't consume him. I'd dare say he loses half of what he used to make employing others to make it for his clients and him now. He just oversees things and trains them, makes sure his clients are cared for."

"She must be something special."

"She must be."

"Have you ever met her?"

"No, just never had to be in the same place at the same time I guess. I've only seen photos.'

"Have you slept?"

"I'm sorry, what?"

"Sleep, we should sleep. I have a feeling we won't be getting much once we get there."

"I can't argue that."

**

Charity awoke and leaned over on her dad. He had drifted off but awoke when he felt her on his arm and the embrace of his arm by her hands as she turned and snuggled up against him with the arms of the seats up. "Dad, how far is it?"

"Let me check? Looks like a few more hours still. Wow, we slept for a while."

"Dad, you need to feel okay leaving me alone."

"Peanut, I can't."

"Dad, you can't expect to keep me safe and save me. At some point you have to risk one to do the other. Which is it going to be?"

"I have someone coming."

"Who?"

"The messenger?"

"Great! A bodyguard."

"No, I think he's bringing a nanny."

"Great! A babysitter. Can't I just hang out with Tumelo? Or can't I just stay in a hotel room? You know, by myself, with room service, food, and a big TV with a remote control? Seriously,

I'll be okay."

"Sure and you'll be even more okay if you have a bodyguard and a babysitter."

They traded snide grins. Charity jumps in with the next comment. "I hope they're fun."

"Oh, don't worry. I'm sure they'll be plenty of fun. Speaking of fun, why don't we play some cards to help pass the time?"

He pulled out a deck of cards and immediately a smile came to Charity's face.

Chapter 14 – The Chase Turns

Flight 1493 from Dubai has arrived to our final destination, Dallas/Fort Worth. Whether Dallas/Fort Worth be your final destination or if you are connecting to a domestic flight or other form of transportation to your final destination we'd like to thank you for flying International Airlines.

"Well, that's stop two of our journey."

"Yep, how many more stops do you think there could be dad?"

"I wish I had an answer for you, best I can say is, as many as it takes Peanut. If it's too much, let me know, if it gets to be too much we'll make other arrangements but only if we have to."

"No, I'm okay."

"All right, I don't know about you guys but after all that sitting and sleeping the last thing I want is a chair or even a bed. Anyone hungry? Maybe hit up something where we can walk a little?"

"Yeah, that sounds great Jon." Tumelo said after a yawn.

"Yes!" Charity responded with enthusiasm.

They headed for the car rental counter. "Yes, I have a reservation."

"Name?"

"Tumelo Le Roux"

"Ah, here it is, we have a full size premium for you. It's a Grey Cadillac. Nathan here will be happy to escort you to the vehicle and see that is it is fueled and ready for your use along with any other special needs you may have."

"Thank you." Tumelo responded as he received the keys from the agent and followed the young man outside.

"Sir, this is our newest model. It should have everything you need for your trip." He opened each door, the hood and the trunk as they stepped up to the vehicle.

Tumelo walked around it examining quickly for minor things others might miss. He then leaned forward speaking a language that sounded like a strange mix of Russian dialects

Jonathan couldn't quite place. Nathan responded with a nod. Then Jonathan watched as Tumelo extended his hand shaking Nathan's and it was clear by the young man's smile, which followed, that there was an exchange.

"Here Charity, let me have your bag."

"Yes, let's each put ours in the car and give me just a moment however, before getting in."

"Anything I should know Tumelo?"

"Oh, you know me Jon, I am versed in many languages. Let's just say I need to have a little talk with the car once our bags are inside. It... speaks a language of its own."

"Oh really?"

"Oh Jon, I, like you, now have what I need available to me in every major city in the world. Especially big conference cities like Dallas where a translator's service is often needed."

Tumelo slid a Bluetooth earpiece into his ear and pulled the keys out touching a button.

"Ignition" Tumelo shouted commands

The car started

"Scan"

Vehicle is clear of any potential hazards

"System Check"

All systems go weight ratio forty – sixty. It is suggested weight be added or shifted to the rear passenger seat to adjust for optimum comfort and handling.

"You heard the lady, Charity please sit behind your dad. So, where would you like to go? I know a great little South American inspired coffee shop on the north side of the city, open all night so we can stay as long as we'd like and the food is good too. Pretty eclectic mix of people as well, you may find yourself feeling like you're right back in the village depending on the clientele of the night."

"Sounds good Tumelo, let's go."

"Whoa! What is this guy thinking? We're just pulling out of the rental lot."

"Careful Tumelo, that's a straight black Suburban. And, it doesn't look like it's the friendly type if you know what I mean."

"I do." Quickly he touched a few buttons on the vehicle which snapped a couple quick photos with the camera built into the mirror.

"Scan."

Scan complete. Rental vehicle. Registered to Elite Lease and Rental.

"They aren't moving dad? Why aren't they moving?"

"Tint windows!" Tumelo commanded the car.

The windows darken. "Great someone is getting out. Jonathan, did you see anyone following us? Do you think someone knows we're here?"

"I don't know who."

"There's someone else. Two of them."

Heads down they walked up, then slowly they looked up.

"Tumelo, can you reduce the tint?"

"Reduce Tint twenty percent."

"I can't believe it. Our timing must be perfect. Wait, the door is locked."

"Jonathan, you know them?"

"I know him. I'm guessing that's a friend as well."

"Are you sure?"

"Well, let's try the easy way. Can you cover me if needed?"

"Sure, but let me, you stay with Charity."

"Too late, you're behind the wheel. You know what to do."

"Passenger door, disengage."

"Thank you." Jonathan opened the door and stepped out. "William!"

"I knew it was you."

"How?"

"As we were loading up..." William points toward a mirror posted to a concrete column behind him. "I saw you loading up in the mirror. I almost missed you but thought I'd make a dramatic appearance instead of picking up the phone. Plus, and it's clear by the hmm, one, two, three people you've brought in now, that we're going to go through plenty of phones on this adventure. Glad I came prepared."

He raised a bag and opened it up. Lined like ammunition on the inside were multiple prepaid phones and accessories.

"Prepared as always I see." Jonathan smiled.

"It's why you hired me."

"That's because you're the best messenger I ever met."

"Being prepared is why I'm the best messenger you ever met."

"Fair enough, who's the friend? I'm assuming someone we can trust."

"Jonathan, this is the nanny. Shu-Ling, this is Jonathan Harris, the man I've been telling you about."

"Good to meet you." She followed with a bow.

Jonathan responded in the same way then she extended her hand to greet him with respect as well, and they shook.

"Where's the girl?"

"A bit direct, don't you think?" He said looking at William.

"I said you could trust her. I always believe direct people are trustworthy people.

"I'm here to help watch a girl. I thought it might be nice to get to know her. Seemed reasonable."

"Fair enough, we're about to get coffee and a bite to eat."

"A South American place, north of town, right?"

"Yeah, how'd you know?"

"I read lips."

"From the mirror?"

"I've worked with deaf children. It's a good skill to have."

"All right, so do you know where it's at?"

"We'll follow you."

The two vehicles pulled out and about 20 minutes later they pulled into the café parking lot.

"Tumelo, this is William he used to be the best bike messenger in all of New York."

"Used to be?" William said sounding a bit offended.

"Well, you moved on, got that sweet ride of yours."

"I still ride a bike, you know me."

"Yep, the thrill of the bike runs deep in your blood."

"Good to meet you Tumelo. What do you do?"

"I'm a translator. I speak multiple languages fluently and many more conversationally enough to get by around the world."

"This is Shu-Ling."

"Good to meet you. you're the nanny?"

"Yes, and this is Charity I assume. Hi sweetie. It's very nice to meet you."

"Thanks. I love your hair! Blue on one side, burgundy on the other."

"I like to have fun. Do you like to have fun?"

"Yeah!"

"Do you like sports?"

"I love 'em but I love dressing up and dancing and--"

"We're going to have a good time you and me. So, are we hanging out outside here guys or are we going to get this girl a piece of that giant cake in there and have some coffee. Milk, for you sweetie."

'Of course!" Charity responded. Then looking up at her dad, "I like her..."

"I think I do too. So, do we talk business or do we just enjoy the night. What do you think Charity?"

"I think we just have some fun!"

"Me too. Family-style ordering tonight? Everyone order something different and be ready to share! It's on me. I think I can definitely call this a business dinner! Seems more than anything this is a good time for us to all just get to know each other. Tumelo, remember that time I had the guy come into the office and speak Romulan, and you looked so baffled by the fact you didn't recognize it."

"That was not right man, had you at least had him speak Klingon I would have had a chance! You know after that, I studied multiple 'made up' Sci-Fi related languages. You know just in case I ran into an Ewok, an Elf or whatever."

"I speak Elvish, that is if you're referring to how Elvis used to talk? Thankya Thankya very much..."

"Oh man," Charity placed a palm on her face and smiled.

"Wow. Jonathan you are now the official Dad I've been waiting to see you become."

"What?" Jonathan said laughing, everyone joined in.

"It's the coffee..."

"What about you William, what's your best story?"

"The taxi and the President."

"The taxi and the President?" everyone asked

simultaneously.

"One time I had a package I needed to get somewhere on time and I had no time for any mistakes. It was for a high profile client. I go out to jump on my bike and noticed someone had hit my front rim, so I open the brakes and take off, no more than 2 minutes down 14th St and I get a flat as I head for the Hudson River Bikeway to fly up town. I go for my extra tube and nothing, I look over and the old bike shop that used to be on that block had closed and relocated."

"What did you do?" Charity asked.

"Shaking my head I look up and think, I'm going to have to call a cab. There is no way I'm making it up town in the next few minutes as I check my watch. Then I look over and from across the street walking out of the Salvation Army in an obviously used suit is a man surely near homeless but having just received this suit he was the spitting image of the President, George Bush Senior!"

"No way!" Charity said.

"You didn't." Tumelo followed.

"I threw my ear piece in, grabbed a suit jacket I had in bag and threw it over my tore up white t-shirt. I was supposed to go out later that night, pulled the rolled up jeans down, switched shoes and put my earpiece in."

"What happened next?" Charity chimed in excited to hear more.

"What happened next, was that I ran across the street told the man, I needed him for a stunt and it was fifty bucks for him if he went along with me. Plus cab fare to wherever in Manhattan he needed to go.

He just said okay, sure. Hey, some of the best actors in New York are homeless."

"And some of the homeless folks I know in New York are definitely great actors." Jonathan said.

"Exactly, Jon. So, I hailed a taxi. I told him the former President was in town and pointed to two limos down the road. Told the guy one was a decoy and the other had broken down. We needed to get him up town in 10 minutes or less."

"No way!" Charity was loving every second of the story.

"Yep, Lucky for me I got a pretty new taxi driver. Fresh off the boat!"

"Did you make it?"

"I always make it."

"Was it worth it?"

Shu-Ling jumped in. "Of course it was. It's always worth it."

"She's right, and it was."

"Who was the client?"

With no response from the messenger all eyes slowly turn to Jonathan.

"What? It was important; I made sure he and the homeless man were well taken care of."

The stares hold. "I'm serious, remember those late night guys who impersonated the President? Well, let's just say that guy isn't homeless any more. Sometimes you're in the right place at the right time. Sometimes things work out for a reason."

Everyone broke out into laughter. Shaking their heads and making a scene at a time of night where everyone just assumed if it hadn't been for the kid at the table they'd all just come from the bars.

As the laughter died down, there was a long lull around the table. Then Jonathan looked up. "Right time, right place, that's what this whole thing is about."

"What are you talking about Jon?" Tumelo asked.

"I don't know. It's just that when I said that, something clicked. I mean, even when we were in the forest, they said you could only find the Cinca at a certain time in only certain places. All this is about getting to the right place at the right time."

"And, do you think we're in the right place at the right time?"

"I hope so William. I hope so. I mean, if nothing else, I think we're close. I think we're on the right track. We just have to keep following the signs we're given. We should get some rest thought. In the next 24 hours I hope to find out more."

"Let's rest, but maybe we can meet up downstairs at the hotel around 10 or so for some brunch if you guys are up for it."

"Yeah, let's do that. Then we can make a plan and I can follow up with my contact as well."

"What if we're up before that? Want us just to wait."

"Your choice. If you're eager, message me, I'm happy to meet up prior and talk." He called for the waitress, "Check please."

Then he continued talking to the group, "Otherwise, everyone have a safe drive back and sleep well. In a little over 24 hours I'm not sure if we'll be chasing them or if we'll be the ones being chased. All depends on how much truth there is to the conspiracy blogs and papers and so on."

They exchanged pleasantries and said good night. Each with a touch of love toward Charity whether a hug or a blowing of a kiss but Shu-Ling got down, looked at her then picked her up on a chair staring her eye to eye. "Charity, you have to know something. Once you're in my care, our lives are not separate. We are one. Your life... is my life." She put her right hand on Charity's chest then with her left hand took Charity's right hand and laid it over hers. "Our hearts beat together. We will share one another's breath. We will see through the other's eyes. I am yours and I will defend and protect you as so."

In awe over her sincerity in that moment everyone just stopped in silence. Charity dropped a single tear and wrapped her arms around her.

Then each turned toward her one by one as they walk out and gave her a nod, letting her know, they each were there in unity for one reason, to save her life and defeat whatever it is that had begun happening inside her.

**

"Dad, I can't sleep."

"Everything all right?"

"Yeah, I just can't sleep."

"Wanna watch some TV?"

"Not really."

"Okay, well honey its three o'clock in the morning."

"I know, I just, I feel like I have all this energy."

"Nervous?"

"Nope."

"Excited?"

"No I don't think it's that. I don't know what it is."

"Well, it's okay. Do you want to take a little walk around the hotel?"

"Can we?"

"Sure, you know it has a roof top and it's such a nice night we could go up and take a look around the city."

"That's sounds good. Let me change."

"Put your shoes on. Let's go up in our PJs, it's okay."

"Okay, yay!"

"Dad, sorry I'm keeping you up."

"Sweetie you're never keeping me up."

As they exit out onto the recreation roof top area, Charity ran out. "Wow it's beautiful. I really love that building with green lights on it."

"Yep, pretty huh?"

"Yep. It's like the lights go on forever."

"Let's walk." The two walk and talk for a short time. "How are you feeling?"

"Better, I think I'm ready to get some rest."

"All right, let's go."

A beep rang as soon as they walked into the room, "Dad, is that your phone?"

"Yeah, I wonder who it could be." Chuckling, "You're not the only one up late." He showed her the phone.

"Ah, Ms. Ruth! Let me send her a message."

Hi Miss Ruth, it's me Charity. We just took a night walk on the hotel roof. I'm doing great!

"Nice honey."

"Let's get some rest."

He added a message to Ruth.

It's Jon. We're just lying back down. Charity couldn't sleep. Did you want to talk?

Ruth: I just wanted to check on you guys and see how things were going.

Jon: It's good and we have a good team here with her best interest in mind.

Ruth: Okay, don't forget about me.

Jon: Ruth, I could never

Ruth: No I mean, don't forget I may have resources here that can help you wherever you go.

Jon: Of course, you know I'm just careful about what I ask for.

Ruth: Ask for anything and be careful.

Jon: Okay, goodnight

Ruth: Goodnight

**

"How is she doing?" Charity asked while yawning.

"Charity, she's doing fine." Tilting his head taking a moment to think, "Get some rest. Never know what tomorrow may bring."

"Okay daddy, good night."

No sooner did Jonathan relax and fall into a deep sleep than he got another text message. Shrugging it off, tired from the need of rest and the comfort of the king size bed, pillows, and comforter that only the nicest hotels provided, he rolled over.

The sun began to rise and the light sneaked through the curtains of the room. A reminder notification sound went off that a text message was waiting. Jonathan rolled over with a groan. "Oh I'm going to need some coffee… soon."

He glanced back over his shoulder to see his daughter still in a deep and peaceful sleep. With a smile she pulled a blanket up high over her chin curling up.

Then he looked at his phone and shook his head… "Of course, William, he's always the early riser."

In response he typed:
What's up?

William: Just wanted to talk shop a little and let you get to know Shu-Ling a little more.

Jon: Sounds good, coffee?

William: Your room or downstairs?

Jon: Charity is still asleep. Downstairs, 5 minutes.

William: Sounds good.

Jonathan opened up the tablet that he had been charging through the night and propped it up to use as a webcam to his phone. Syncing them through an application where he could keep an eye on Charity. He then threw on some shorts and a shirt with his shoes to go down to the coffee bar by the breakfast area in the hotel.

"Good morning guys."

"Good morning."

"So Shu wanted to let you know a little more about her credentials."

"Mr. Harrison, I'm guessing before last night you knew nothing of me?"

"You assume correctly."

"Okay, that's my cue, I'm going for a short run and I'll be back." William said stepping away from the table.

"Of course you are. Enjoy!" Jon exclaimed.

Shu-Ling continued, "Well, I grew up in a family that would take in anyone and often, well mostly, it was other children. I was the oldest however. The only thing is some of the children we took in before we came to the US had been part of an underground black market. I became very good at caring for children, understanding them, breaking down walls of fear and lifting them up and strengthening them. However, I had to be more than all of that for them. I had to be their protector while my family worked. And so I did."

"How? I mean it sounds as if, well, I'm guessing there were some people who were after these children and from the stories I've heard of these kinds of things, well they don't let a young girl stop them?"

"You're right. So, let's just say I'm creative. I found ways to slow them down, ways to throw them off the scent of that which they chased. And if necessary, I found ways to stop them for good. I say this to let you know, that I am a born protector. My great, great, grandfather is from a long line of men in India who were well... Do you know the story of the Musketeers?"

"Yes of course. All for one and one for..."

"All... and one of those men, from a similar group to those like the Musketeers, in India was my great, great grandfather. They say he received a special visit from the god, Sendan Kendatsuba. It is said that he touched my great, great grandfather and that that power of protection was passed on.

In addition to being known as a guardian of children, it was believed he was there to keep the young safe from several malicious deities."

"Why do you share all this with me?"

"I just know if someone was taking care of a child of mine or of my responsibility I'd certainly want to know who they were. Sendan Kendatsuba was much known for the use of music and illusion."

"So, I can't say I'm quite ready to see these different forms but I will say there is one part that makes me quite curious."

"I'm skilled in various weaponry and martial arts styles. I can ride an actual horse or a steel horse all the same."

"Right. But, both of the gods you mentioned have associations with music."

"Music is the first form of illusion and deception Mr. Harrison."

"How do you figure?"

"Simply consider the Mockingbird Mr. Harrison. Many after seeing my brothers, sisters, and I, and how I taught, cared for and protected them said I had been visited too. They said the goddess originally known as Sarasvata had touched me. She too was a protector of Children dating back into the Middle of the Seventh Century in China and later known as Benzaiten in Japan. They say I reminded them of her because of the various forms I took as a caretaker of children."

"Well, I'll be curious to hear you sing."

"Please do not take offense, but be wary of your wishes. If I'm singing it'll be to call on all the powers, it will be to warn, and protect. In that time, I hope your ears hear what you are meant to hear and do not fall like the many men before who have heard the instrument given to me. Consider the flute player Pan. Music can be a weapon, just a very subtle one."

"Fair enough. I know the hard rock and high-pitched guitar playing I listened to when I was young was arguably a deafening instrument."

"Sir, may I beg you to please..."

"No, my apologies. Please do not mistake my silly responses for me not hearing you or taking you seriously. I'm just a dad. I'm very glad to have you here. I feel better knowing you'll be watching over Charity. With all sincerity, thank you for coming."

"It is my honor."

"It is mine. I fully believe when the time comes my dear Artemis, you... you will more than be able to handle it."

At that moment, with his reference to the Hellenic goddess, both protector and hunter, she realized he certainly understood and they exchanged nods and then she began to laugh looking just beyond Jonathan.

Confused he turned his head to see that it was William just jogging in place as if to be waiting for a signal.

"Whew, I've been out there waiting for you guys to finish this little bonding exercise for a good ten minutes. We good?"

"Yes, we're very good. I know I have the right people for the job."

"Just as you have always been very good at finding, Jon."

"Okay I have to make a couple calls. Let's meet back down here in, say an hour?"

"That sounds good."

"Good for me as well."

"William, do you mind reaching out to Tumelo for me and letting him know?"

"Of course, what's next?"

"I'm pretty sure it'll be a meeting. I just can't tell you how that meeting is going to go or if the other party is going to welcome it."

"Understood."

**

Back in his room Jonathan got a call as he stepped out of the shower. "Bill any word?"

"Yes, Zhang will be here later today actually. I'm going to probe a little. No one knows about what you guys are looking for, do they?"

"No. I mean, not that I know of outside of our contact from the rain forest that led us to the medicine tribesmen."

"Okay, I'm going to be delicate yet still try to work it into my conversation."

"Thanks Bill. I think I'm going to show Charity around Dallas some but you can reach me anytime."

As Jonathan hung up, Charity rolled over. "Dad, who was that?"

"Just the man I'm asking to help us find what we need. How would you like to do some sightseeing until I hear back from him?"

"Sounds great!"

As they came out of the elevators downstairs his team was waiting. "So, what's first, Cowboys Stadium? Downtown Dallas? Las Colinas? Southfork?"

"What's South… Fork?" Charity worked to sputter it out.

"It's a famous ranch that used to be used in a TV Show."

"Really? Can we go?"

"I'd rather we stay a little closer to downtown honey, just in case we get a call to meet up with my client."

"Well, what's Las Colinas?"

"It's a cute little area. Has a nice little canal with water flowing through this little village type shopping area."

"That sounds nice."

"It is. Let's maybe go there and walk around. Afterward we can walk around downtown and maybe go up in Reunion tower for a nice view of the city if we have a chance."

Everyone nodded and they headed out.

Over the next few hours the group laughed and bonded with fun photos and a general good time around the Dallas area. Then while heading for Reunion Arena, shortly after having dinner in downtown Jonathan's phone rang.

Everyone suddenly stopped, as if an entire city had gone silent at the drop of a pin.

**

"Hello, Bill, how'd it go?"

"Hey Jonny Boy, how are you?"

"Bill?"

"Good, Good. Listen I have a potential new client for you."

"Oh, you do, do you?" Jonathan began to play along.

"Yes, yes, he's here with me now, you might know his name, Zhang, Gerald Zhang of Zhanger Enterprises and Zhanger Pharmaceuticals."

"Yes, of course. I've heard of them. I'm a big fan of their stock production. You may not know but they've made you quite a bit of money Bill."

"Well, let's not tell them that now." His bellowing laugh ensuing, then he continued. "I know you aren't looking for any new clients but I told him if he ever needed someone in your line you are not only a great guy, you are the ONLY guy."

"Well, thank you Bill."

"Of course, of course you know I mean it too. Well, he is here and said he's only in town one more day before he has to visit a research facility they have here in West Texas.

He was thinking maybe you guys could do a little breakfast before he heads out tomorrow, well hell, let me get him on here."

"Mr. Gerald Zhang, my financial guru Jonathan Harris, Jonny, Gerald Zhang."

A pause, as if it's a contest of ram horns to see who will speak first loses. Jonathan knew the game. He always won, however, he quickly conceded after just enough respectful moments passed. "Mr. Zhang, it is very good to speak to the man behind such a successful company."

"I have one question." Zhang moved quickly like a mercenary on a target. "Why has your group never attempted to work with us in the past? For that matter, while we were waiting I did a little research and as I see you've never worked with any clients related to pharmaceuticals. Why?"

"Mr. Zhang, with all due respect. None have asked, and in my business I can make my money and my clients more money by knowing what companies like yours do than having heads of said companies as my clients. I have to be careful of how my web is woven."

Zhang nodded with a look of agreement. "What do you like for breakfast?"

"There's a wonderful French Bistro that opens early for breakfast in Las Colinas with seating by the canal that I favor."

"Well then, a little, Eggs Benedict it is. It'll have to be short and early. How's seven sound?"

"Seven sounds great. I have a meeting mid morning as well in Tyler then may have to make my way down to Waco before close of business."

"Yes. Well, then." Immediately Zhang could not help but wonder what was happening in Tyler and Waco that he was not familiar with, a competitor maybe? "I'll see you then."

"Good day Mr. Zhang."

"Good day Mr. Harris."

Bill hung up the phone and Zhang motioned toward an interesting piece of what appeared to be Asian art behind him near a bookshelf full of books of inspiration, psychology, and communication focus. "Bill, may I ask where you got that?"

"Oh that, it was a gift."

"Quite exquisite for a gift? Nothing in exchange?"

"Oh you know, in business there's always gifts and there is always an exchange Mr. Zhang. This one is called The Watcher. I forget what she called it in Chinese."

"Chinese hmm, may I take a closer look?"

"Why of course… here let me open the shades for a little more light."

"The 6 branches represent the 6 heavenly stems of Da Liu Ren. While it appears these 4 clocks are each designed to represent a different aspect of Bazi. See, each has different carvings representing childbirth. And even here while the eye is the largest of features each of the facial features are enlarged to draw a focus to them. This reflects that while she is a watcher she watches each part of a persons face in order to see their future. Finally and appropriately she holds a bamboo cylinder in her one hand with the other hand palm up. This represents Kau Cim and Zi Wei dou shu.

Ah, she is truly beautiful. It is as if she has already read me like a book in a moment knowing my past before birth and my future beyond death." Zhang simply stopped to stand in awe respecting it too much to touch but feeling drawn to it through his understanding.

Then he shook his head and turned about to ask Bill a question, Bill jumped the gun with, "Well damn friend, all I ever got was that it has a big ass eye and that it is used it to watch everything. That's why I liked it behind me. It's as if she was the one behind me watching over me."

A little nod, and a grin appreciating Bill's comments, appreciation for what it meant to him and even a little appreciation of the Texans ignorance. Zhang then continued with his thought after reflecting. "Bill, I have to ask. Can I get the contact of the person from where you got it?"

"Tall order, after all folks who give you gifts like this... well let's say it comes often only after a tall order follows."

"I see. What is it you want?"

"Oh it's not me. It's what she may want." Bill reaches in a drawer and pulled out a card. It was a simple card with a name and a number on the front. On the back: 恐惧之美, which is Kǒngjù zhīměi or Fear Beauty.

He grinned. "Thanks Bill. It was good seeing you. Hopefully next time you come to me. And maybe I'll have something nearly as beautiful watching over me as well. Let's see how this deal works out."

"I'd like that Mr. Zhang."

Zhang left with two security guards shortly following just beyond the closed doors of his meeting with the Texan.

As they exit the building, Tumelo was nearby. "Will, are you around?"

"Always."

Suddenly an envelope dropped on the table where Tumelo was sitting outside of a coffee shop. He opened it. Four words: 'always watching, always close.'

"Nice, I got your message. Now turn those eyes toward Lamar and Elm. The trio will be headed your way. They're all yours."

As they exit a Silver Mercedes pulled up, one of the security guards got in, the other held the door watching the area and Zhang got in the back. A moment later the second security guard got in a taxi to follow them.

"An interesting way to have 2 sets of eyes but I guess it works." Tumelo pulled out a few cars back. "Where are you Will?"

Meanwhile William slipped into the chair where Tumelo had just been sitting and took a sip of his coffee. He followed with a text message.

Caramel Latte Tumelo? Really and with whip cream and sugar?

Where are you? Wait! He's drinking my coffee! He shook his head, he followed the vehicles to a hotel just outside downtown, *and they're headed for...* Mid thought his phone interrupted. *It's Will*

"Las Colinas."

"Wait, how do you do that?"

"I was just in that cab."

"Of course you were."

"And in just a moment we'll have what we need next. Jon is your girl with you?"

"Yep, and yours is on her way."

"Perfect."

The two vehicles pulled up to the Omni Mandalay Hotel.

"Amazing, I mentioned doing breakfast there tomorrow morning, and he didn't even blink. It was perfect for him because it's where he's staying. Why wouldn't he say anything? Typical."

The Mercedes stopped and Zhang waited. The taxi pulled up, the security guard paying the driver and getting out. There was a young beautiful woman running from the hotel door with a shopping bag a large hat and sunglasses toward the vehicle.

"Taxi, Taxi, wait! OMG I'm running so late, my new boss is going to kill me. It's my first day and I can't believe this is happening," she continued to mutter with a southern California accent. "I can't screw this up. It's my first fashion gig!"

Then perfectly timed, she bumped the man as he turned to head towards the door to open it for Zhang.

"Oh my... Hello."

"Excuse me?"

"Oh, nothing, I thought you were you know the big handsome Texas cowboy type I'd heard so much about."

"Not me miss."

"Well then, I guess, I'll be, oh shoot! Taxi!!!" She yelled and the driver stopped. She jumped in and the taxi pulled away.

She pulled out her phone and with a couple of taps. She saw a simple map and a green light.

"Where to miss?"

"The Galleria."

"You got it."

She sent a quick message to the team: The packages have been delivered.

Jonathan's phone rang.

"Well what do you think Jonny?"

"Bill, I think we're set for our next step."

"What if I could help you have an ace in the hole?"

"Well, I guess I'd be the one owing you from here forward."

"Nah, I'd rather do business with you then well you know. I'd just rather do business with you. He liked the statue your friend gave me."

"The Watcher?"

"Yes, that's the one. He took to it, like it was a young naked virgin in full bloom waiting for him in bed. I don't know what it was but something about it meant a hell of a lot more to him than me. He asked for her card Jonathan. I have a feeling she should be your next call."

"Thanks Bill, all right guys, back to the hotel. We have work to do. Charity, what if Shu-Ling takes you horseback riding?"

"Really?"

"Shu-Ling, that okay with you?"

"Of course! I'll have the driver circle back to meet up."

"All right sounds like a plan. Will, since you're just sitting there finishing Tumelo's coffee maybe you can grab us a little Tex-Mex on your way back to meet up?"

"Sure," shaking his head. "I guess it doesn't always pay to be the messenger."

They all laughed and headed back. Tumelo picked up Jonathan and Charity at a rendezvous point along the way and Jonathan took the chance to make a call to a woman he hadn't spoken to in a while.

"Hello, Jonathan. It's been a long time."

"Cai, I don't have much time and I need you."

"Jonathan, you wait all this time to call me after that night and it's with a desperate plea, so unmanly."

"Cai, do I need to play the game or can I just call it how it is."

"Jonathan it's never been about the game."

"Cai, you're going to get a call. The man is going to bring up The Watcher."

"The Watcher? The one I gave that man in Texas back in '08 for his help with my dad?"

"Yes. By the way, how is your dad?"

"He's fine, well, not really but we have the best doctors and wait, who is this man and why did The Watcher make him want to talk to me?"

"He was touched by it and he wanted to know who and where it had come from. Bill gave him your card.

His name is Gerald Zhang and he's staying at the Omni Mandalay Hotel in Las Colinas outside of Dallas. He leaves tomorrow morning for what I think is…Wait, Cai, I, I have to know where we stand."

"Jonathan you were always the one, always my Bowler and I your Catherine." She referred back to their shared love of the movie

'The Thomas Crown Affair.'

"Cai, we may have many a shared interests these days. The man who is going to call you is…"

She cut him off, "Zhang of Zhanger Enterprises. Yes, I know of him and about his companies work."

"I believe he is headed for a secret facility that is working on a regeneration method for quicker healing based on a berry derived from the rainforests of Tanzania."

"Oh. I love how someone always finds a new berry for quicker healing. Remember I'm Japanese. In Asia we know all about herbal healing power. If there were something like this my dad would have already been bouncing back. After all, I believe it's why he's still alive. It isn't your so-called American Doctors that is helping him."

"Cai, I need a minute."

They pulled up to the hotel, Jonathan clearly emotional; he could see Shu-Ling walking over.

"Should I take the car, the SUV or my bike?"

"I'd say the SUV, never know which roads you may end up on. Charity go with Shu-Ling, get changed into some jeans and you guys go have fun. Make sure to take lots of pictures okay?"

"Okay dad, you sure?"

"Yep, and Shu-Ling, please, buy you both a nice cowgirl hat and have a good time?"

"Yes Mr. Harris, we sure will."

As they walked away, Jonathan remained in the car, closed the door and put the phone back to his ear, took a deep breath. "Cai, this is real and I know it's real. My daughter is dying but didn't die at birth because this saved her. We need to help find a way to keep her from dying now."

For the first time his strength was gone and tears began to fall. "I'm scared Cai, I'm scared I'm going to lose her."

"Jonathan, do you still have her?"

"Yes Cai."

"Then do not be afraid of a future that cannot be told."

"I know Cai, thank you."

"What can I do?"

"Whatever you can."

"Fair enough. We need to get what he has in the facility we need to know if it is what you say it is and if so we need to find a way to get it for you to use. Sound about right?"

"Yes. Why is it you say it like it's simple and easy."

"I see these things the way you see making money from symbols and trends. I just see the way."

"Like the watcher?"

"Well, you might say that, but I wouldn't dare."

"Expect a call back in the next 12 hours."

"Okay, I will."

**

"Jon, you okay?"

"Yeah Tumelo, thanks."

"Who was that?"

"Do you ever remember me telling you about the one fish I couldn't seem to catch but instead always found a way to not only catch me but would remove the hook, put it in me then remove it as if to teach me a lesson and throw me back in the water so I couldn't forget her?"

"Yeah, that's not exactly the kind of analogy a man forgets about another man's experience with a woman."

"Well, that's her."

"Oh." After a moment of silence, Tumelo spoke up again. "Look, there's Will, let's go have some Tex-Mex!"

"Yeah, let's do that."

Chapter 15 – A Way In

A few hours later, Cai was surprised she hadn't gotten a call and knowing she needed to move, decided to get aggressive.

She made a quick call.

"Omni Mandalay."

"Yes, I need to get a message to a Mr. Gerald Zhang."

"Yes Ma'am, let me check for him."

"Oh, you won't find him on your list but you tell the men in black suits standing with ear pieces that they need to get him a message."

"Ma'am… I don't believe we can do that."

"Of course."

"Oh wait, miss we do have a business listed here, a representative of Zhanger Enterprises? Would there be a connection?"

"Yes, perfect. Thank you."

"Please hold."

"Hello?"

"Yes, I'd like to speak with Mr. Zhang."

"Who is this?"

"Tell him it's Kǒngjù Zhīměi, he has my number."

The man walked out his door, took a turn and knocked, "Yes?"

"Kǒngjù Zhīměi called; she said you have her number."

"Yes, indeed I do." The man said without looking up at the assistant.

**

"Hello, Kǒngjù Zhīměi."

"This is Gerald Zhang."

"Hello Mr. Zhang. I heard my card had been passed on. I was only surprised that if you really knew about The Watcher you didn't call me."

"Oh, but I was going to call. It is much to my surprise you have called me."

"I think we may each have something the other wants."

"Oh?"

"Yes, I have the original and each of the pieces that accompany it."

"Oh?"

"Yes, maybe we could do a bit of a, shall I say, gift exchange?"

"What exactly could I give someone who clearly already has everything?"

"Life. An extension on life to be exact. My father's aging quite rapidly it seems these days. I've heard your company might have something in the works that could help him. His cells aren't repairing as fast as they need to be for the drugs they are giving him to work. We've tried so much Mr. Zhang."

"Oh Miss…" Cai did not respond. "Miss we all die."

"Hmm, yes…"

"But, say I was able to get you something that could help him just enough for him to have a little more time. I can't give you life but I can give you time, at least a little more time. Would that still hold enough value for such a gift exchange?"

"Yes, yes it would but I want some for me, let's call it an emergency back up supply. After all, things do happen."

"Well, shipping can be a problem."

"Oh, not to worry. I'll send you my gift complete with a return package pre-labeled for your convenience."

"Okay, I'll be looking forward to it. When can I expect it?"

"My collection is stored stateside. You will have it tomorrow afternoon. Where should I send it?"

"You can send it to my office."

"Will you be at your office tomorrow afternoon?"

Mr. Zhang paused, thinking on how to respond, "No."

"Well, then I'd strongly suggest you give me an address where you will be because I would expect you to respond in the same way as I have to you, with respect to business and urgency in the highest manner."

"Yes. However, there is no address I can give you. Take

note…" Zhang spoke a few numbers quickly.

"Done."

"Good."

**

A few moments later, Jonathan's phone rang. "Hello."

"It's Cai, do you have anyone who can pull off the Trojan horse tomorrow?"

"Seriously?"

"Yep. It's old fashioned but it works so well."

"Sure, I think I have the right people for the job."

"There will be a crate arriving at DFW airport tomorrow morning via my private transporting company. I'll have someone to unload it and bring it through security. There is a cargo delivery building that is shared amongst importers like me.

I'll send you all the details. I need you to have a driver in a truck there to pick it up. A delivery van of some sort should work. It's large and inside will be some original pieces of work. One of them will be hollow. She or he should hide inside that piece.

Once inside she has to find out how to survive for 24 hours then the truck should return for pick up, to pick up said hollow piece. It's going to be sent 'return to sender'."

"I'll set it up."

"Be careful Jonathan. And make sure whoever is with you is so as well."

"We'll talk tomorrow." He hung up and turned to Tumelo.

"Tumelo, it looks like we may have a game plan and we made need Shu for it."

He tapped his phone. "Will, let's meet somewhere for a bit, hungry?"

They pulled off and met up at a quiet café. After he explained the plan, Will was the first to jump in. "Jonathan that all sounds great, but I have one question. What does she do once she's inside?"

"She waits."

"And, what if they open the container?"

"I'm sure she can handle herself."

"Jonathan," Tumelo added, "you're not thinking man. Seriously Jon, I get it but if it goes as planned I'm guessing this hollow piece becomes the so-called return package she mentioned to Zhang. He puts the items in and we pick it up next day. If this is his Cincaberry garden of sorts, then it sounds like we'll have what we need right then."

"If not then we can wait, see what his next steps are and if we need to get in we look at it then." Jonathan finished.

"How are we going to get in?" Tumelo asked.

"I am a messenger. There is always someone expecting a message or someone who is in desperate need of receiving one. We just play to that."

"Okay guys. You're right." Jonathan said shaking his head.

"None the less," Will continued, "she should join us. Tumelo can ride up front and she can remain in the back, in a second box so she's unseen but available. Her skills maybe useful and it keeps you away from the scene.

Also she's been seen before, at the hotel. We need to make sure she's prepared."

"Of course." Responding to a text, he lets Shu-Ling know they'll be meeting back up at the Hotel and that they have an early day the next day.

The following morning Jonathan met briefly with Zhang. They discussed the business of Pharmaceuticals. No matter how subtle the questions and the interest about possibly taking on the financial investments for Zhanger Enterprises Jonathan couldn't squeeze anything from his counterpart. It didn't take long despite Jon's best efforts that Gerald Zhang could clearly see he despised the business of drugs, legal or not. It was clear there was no deal to be made here. The only thing that came from the breakfast was a hand shake that left both curious about why the other even took the time to meet them.

As soon as Jonathan returned from the meeting with his group he informed them that the meeting had not produced anything for them and that they would have to make the delivery and the pick up going with Cai's setup.

Just after Will and Tumelo leave the Import and Export Freight building at the airport, Tumelo speaks up to Will.

"And good, the first part of this is done."

"Jonathan, where are we going?"

"There are no instructions?"

"She didn't tell you?"

"No. She was going to send me a message but she only messaged me with information on receiving the package and getting it on the truck."

"I thought he was going to send her directions for her driver."

"Yes, that is what she said."

"Wait guys, in my business there are many ways to send a message." Will began to navigate his way around the custom box container. He noticed numbers and arrows often one would associate with the height and width of the container. "Hey Jonathan, any idea how big this thing is supposed to be?"

"From what she explained, there is a total of five pieces each about four to six feet in height and one foot wide. So packaged, maybe two or three feet wide and six or seven feet high. It seems longer than needed. That is according to these markings. Why, why not use the smallest container possible?"

"Maybe this one was lying around? Yes but it's also only about 4 feet high. One second." William brought up a GPS and began typing in the numbers until he recognized something. "I've got it!"

"What?

"How?"

Tumelo chuckled in the background. "They're coordinates Jon. 29 90 103 85. Wait these numbers look familiar… Richardson! Jonathan these are the numbers Richardson gave us.

"When, wait, the deposit you received was…"

"Yep. This guy is good. It took me a minute but this lands us west, northwest about four to six hours. We better move."

"I'll follow you." Jonathan said the moment Tumelo stopped talking.

"No."

"What do you mean no?"

"Jonathan, stay here. We don't all need to be in the same place, in case anything goes wrong."

"I'll follow behind then. At a safe distance, of course."

"Look, I know there is no deterring you but here is what we're going to do. We'll watch for a location on the way where you can stop off. Otherwise you get no closer than that."

"Tumelo, I want to argue with you but you're right."

"We're already on our way. Give us no less than 1 hour before you even begin to follow our signal. I'll turn on the truck tag in twenty to thirty minutes."

"Okay. Charity, let's go get some breakfast."

"Sounds good!" she said with a smile.

**

Over breakfast Jonathan picked up his phone. "That's it. A text should be coming shortly. How's your breakfast?"

"Good."

"How was horse back riding with Shu-Ling?"

"Oh, it was amazing! Didn't I tell you?"

"No sweetie, I think we were both a bit distracted afterward yesterday for you to go into detail."

"It was so much fun. It was a real ranch and real cowboys and everything! We even saw some cows and pigs when we were riding. So great!"

"That's awesome. I'm really glad you got to go."

"Me too, and that girl can really ride!"

"Oh yeah?"

"Yes, she really surprised me."

"Why?"

"I don't know? I guess I don't really know what a rider looks like?"

They laughed and continued to eat. A beeping from his phone interrupted them. "That should be it."

"All right dad, do we have to go?"

"Well... we... I..."

"Yes?"

"No. I guess we really don't need to."

"Then let's just wait. Is there anything else we can enjoy until they head back?"

"There's always something."

"Well let's do that." He shoots a quick message to the team, **Plans changed. We'll wait and enjoy our time.**

**

"Ok Will, we pull off here."

"Are you sure?"

"I'm positive."

"Wow, talk about secret research facility."

Half way down the road there was a large fence, gate, and security, yet no building or structure of any kind. Slowing down, they pulled up to the security speaker.

"Delivery?"

"Yes, C & I Importers, special delivery for Mr. Zhang."

"Please take the security card." Immediately a card came from a dispenser. "Keep the card and return it when you exit. To open the gate and enter wave it over the adjacent reader."

Will did so and they continued forward. "Okay, here we go."

Tumelo tapped the rear of the inside of the delivery cab two times to let Shu know they were in. As they arrived they were directed to a delivery bay for trucks. Will backed the truck against it. They opened the rear door.

They put it on a furniture mover and rolled it out into the loading dock.

"We need you to open the crate."

As they scanned the room they quickly noticed cameras and armed guards as well just beyond the men who had approached them. "There are 5 pieces."

"Yes." Tumelo walked along each, and knocked on each piece.

"Excellent. Wait here." The men called two other men to assist with rolling the crate away.

Nervous, yet, patient they waited. They began pretending to check their load and made sure all the boxes in the truck were secure though most were empty, simply filled with foam peanuts and discount store statues.

"Gentlemen, we were asked to return this piece. Mr. Zhang said thank you, but no thank you and that he'll only be keeping the four originals."

Unsure if they fully understood. Tumelo walked up. "Is he sure?" He then proceeded to knock on it much in the same way he had prior when they unloaded it and the other pieces.

"That's what he said sir. And we do not question him."

"Understood." He turned to William. "Dave, let's put it in that crate that was for tomorrow's pick up."

They popped off the top and lifted the piece up. William nearly slipped, not prepared for the weight of it.

"Dave, you gotta start working out man."

The guards snickered toward him, and William scoffed getting a look from Tumelo that said, 'keep it together.'

They lifted it up and over and slowly slid it into the crate.

"Thank you gentlemen," they put the top loosely back on top, closed the cargo door, and lock it.

Driving away, they heard some noise in the cab. "Should we stop?"

"Nope." William pulled out his phone. Bring up the app labeled: Camera 2. Now touch option: Cargo. Immediately they noticed the lid on the crate moving.

"Text her."

"Already on it!" A moment later the movement stopped.

As they pulled up to security and stopped, "please open your cargo door for inspection."

Tumelo hopped out of the truck, opened the door. They took a glance, and then compared to a photo captured from the video taken at the loading dock. "Okay, just re-insert your card to exit."

As they pulled out they took a deep breath hoping they had what they came for. They went back to the cargo camera. The lid moved and Shu-Ling came out.

She moved the statue inside the crate, twisting it when suddenly she removed the top quarter of it. Styrofoam peanuts burst out. She shined a flashlight inside. Pulling peanuts out until something fell to the floor. Quickly Shu kicked her foot out and stopped it. It was a small pharmaceutical drug container.

Curious, she continued. In addition to the peanuts, there appeared to be plastic bubble wrap and air packaging. "What'd they do, just use whatever they had lying around to fill this thing?"

As some of the air packaging pulled out a light came on.

"Hopefully that'll help her."

"There was a cargo light and you didn't think of that earlier William?"

"Hey! I'm a messenger, I was driving."

"Ah, much better, thanks guys." She looked down. One of the air bags seemed to be filled with something that appeared to be shredded leaves of some sort. "Oh boy that looks awfully like..."

As she held it up and shook it, she wondered if it's what they need or just an herb of some sort, a mix of nutty, fruity and leafy texture inside.

She gave a thumbs up as it appeared the mission was complete, at least the first mission.

A sigh of relief as night began to fall on their way back to the Dallas Metro area. About halfway back there was laughter and good music as William and Tumelo had bonded and were feeling good.

Then suddenly they looked up and saw a roadblock. "Ahh Crap!" Slamming on the breaks, they came screeching to a halt. Upon instinct William decided to hit reverse and make a change of plans. One problem.

They felt a tap to their back end. "How did we not see this coming?"

"We got comfortable."

"Well, I have a solid record of deliveries and I'm not about to end my streak like this."

"Do you have a plan?"

"William?" Tumelo looked over and William was gone.

"Get out of the Truck!"

"Sheesh, leave me high and dry."

"We're going to have to inspect your cargo. We got word you may have stolen some confidential paperwork and experimental secret drugs from Zhanger Pharmaceuticals."

"No, we have a bill of lading showing we did a drop-off and made an authorized pick-up."

"You do? Can I see that?"

"Of course, here you go sir."

"There's nothing on this."

"What?"

"Get out of the truck."

"But I swear, that's it. Maybe I grabbed the wrong paper."

"Get out of the truck before we take the door off and yank you out!"

No doubt these guys weren't kidding. He was in the middle of nowhere in the Eastern half of a dead zone in Texas where no one would find him. As far as these guys knew, that was.

**

An alert went off on the vehicle tracker. Jonathan was having dinner with Charity when he saw it. "Hmm, let's see what's happening with those guys. Looks like they stopped."

"Should we be worried dad?"

"Nah, probably just getting gas, or a snack. Let's take a look where they are. Well, maybe not. There doesn't appear to be anything for miles where they are. Maybe Tumelo needed to um…"

"Take a leak?"

"Charity!" Jonathan responded in surprise.

"Sorry dad, let me re-phrase. Take a pee-pee?"

"Better," He shook his head, "they're still in the same spot, says they've been there for a short bit. If they don't get on the move in the next 5 minutes, I'm making a call."

"I thought you could access the cameras on the truck?"

"I can but… yeah, I can." A moment later, "It's dark. Wish I had sound but I only have video. Wait, I don't see anyone in the front seat or a shadow or anything." Suddenly there was movement.

"Open the cargo door."

"Sir, I just have my packages."

"I'm sure you have packages. That's exactly what we're going to take a look at."

"Yes sir."

"Hey, if there's nothing unusual we'll write this off as a prank call by some goof just wanting to mess with Zhang or us. You know there's always some conspiracy theorist that doesn't like that spot they took there outside Amarillo."

"Amarillo?"

"Yeah, that's where you were coming from right?"

"Um, yeah, yeah. Let me open up the cargo door." All he kept thinking was, *I hope you know what you're doing back there.*

"There you go. Cargo light?"

"Sure, sure, one second, it's in the cab."

As he stepped into the cab to click the light the men climbed in and started sifting through the packages, finding classic art pieces of all kinds.

"Who do you work for?"

"C & I Importers."

"Hmm, that makes sense. Looks like some crazy Asian sculptures and such in here. Nothing else."

"These guys are clean sir. We scanned everything and found nothing." One of the other uniformed men said.

"All right. Let 'em go. Sorry to bother you but you know we gotta check these things out. Zhanger pretty much owns the governor these days. Plus Homeland is on these guys like a cowboy on a horse."

"I get it, we all got a job to do. Have a good night." As Tumelo closed the rear door there was a thud and the truck shifted.

"What was that?"

"I, I don't know?"

"Open it back up!" The men pulled back their guns at the ready.

Tumelo took a deep breath, ready for whatever was about

to happen and opened it up, but nothing new.

"Search it again!"

Tumelo tilted his head, as the men got ready to get back in when he suddenly noticed something. "Ah Man! Wait! That's one of our most prized pieces. When it was sold I was told it was priceless so don't even ask what would happen if something happened to it!"

"Excuse me?"

"Look, clearly that piece fell over, that larger skinny box there. Did you guys knock that over?"

Not remembering what was left or moved, not one of them wanting to get in trouble for damaging a 'priceless piece of art' they responded. "No, no, nope, no way."

"I saw it standing up when we got out that must've been what fell and made the noise."

"All right, let's go but if we get another call, we're pulling every piece one by one and tearing them apart."

"Okay, you just let me know who to have my boss talk to about that."

"That's easy, you tell him."

"Her."

"You tell, ahem, her to talk to Mr. Zhang."

"Who do you think made the deal? Sir, deals over pieces of art worth millions have no middlemen."

At that very moment, blinding lights overhead shone down. They couldn't tell what it was but it had impeccable timing.

"Right, I'd say it's time we were all on our way. No reason for the pawns to have to be the first to take one another out. Let's just leave that to the Kings and Queens to go one on one. What'd ya say?"

"I'd say you have excellent judgment sir."

Each of them got back in their vehicles. The light vanished and each drove away.

Tumelo dared not stop but he couldn't help but ask himself, aloud, "Where are you guys?"

Shaking his head, "They're still following me it seems. Steady. Man, William, you're the messenger. Where are you and how did you secure your package?"

Suddenly, a sliding door behind him opened up and both William and Shu-Ling fell through with a thud.

Tumelo yanked the truck slightly shocked a bit from their sudden appearance.

"Go!" William struggled to let out with the bit of breath he had. "And for God's sake, roll down the windows."

"What?"

"Roll, down, the--" William passed out.

Quickly Tumelo rolled both windows down. Still the headlights of those who had stopped him were following but it appears it had scaled down to just one car and no longer three.

"I gotta call Jonathan. Ugh, what if they put a trace on us or a bug."

He turned up the music and pulled out his phone to text him: Changed plans, two down, Abilene.

**

As soon as Jonathan got it, he made a call, "I need Dr. Samuel Brodowski."

"He's unavailable right now."

"Tell him it's Harris. He'll make himself available."

"Sir, I'm sorry."

"You will be if you don't page him, now!"

"Sir, he's on rounds."

"My name is JT Harris. Sam and I go way back. If you page him one time and he doesn't respond in two minutes I'll hang up and stop bothering you."

"Hold on Mr. Harris," the voiced sounded annoyed at Jonathan's request.

"Harris. What is it? Where are you and what's happening?"

"I need your help. I have three friends and I think something has happened to two of them and they should be in Abilene in the next twenty to thirty minutes."

"They can't come here. If they're trying to lay low this isn't the place."

"Then where?"

"Will they be discreet?"

"I doubt it. They're in a box truck returning from nowhere. And my guess is they're being watched."

"Oh boy. Which direction are they coming in from?"

"East, a little northeast, but I think they'll be headed in on I-20 once they get off the state highways."

"Okay, here is what we're going to do."

**

Tumelo got a text, I20 X277. He looked down at the two who appeared to be unconscious on the floor to his side. "Jonathan, I hope your plan is better than William's."

Tumelo pulled into the truck stop and saw that many of the fuel pumps were coned off, but one was open, he pulled in. An ambulance was on the other side. An EMT came around.

"Nice night."

"Yep."

"Late night for finishing up deliveries."

"Well, you know, we're private so we get worked hard."

Who is this guy? Tumelo thought.

"Yep, me too. You ever drive an ambulance?"

"Nope."

"Well..." He reached out to shake his hand, "maybe tonight you'll get a chance." The man spoke with a chuckle and a grin.

Immediately Tumelo knew what was going on. "Yep, maybe. You know we got a couple extra packages in the back I think would look great in any hospital. Maybe, call it a gift from our company to the locals?"

"Yeah?"

"Yeah. Hold on I'll go through the cab and meet you back there," he said as he unlocked the rear cargo door. Going through the inside he slid Shu-Ling into a box and pushed it toward the back.

"Thank you, this is awfully nice."

"Well, delivery was refused for this one, may as well do something nice with it."

"Thanks." Meanwhile, the other EMT had sat William up in the driver seat and changed jackets and hats with him and then took a seat on the passenger side.

After Tumelo and the first EMT put the long box in the back of the Ambulance, they too went in the back of the Ambulance and traded jackets. Tumelo walked over and looked up at William. "Ah man, he's been working way too hard. C'mon buddy."

William didn't respond.

"Looks like you're gonna have to help him into your ride and get him a large coffee from inside."

"Yep, Mind givin' me a hand, he's really out."

"Sure thing."

They picked him up and sat him down in the back of the Ambulance. Each group replaced the gas nozzle and the drivers hopped into their respective vehicles. The EMT's now appearing to be the delivery guys, they headed off in the truck and Tumelo hopped into the Ambulance.

He started up the Ambulance and out loud, "3, 2, 1…"

"Hi, I'm Dr. Brodowski."

"Hello Doc, I'm Tumelo. Where we headed?"

"East."

"Good enough. Can you help my friends?"

"That's my plan. Let's get moving. They'll take your truck to its destination and Jonathan has transportation for them to get back to me here. They'll be on I-20 around Abilene. To be safe, I'd suggest you exit and take 84 toward South 1st Street straight through town. Also, if we have to stop off for anything we can drop south to the hospital."

"You got it Doc. For now, you're in the driver's seat until we can get things back on track." A few minutes of quiet later, "Hey Doc, should we drop south?"

"Doctor Brodowski? How's it going back there? We're nearing the split for 84 or taking South 1st Street straight across town." Still there was no response.

Tumelo pulled over quickly to the side of the road and jumped out of the driver's seat and looked to the back. "Doc!"

"Pipe down Melo, we're going to be okay."

"Thanks Doc."

"Melo?" Tumelo replied, recognizing the voice.

"Yeah, as in mellow out!" William spoke jokingly but showing pain as he woke up.

"What, what happened?"

The doctor pulled headphones out of his ears and turned his head. "I'm sorry did we pull over? Is something wrong? Oh good, they're waking up."

Tumelo shook his head, "No, nothings wrong."

Just then Shu-Ling raised her head. "Ouch, I feel like I woke up in the afternoon after a night collided with the morning, as if I'd had shots of Black Dragon followed by breakfast that called for a Bharat Mary with Baijiu. Either that or I actually did get hit by a truck." She shook her head. "Ow!"

The doctor responded, "You'll both be fine."

William couldn't resist being quick, "Who's the guy in the white coat?"

"That's you're first question! Not how did we end up in this ambulance or why is Tumelo driving one?"

"Yeah, those were next... Ow, my head really hurts as well. Tumelo, you drive, I'll explain."

"Sure." Tumelo jumped back into the driver seat, "wait, Doctor B, where we headed?"

"Jonathan had options on standby. Before we head out we should let him know we're dropping off the vehicle outside of ARMC. Head south on 84 where it merges with 83 and you'll see signs."

"Sounds good, I'm personally ready to call it a night. I have a feeling it doesn't end here."

"You're right about that son, it doesn't. You made a pick up from Zhanger Pharmaceuticals?"

"Yeah."

"Did it not even occur to you that the world's top drug maker might have a way to get what they gave you back through the use of a drug?"

"But how, I didn't take anything."

"Me either, I don't get it."

"Young lady, did you open up anything they gave you?"

"Sure," she pulled a small sachet out.

"Careful."

"No, it's just a mix of things including a couple of these strange little nuts or cherries or something that resemble a coffee cherry but a much darker reddish brown color."

"No, something else. There must've been something else."

"I, I don't remember doc. My head really hurts." A half of a plastic capsule fell out from somewhere on her clothes.

"Wait, what's that?" The doctor picked it up. "Did you open some sort of capsule when you were looking through these sachets, was there like a container of some sort?"

"It was a mix. These, what appeared to be tea sachets with some that only had these cherry type nuts and then a few capsules. One must have opened up as I was rustling through in the dark looking at everything."

"Well, that's you're culprit. What was released was a gas meant to knock out the guys in the front. Instead, you took the brunt of it."

William added, "And when I went back to check on her there was just enough in the air to get me."

"Especially since you were likely breathing much heavier than normal at the time from seeing her on the floor unconscious."

"You nailed it Doc."

"Okay, so how did we end up here?"

Shu-ling, looked up. "Ouch, Melo? Ugh." Still feeling a pounding headache as the result of the gas she had inhaled.

"Mr. Melo, would you like to expand on that?"

"Jonathan arranged it. Two texts, followed by a short meeting with a couple of EMTs at a truck stop just outside of town and next thing I know I traded vehicles and this guy popped up and revived you two."

"Oh, simple. Just another day in the life of our little rag tag crew." They all shook their heads.

Chapter 16 – One Plus One

Tumelo pulled into Abilene Regional Medical Center, "all right Doc. Looks like this is where we split up."

"Yep, listen, I wasn't kidding when I said it isn't over here. You kids watch your back. Zhang and the drug lords of the pharmaceutical industry are really no joke. You never know what they might have lurking or what they may be capable of."

"We'll be on watch. I think we all knew if we made it this far, things were only going to get, well, for a lack of a better phrase, more interesting. Thanks again doc."

"You bet, turn right here, there's a place where the guys often line up and I have a feeling... yep." Just then a helicopter dropped down on the helipad. "You guys go, that's your ride."

"Are you kidding?"

"You know Harris. That's how he works. He takes care of his friends. Let him know I said thank you, again."

"Will do."

They shook hands and the group boarded the helicopter. "We'll be touching down on at a nearby spot from your hotel. Mr. Harris has arranged to have you picked up there."

"Thank you."

The helicopter touched down. As they stepped off, a Lincoln town car pulled up. As they stepped toward it, the helicopter flew away and the rear passenger door of the car opened.

"I say we go low key the rest of the night. I'm guessing you guys are famished. I'm also guessing you've got quite the story to tell." Jonathan smiled from the inside of the car.

"Yes." They all said at once.

"What about the Nut?" He asked while sliding over further into the car to make room.

"You mean the guy who picked us up?"

"No!"

"The nut we were supposed to pick up?" William said.

"Well, did you get it?"

"Yes." Tumelo said.

"Yes, we believe so." Shu-Ling added.

"Well, great. Right now I'm concerned about my team, scratch that, I'm concerned about my friends. You guys ok?"

"Yeah, but I could still take you up on that offer for some food!" said William.

"Then let's do it! Jerry, can you take us to that new BBQ place off of Royal and MacArthur."

"Big Star?"

"Yep, that's the one."

As they filed in Jonathan had called ahead and reserved a private booth toward the back. "Okay guys, talk to me."

Slowly they each told their part of what had happened until Shu-ling pulled a small bag out of her inside pocket. "And we think this is…"

"That's it. I know it is. The color is near ripe, exactly as we need, but that close to being ripe and ready for what we need means we have to move quickly. In one to two weeks, it'll be at its best. A week or two after that and it'll start to dry up."

"How did they use it before if it has such a temporary life span?"

"With the right technology and chemicals you can stabilize it safely so that it can be held in a holding facility at the right temperature and humidity, of course, in a very specific type of container as well. This is what had to have been done, but we do not have that luxury. The time we'd spend to do that would likely take the very time we need to use focusing on getting the remaining items we need."

"What's next Jonathan?"

"Next is a good night's rest. Are you guys cleared to sleep?"

"Yes, he just said we needed to drink plenty of water to help flush the effects of the gas from our system along with a couple aspirin."

"Pretty much like a standard hangover cure from an old-school doctor."

"Pretty much."

"Alright, well tomorrow we need to split up. I have a

strong feeling we'll be watched. Each of you will have your transportation details by 10am under your door. Do not answer for anyone. Not even me."

"Seriously?"

"Yes," then Jonathan looked just beyond the private room they were in. A man walked by, leaving the restrooms located nearby.

"That's his third time in the past hour using the restroom. And he has a strange familiarity. I don't think this is my first time seeing him on our expedition."

"Jonathan, you can't let yourself get paranoid."

"He doesn't look like one of Zhanger's men."

"What exactly would that be Will?"

"Well, I mean, just going from what we saw at the facility."

Then Tumelo jumped in. "Wait, remember when we were in Dubai?"

"Yes."

"There was a man who, nah, I'm sure they just look a bit alike. It's been a long trip."

"Tumelo, if you even think for a moment…"

"Let's just stay aware, okay Jon."

"At the very least we will be doing that."

"Gentlemen, I think maybe I should take the young lady for a little sight seeing."

"Why is that Shu?"

"Because in fact, we already seem to be part of the local scene ourselves. One, Five, Nine."

Each of them looked to their right and correctly positioned at her positions of One o'clock, five o'clock, and nine o'clock, it appeared there were at the very least some suspicious eyes looking their way.

Charity picked up on it quick, "Oh boy do I have to go to the bathroom."

She turned to her Dad, "you were right," she exclaimed, "Wings and Beans were a bad idea! Why are you always right? Sheesh, Shu would you join me?"

"Big girl, Jon, big girl drama."

"Of course."

"Men, they don't understand us girls."

"Hey…" Jonathan replied, but they were off just a few feet away.

"Looks like you're really in for a whole new world ahead of you Jonny boy."

"Oh yeah 'Melo, you think so?"

"Yeah man, the life of a single dad with a teenage girl is not that far away."

"Ah, come on she's only… You're right she's getting awfully close, nearly pre-teen already I guess those hormones are kicking in."

Suddenly they were all on the same page.

"You know what boys, it's time to be boys and let those girls be girls. Let's get outta here."

"Okay, but I have a delivery to make." William pulled a small bag resembling that of the one Shu had held with the Cincaberry nut mix in. "I need to get this to the mustang owner."

"He's in downtown, right?" Jon asked.

"Yep. Okay, let's meet by the Mandalay Canal and grab drinks. We can meet the girls back at the hotel and part ways in the morning."

"You boys leaving?" The waitress came around overhearing their conversation.

"Yes. And you were wonderful," Jonathan quickly pulled from his years of womanizing like a boy who hadn't been on a bike in ages but never forgot how to ride. Before she could hand him the check holder, he pulled a $100 from his wallet, slid it out to her as she opened it. She closed it and as she pulled it away he replied, "no change."

"Well then, thank you boys…" and looking down at Jonathan, "I sure hope you will be back."

"Oh, we will. I like a good sauce on my brisket."

"Well, I make a homemade sauce. If you like that one well, you come back now, ya hear?"

"Loud and clear Ma'am," Jonathan threw in an effort at a Texan accent and pretended he was tipping a non-existent cowboy hat.

"Oh, you city boys are cute when you come down our way. Have a good night."

The men walked away.

"Hey Jonathan, let me grab you that box from the back of the truck."

"Okay, thanks William."

He opened up the back of the Suburban and the motorcycle was gone. They knew Shu-Ling and Charity were safe. Or at least they believed so, as it had appeared no one had followed them.

**

The girls were heading down the back roads of North Dallas.

"Hold on Charity."

Charity wrapped her arms around Shu-Ling knowing very well that not only her life relied on it for the long term; it might very well rely on it to survive getting through the night.

Heading into a shopping center and into a loading area they stopped. Charity relaxed for a moment.

"Don't relax just yet sweetie, just making a note and sending your dad a message."

A couple of taps on an onboard touch screen and they eased out, lights off, from around the building which came out along side a dumpster next to a gas station. "Ready?"

"Yep," Charity took a stronger hold.

They shot straight across the fuel island lot into the street, jumped the median and took a sharp left. It was a steep downhill. Just as they neared the bottom they circled around near the Movie Studios at Las Colinas and up to the gate. "I'm late for a shoot!"

"You are?" A guard said.

Raising her visor, "Dragon lady, the latest bad girl to take on the rebooted Texas Ranger."

"Of course... So you're here on behalf of?"

"Set Ten, Jerry Stiles."

"You know, I thought I saw those guys pull in. I was wondering why so late. Pull up forward a couple feet."

"Yep, just got in from a direct flight from LA that was delayed five hours. I'm in the final scene and the Executive Producers said if it isn't ready for a first viewing in the next 48 hours it was out of the running for this season." She pulled forward. Two cameras went off, one of the girls, the other of her plate.

"Who should I list as your guest?"

"You shouldn't," she replied, dropping her visor and shooting off. The gate stopped but it was already open far enough for her to squeeze by. Two men in a black Mustang came just around the street corner and looked up as she sped off.

"Where'd she go?" One of the men in the car asked.

"I don't know. There's not far for her to go."

"What else is down the road?"

"There's an Army Facility and a park."

"Head for the park." The first man barked. They took off.

Shortly after, the girls found an emergency exit out the back of the studios where they crossed some land and headed back to the street on the original route they were on originally.

Just then a pack of motorcycle riders came by, dropping two fingers to her left, the pack responded in kind and she tapped Charity's hands with one of her hands. Charity pulled close, tight to her, and Shu-Ling braked hard and caught an opening in the median so she could make a quick u-turn. She jumped into the group and pulled into the middle. She taps the on-board touch screen a couple of times.

**

Jonathan received the message, "She's okay!"

William pulled up next to two staged-vehicles in a shopping center lot in Valley Ranch near the Dallas Cowboys administrative facilities. Jonathan caught a glimpse of two men he recognized from Sundays. William pulled up alongside them.

"Here you go, Willy." They each glanced behind them at the vehicles they were leaning on.

They tipped their head with their hands as if to 'tip their hat' to William and then entered a luxury SUV and drove off.

Jonathan was in a bit of awe fairly sure he recognized the men from their play on Sundays… "Was that?"

"Customers of mine? Yes, yes they were. You're not the only one with favors to call in. From time to time, I, um, you might say… lend, vehicles to customers who in exchange deliver them to me, if I have a local delivery to make. Your thumbprints are each already embedded. Upon activation you'll have access to a single compartment with what you need. I assumed this was the right time Jonathan?"

Then turning to an express shipping box he dropped a package inside. "Let your friend know she'll have what she needs for her dad by 9am tomorrow."

Just then a Police car went by slowly, activating its lights. As if it was a warning for folks just loitering in the area after hours.

"Yeah, I think it's probably time we split up. When you say what we need is…"

"J, everything you need is in place. And there's room and provision for any of us to have a companion of our choosing."

"And Shu-Ling?"

Looking over to a trash can, William pulled out the phone he'd been using, opened it, pulled the SIM card and tossed it in. He replaced it, and in a moment looked up. "She's abreast of the situation."

"Convergence in forty-eight hours. Location TBD."

Jonathan knew what was happening, he couldn't help but feel anxious and afraid all the while knowing he had the few people around him that he would not only trust his life with, but everything he'd ever given his life for, most of all his daughter. No matter how much you trust someone with a life that you are responsible for, actually letting go and doing so is one of the hardest things there is to do, and he was feeling the pressure and intensity of what was ahead.

"J, we don't have time for reflection my friend. You pay me to make sure your most valuable documents and materials are delivered safe and sound to their intended destination. I have never failed you. I will not fail you now." Jonathan nodded his head. "Let's go."

William returned to his vehicle and immediately headed for I-30 west, with one stop first.

Tumelo touched the activation pad with his thumb. Though the trunk opened, there was only access to one small area. The rest was closed off. He raised it and pulled out a box. There was a small piece of recessed carpeting under where he picked up the box, he pulled it up and it was a key.

"That sneaky…" Shaking his head, "he didn't even tell us there'd be a key."

He opened the box and inside there were two plane tickets leaving from Dallas Love Field. Each of them was headed to areas near nuclear power plants. William went to one nearby, on the border of Texas and Arkansas. Tumelo headed for an international flight for the other.

Shu-Ling and Charity drove to Shreveport, while Jonathan headed to a Mid-Atlantic location. The next item on the scavenger hunt was radioactive aloe.

**

The men who were after Shu-Ling were still at the park. William was looking at his GPS tracker, reviewing Shu-Ling's path and headed toward where she had let him know she lost her pursuers. He made a call along the way.

Arriving on the scene, two undercover cops were leaning against the men's vehicle and clearly they would be detained for a while.

He sent a group message:

I can't speak for them all, but chase one is going to be delayed a short while. Move quickly. I'll get your stuff from the hotel.

He made another call. Moments later he pulled up around the back of the hotel, loaded everyone's bags and then made a click and slid into the back seat. Another man slid in and drove away.

They pulled into a garage in downtown. William got out, and got into a silver sports car and pulled away. "I've got some time to make up."

**

"Where are we?" Charity asked.

"Shreveport, Louisiana!"

"Shrevewhere?"

"Don't worry, we're not here for long." Shu-Ling parked her bike and the two of them headed inside a small Greyhound Bus station. "We're not in a hurry. Everyone else is but we need to lie low. Nothing better than a Greyhound bus for that."

"Two tickets to Lafayette please." She paid, got the tickets, and they headed for the bus. "Hold up, I need to make a call." She stepped into a phone booth and placed her motorcycle key into the phone change slot.

Stepping away a man walked up. "Are you finished with the phone miss?"

"Yes."

"Would you happen to have any change? I need to make a call?"

"Where to?"

"Lafayette."

"Why, of course."

He put out his hand and she pretended to place coins in his hand and kept moving. Shortly afterward, he picked up the phone, placed his hand in and pulled out her key and headed for the bike.

**

The next day, everyone had made it to their destination with one goal, to find a four-leaf clover, in a radioactive field you might say.

Tumelo began hopping between locations, making friends

along the way in places where each spoke a different language. He was not sure if this scavenger hunt had become more of a goose chase at this point.

William had made it to the location on the state line and it was clear nothing of the kind was here. He had checked the soil. He had asked the right people. And nothing. He headed for Jonathan.

Jonathan was in a small North Carolina town, by the outer banks. At this point he was probably as much a pirate himself as those who had sailed these shores.

He pulled up to a bar and decided he needed a drink. This had been a long road and he knew as well as anyone, *find the right bar, find the right guy, you can find anything.*

"Stella, please." He took a seat at the bar ordering his favorite beer.

"I'm Stella. And you are?"

He laughed about to respond with, 'Not Interested', when he realized it might be a perfect time to play the game again, this time for a different prize.

"Some call me Green Beard."

"You don't have a beard."

He pulled out a fifty and laid it on the bar. Pointed at the picture of Ulysses Grant on the front. "I have the green. He has the beard."

She cocked her head with a half smile. "I see. And what brings a self-proclaimed pirate to these parts?"

"Well, like any pirate, I seek treasure."

"Well, have you found it?"

"No, I can't say that I have."

"You know, sometimes you have to be careful. You can have gold right underneath your nose," She scooted closer and leaned over the bar where a necklace and a gold coin revealed itself between her breasts, "and you don't even know it."

"Well, when you put it that way. I wouldn't be much of a pirate if I weren't sure to try and uncover the treasure right in front of me."

"You also wouldn't be much of one if you didn't get the girl a drink."

"What would you like?"

"Looks like you're having a Rum and soda," She prepared it as she spoke then pushed the glass in front of him. "and I'll have the Captain with ginger." She called someone over to cover for her and swung around and grabbed the stool next to him.

"Appropriate." He knew from her follow up she was still playing along.

After a couple drinks he asked, "So what do you do? Or are you like me, just looking for something buried in the rough."

"No, I'm a botanist. Well, when I'm not tending bar here. I used to work on some of the nearby shore land but after the double disaster, not much to work with. So now I'm a mixoligist, at least on summer weekends. Biology teachers don't make much."

"Double disaster?"

"We had a pretty nasty hurricane, Hurricane Molly, come through recently and did a real doozy on these parts."

"Oh, I heard."

"Well, what you probably didn't hear was it caused some minor damage to the ground work near the power plant. Something pierced something. All I know is within twenty four hours there was an emergency fence one hundred yards out surrounding that place."

"Really?"

"Really. Too bad too, there are some amazing plants around there that only grow in the outer banks. They say, when pirates would sail they'd each bring seeds from their favorite exotic remote islands to transform these shores into those that would become known as The Islands of the Pirates themselves. Legend is they wanted a place on the mainland that still felt like their home at sea."

"That's quite the history lesson."

"Tell you what, it's getting late, let's get some breakfast and I'll take you to a spot. A spot where the fence, let's say isn't so good. No one seemed to care after several months went by, they just moved down shore."

"Okay, sounds good."

Then suddenly she leaned in for a kiss. He took a breath and followed through. When she pulled away turning her head for a moment, he shook his. She looked back, "Ready?"

"Yeah."

**

Tumelo looked up as he walked through the local village, stopping to read the sign on top of an old wood building, **Herbal Store** 'Let Mother Earth Heal You'

"Well, that sounds about right, but way too easy." He walked in. "Do you know where I can find some Aloe?"

"Sure, we have some right here?"

"Do you know if there is any place where I might find some that has been grown near heavy sources of radiation?"

"Why? Who are you?"

"Whoa? Really?"

"Who are you," the little lady from behind the counter pressed a button and two men came from behind the curtain that hung just beyond where she stood.

"I'm no one. Just a guy who has been sent on a sort of scavenger hunt, I was asked to see if I could find some aloe plants that have been affected by radiation."

The woman and the two men turned and talked. They spoke low and in mixed languages to do their best to keep Tumelo from understanding. He picked up one or two of every few words, doing his best to make sense of it.

"How much can you pay?"

"Money isn't the question. If you have what I need, is the question."

"If healing is what you plan to do. The aloe will not work alone."

"What do you mean?"

The woman shook her head, "ignorant man of chase," she said in her language. "There is a special bean that is grown in a pod. The pod and beans must be grown and made strong into a tea to help the body accept the aloe. Otherwise, anything it is used with will likely only create a temporary effect but not a cure."

"So, do you have the aloe?"

"No, no, no, very rare that is. Must be grown in soil rooted deep in radiation or grown in a radiation nursery."

"So you have this pea pod?"

"Bean pod." She corrected him. "Yes, fresh, you come back tomorrow," she slid a paper on the counter with an amount he would have to pay.

"I go today," and he handed her a large amount of cash in an envelope. It was almost all he had left.

"Excuse me."

She returned with a very small bag. Tumelo looked at it and decided it was too small for his payment. He began to place his hand on the cash.

"Wait." She looked back at the men accompanying her. "They will take you to the edge of the horizon. Where the mountains meet the sky, behind the waterfall where you can find more."

"Let's go."

They drove him along the edge of a mountain, and near the top they stopped suddenly. Looking outside, the men point to a walk way with a wooden bridge and a waterfall. "Go."

"Go?"

"Go. We wait here. You go. Take as much as you want. And some advise…" they handed him a small container, "put it in here with some of the water. The water from the falls is known to be quite powerful as well. An essence you might say lives in it."

Then he noticed it. As the water hit the rocks he could see something, someone. For a moment in time it seemed time stood still and the image he had seen was etched in his mind for eternity.

Tumelo took the container, threw it in a small pack and wrapped it around him. He headed off.

**

"Nice place." Jonathan stepped into what he hoped could be, the beginning of a lead to what just may save his daughter's life. He hadn't stepped into this part of his life in a very long time, he felt out of place and comfortable at the same time. *Like they say, once you learn to ride a bike, it doesn't matter how long you're away...*

"Make yourself at home."

He stepped in and took a seat on the couch.

"Would you like a drink?"

"Um sure…"

"What would you like?"

"Anything… Anything refreshing sounds good."

"Oh?"

"Yeah."

"Well then…" She came from out of the kitchen in nothing but her top hanging just down past her waist. "How about a glass of water?" She handed him a glass of cold water filled with ice. Condensation dripping down the side, she slowly ran her hand up the glass, then sat across Jonathan's lap and ran that same cold hand down his cheek.

"And another Stella…" She leaned in and kissed him passionately, pulling the shirt off of his body. The game was about to run its course, and she was no stranger to playing it.

Sensual and powerful, Jonathan was drawn to her. Soon, they had moved from one room to the next, a string of clothes along the way, they fell side by side and she went to crawl on top of him. But when he looked up, it wasn't here he saw there.

Jonathan shook his head and looked again, nearly blinded this time, he repeated himself and then he said it, something he had never said to a woman.

"Wait. I can't. Stella. You are… beyond words. And I am no man who is short of speech."

"I believe that. So what is it?"

"I have a daughter."

"Oh, that's sweet. And you're married?" She shook her head and fell back to his side. Her head hit the pillow next to him.

"No. She's adopted."

She rolled over looking at him. "Wait, you're a successful man, never married, and you have an adopted daughter?"

"Yes."

She drew near him. "Tell me more."

He told her the part of the story he felt safe enough to tell. Amazed and compelled by the story, as the moonlight shone through the window, she looked at him. "Jonathan, you could have just asked. Let's get some rest. The sun will be up soon and we should get a jump on its rise." And a moment later they were fast asleep.

**

Tumelo saw the pods. He recognized them from the few in the small bag, and he began to fill his bag with as much as he could get and then remembered what the men said. He took the container and filled it halfway with water and placed a greater amount into the water. It was the first time he could ever recall a warm, very warm waterfall, like what he saw in the hot pool of the natural warm baths found around the world. But waterfalls were usually cold. Quickly he saw the change in color from the pods.
He approached the off road trail vehicle driven by the men. He saw them to the side fishing over the short cliff.

"Gentlemen, this is no time to be fishing. I'll be happy to buy you dinner upon our return."
"Who are you?"
"I told you I'm…"
"Three men came. How do they know why we are here?"
"What kind of men?"
"Two Americans. They appeared to be government officials or something. We just told them that we come here to fish for the fish of the cliff. They jump for the food."
"Really?"
"No, not really, man of travel and ignorance. We bluffed. Let's go!"

Quickly they jumped in the vehicle and left. "If they come back, here is how you can reach me. I know someone. He can vouch for you and your business… as fishermen." He handed them a card.

The driver hit the brakes. He took the card from the other, tore it in two and threw it off the cliff and it drifted off into the river below. "We do not need your help. You need ours. The price has doubled."

"Whoa, whoa guys…"

"No whoa, oh, oh guys."

"Okay, the money isn't a problem but I don't have it with me. Just get me to a phone and I can have it wired to you though."

"Who are you? I say price double and you do not even ask a question."

'It's simple. I'm one part of many trying to save a little girl's life.'

"Little girl?"

"7 years old, and without this…" suddenly it hit Tumelo and he thought back to the hardest years of his younger days, "without this," he held up the bag shaking it. His eyes began to water with tears he attempted to hold back, "without this, she could die any day! And every moment we discuss money is a moment closer to her death. So, if it's okay with you, I'll pay if you will just get me back so I can help her."

The men, overtaken by the sincerity of Tumelo's near break down seemed speechless, nearly breathless. "No, you will not pay. But we cannot take you back."

"Why? I won't…"

They cut him off. "They'll be waiting. If they have any connections at all, they've already been to our store or are there now. They will know. There is a small fishing town near here. There you will take a boat up the river. There is a small town with a very small airport. Ask for Zandin. You give him this. He will fly you where you need to go so that you can get to her."

"It's far from here. I'm going to need…"

"You're going to need to avoid being caught. If they ask, we will say we saw a man coming from the cliff. We stopped him. Where should we say you are going?"

"Tell them… New Delhi."

"India?"

"Yes."

Quickly they sped away.

**

"Jonathan, wake up."

He rolled over. "Stella…" He smiled, "I've never just slept with a woman."

"Well, seems you slept quite well."

"I did. My point exactly, I slept."

"Wanna know something? I've never woken up next to a man. Wanna know something else? I've been lying here a few minutes surprised by the fact you were here when I woke up."

They exchanged smiles, and then Stella giggled and continued, "We should go."

Moments later, they headed out the door with a bag full of snack bars and water along with a few tools. As they drove along she told him about her story, and he expanded a bit on his. She also began to explain about where they were going in more detail and her plans.

"There is a public park that connects to a beach nearby. We'll park off the beach, work are way through to the trails in the wooded park and up to the fence."

"I'm getting the feeling you've done this before."

"Look, I may be a bartender but this was the land I had given my life's work to. I didn't walk away from it nearly as easily as I may have alluded to last night at the bar."

"Fair enough."

They parked near a shaded area among the cars but closer to the tree lined section.

"Okay. I haven't been here in a while. I don't know what to or not to expect. If this stuff is as valuable as you say it is, we may need to be prepared for the worst." She handed him a large knife.

"You think we might encounter some resistance?"

"I think this place is overgrown and tearing it apart might not be as easy as cutting it." She also pulled out a couple of special bags. "Two for each of us. These are from my lab."

"Lab?"

"In my basement. When we get back we can analyze the plants. Make sure it's what you need."

"Okay." He glanced at his phone. It was a text from William, I-40 TN ETA 8H.

"Everything okay?"

"Yes, everything is good."

"There's more to all this than just the Aloe isn't there?"

"Stella, I hope you'll understand if I don't tell you…"

"Jonathan…"

"No, I can't…"Another text came through. 'She's clean.'

"I take that back. Maybe I can. But I just don't think it's best, for now."

They began to move into the wooded area. "The trail is about one hundred yards west then about fifty feet north as I remember."

"This is amazing. Almost like a rain forest by the uniqueness of the land and the foliage, yet not as green or as lush."

"It's changed a great deal. Oh, I almost forgot, close your eyes."

"Why?"

She broke out a small spray container. "This is a special solution I conjured up to keep the bugs in this area away. The accident did more than mess with the plants, it messed with the bugs as well. The ones that didn't die were only the ones that were deep in the soil. Seems they mutated a bit and let's just say the regular stuff doesn't have much impact on them." She sprayed him good from head to toe and followed on herself.

"Alright, let's keep going."

Shortly thereafter "There it is." She motioned toward a small wearing of the ground foliage.

"There what is? That's the trail?"

"Well, as I said, I haven't been out here in a while and my guess is no one else has been either. Be careful, no telling what's crawling in these woods."

"So, how far again are we looking to get to the site?"

"Maybe a hundred yards or so."

"When should I be on the look out for it?"

"No need, I'm not going to miss it."

"So, just follow you?"

"Just follow… Wait."

"Wh…"

"Shhh!" She put her hand back and froze, implying that Jonathan did exactly the same. Everything went quiet, then suddenly several deer went by, jumping across the trail just ahead of them.

"Careful, they may have just been going along or something may have scared them."

Walking along, she slowed her pace. "Look up ahead, do you see that?"

"What, that ivy vine?"

"It's not ivy, or a vine. It's the fence. The growth has overtaken it so that it can barely be seen. Come. Let's take a closer look…" her pace quickened.

She moved close and took a knee. "Amazing."

"What? What is it?"

"The power of nature, the power of plants, is really amazing. There was a time this fence was here to separate the affected area, and when it was first put up it was as if the fence lined a separation of life and death. But now, look!"

Jonathan kneeled down and noticed where the plants had not only overgrown the fence, but as they grew they had pulled the fence up nearly a foot in the air with them.

"Wait, look at that tree!"

"What tree?"

"Down there."

"What about it? It's not like it's a big tree… oh wait, does the fence, does the fence actually…?"

"Yes, I think so. That could be our sweet spot."

As they walked along the fence toward the tree, the fence continued upward slowly until near this tree that had grown along side it, it had actually caught the fence with a growing limb and pulled it over two feet from the ground. "Well, this makes our job easier." Immediately she began to slide under the fence.

"Okay, here we go I guess."

"On this side you'll notice much is just beginning to re-grow. But like in any great disaster, not all is destroyed and you'll see some life that remains from before. Look for that which is green, thicker and larger. That will likely also be what is older."

"Got it." They moved along slowly and carefully. "Wow... is that it?"

"Yes, that's the old power plant. I don't know if they still have any cameras or security so we should still be cautious."

"Oh, how cute."

"What, what's cute, are you calling me and my caution cute?"

"No, I just saw a frog."

"A what?"

"A frog. Why?"

"Where?" She responded with urgency, yet somewhat quietly not wanting to frighten it.

"There, there it goes."

"We may be close."

"Because frogs like Aloe Vera plants?"

"Because frogs are amphibious, and we might be near a patch of wet soil where things are likely to grow and to have been less likely to have died fully. Let's wait."

"He's headed in that direction. Let's move that way and see what we come across."

A squish under Jonathan's boots told them they were close to the spot the frog called home. "I think we found the little guys' swampy home."

"And, I think I may have found your plant." She pulled out some weeds revealing two, tall, aloe vera leaves coming up from the ground.

"Wow."

"We're about a quarter to a third the way to the plant. This area was surely affected. We better get them and go."

They both pulled out their knives and cut several as close to the root as possible and then began to head back quickly. As they moved quickly through the wooded trail they were nearly running when suddenly he stopped, "Ow!"

"What is it?"

"I think, something bit me."

"Let me take a look." Then she noticed it, a fairly small light brownish snake scurrying away. It appeared to be a small copperhead.

Jonathan peered over his shoulder to follow her eyes in the same direction.

"I think I know what bit you."

"Is it venomous?"

"Yes, but typically not too bad, and in this case it looks like it was just reacting out of fear, just caught your skin pretty good. Plus it was small, probably a young one." She went to work with a small first aid kit. "I really don't think he got his teeth in deep but he did tear your skin pretty good."

"Try the aloe."

"Huh?"

"Look Stella, I'm looking forward to your lab results but if this stuff is as quick acting and potent as I need it to be, maybe we'll have our results by the time we get back."

"Okay." She cut one open cleaned the wound with alcohol and put some of the liquid on the bite and began to bandage it. "And they say a little venom can rush to the head and mess with the mind."

Jonathan was already trying to discern if these feelings were just the effect of being cared for by a woman or if there was something genuine. Her hands were so gentle and yet skilled. She worked carefully while taking a moment here and there to look up at him, as if to ensure him everything was going to be okay. "You good to go?"

"Yeah, okay let's take it easy, just in case, I don't want it to move through your system so quickly that you pass out or anything."

"I thought you weren't worried about the venom?"

"I'm not. But even a little if it gets pumped through you too quickly can mess with you. It also depends on your body, everyone can react differently. Let's at least give your body time to put up a fight to what little is in there."

"Right and it feels like we're getting close to the fence."

"Yes, just a little further."

Chapter 17 – Found

"What is that?"

"What is what?"

"I thought I saw movement."

The two men reviewed the security tapes, "Look once a month, when it's our turn to watch the screens, every month it's the same. You order the pizza, I bring the popcorn and we fight over which would be really better to watch, the 3 Stooges or old Hitchcock films."

"The 3 Stooges, but that's not the point, I really think I saw something."

"You know if you stare at anything long enough, the mind will make you believe it moved."

"Can you just take a look?"

"Sheesh, okay I'll humor you. Meanwhile, pass me the soda would you?"

"Look, there's nothing… wait."

"Uh huh, eagle eyes, I tell ya. You better get on the horn and report that."

"We gotta be sure. Anyway I think it was just a couple kids."

"Why?"

"Take a closer look."

Stella had just wrapped the bandage. The men watched as they sat next to each other in the overgrowth. They watch as the conversation unfolded, only being able to see them and not know what they were saying.

**

"Okay, are you ready to get up? The fence is just ahead. You can see the tree and the rise of the foliage."

"I, I think so."

"Careful."

As he put his hands out, he put no weight on the hurt leg,

he fell toward her and they rolled.

**

"See! Look at 'em! I think they're just having some fun. Pass me a bowl, I want more popcorn."

"Here, yeah, this is better than Hitchcock. Well, if she's out to kill him. Boohahaha."

**

"Sorry about that."

"Are you?"

His hand had found its way around her and was sliding downward slowly. "It's just, I, um, you…" he shook his head

"What was that?"

He shook his head a little more and pulled his hand away quickly but without being harsh. "Wrong, I was going to say I don't know if this is right, I just…"

She cut him off. "Jonathan, I'm just here to help you. That's all. You're a good lookin' guy and I'd be lying if I said I wouldn't be okay with this going somewhere. But I get it, wherever you're coming from, it's clear you're not sure how to get to wherever you want to go. At least not until you have taken care of her."

"Thanks."

"You're welcome. Now, let's take it easy and make our way over to the fence. But, let's stay low."

"Why? Cause you see that branch?" She said regarding a small tree nearby. "Do you see what I see?"

"I think so. That's not a squirrel."

"Nope. We're either being taped or being watched."
Suddenly she leaned in, kissed him, and rolled into a nearby bush.

**

"Ah man, where'd they go?"

"Ah, show's over, let's put on something good. After we

settle in, we'll check back and see if they come out."

"Three Stooges?"

"Hitchcock."

"Look we already agreed we got to watch some live Hitchcock tonight, plus it's my turn."

"Fine."

**

"Look, sorry, not trying to send mixed messages, but I'd rather it look like a couple just fooling around than like we had anything more going on."

"Yeah, yeah, good call. One problem, I don't feel so good."

"Oh no, your heart is racing. Sorry, take deep breaths. Think relaxing thoughts."

"Okay."

"We gotta move though. I have an idea." First she took some of the large leaves from nearby and put them under him, then she made a rope from some of the thicker vine, tied it around his waist and then to hers, and got into a low position and began to pull him forward. "Just relax."

A few minutes later they were at the fence.

**

"They come out yet?"

"Nope, just a mess of leaves and some branches. Looks like they either left, or like most of us, he fell asleep and she left him there."

"Oh, that's good. That's definitely quality Hitchcock." They laughed and each grabbed another slice and looked back to the screen with the 3 Stooges playing.

"Hold on, hadn't we better send it in?"

"All right, I guess we should." A couple clicks and a quick note, they tied the clip of the kissing couple, and sent it off to their security head.

**

"Alright, we're here. How do you feel?"

"Better."

"Good." She pulled out a knife and cut the vine and rolled under the fence.

"Oh boy. It's like I can feel everything in my body."

"Its short term, you'll be fine."

Jonathan rolled under the fence. She helped him up and as she turned they shared a glance again, deep into each other's eyes. She turned to walk away and he shook his head. Under his breath, "Ruth," he said to himself. *Ruth? What, why, I guess I do need to call her. The mind does play tricks on you*, he thought. They made their way back and headed out.

**

"When did you guys find this security footage?"

"We just caught it about 2 hours ago. We sent it to you as soon as we confirmed it was something worth sharing."

"Well, it looks like nothing, but it's documented. If it needs to be pursued, it'll be pursued. Anything else I should add to my report gentlemen."

"Nope, we watched and the guy was like woob, woob, woob then boink, if you know what I mean," while he was actually referring to Curly from the 3 Stooges holding back his laughter. "Yes sir, that's all, Good EVENING," he said with his best Alfred Hitchcock impression.

"All right, get back to work. And just in case, keep an eye on those screens."

"Oh, we are sir."

"Yes sir, we won't take our eyes off 'em."

**

They were back at Stella's home, "How ya' doing?"

"I'm good actually. You were right, evidently it was just enough to mess with me, but I think I'm good."

"All right, let's go take a look." She walked in, and down the hallway, she reached down. "Step back." She pushed down, a

---

handle popped up, and she pulled up a section of the floor. There was a staircase and they headed down into a full basement with her lab.

"Wow, this is amazing."

"Yeah, you can take the girl out of the jungle, but you can't take the jungle out of the girl. I love plants."

"I can see," he responded as he looked around at little green houses and bottom-up moisture growing contraptions she had built for indoor use. The lamps combined with the moist basement created the right kind of heat and light over each and made it feel like they were in a tropical zone.

"This should give us the radiation levels, if any, in the aloe."

The meter began to jump as she placed drops into a container that pulled it through and created a reading for radiation. "Jonathan, I think we found it."

Suddenly there was a pounding at the door. She came up, and then heard a light knock at the back door. She looked toward the front and then the back.

Jonathan got a text from William, 'Back not Front!'

"Stella, get the back door first."

"Wait, how does he..."

"Quick!"

"Coming, just a minute!" She opened the back door.

"Take your clothes off."

"Who are you?"

"I'm a friend of Jonathan's."

"Well, I..."

"I don't want to look, there's no time. Do you have a robe? Something just to make it look like we were... you know?"

There was a loud knock at the front door. "Wait, Gimme your shirt. I think I know what you have in mind, the bedroom is that way, wait for my cue."

The knocking continued.

"Coming!" She opened the front door, "Can I help you?"

A local cop and a man in a suit stood outside.

She opened up the door completely, "Hello Officer, can I help you?"

"Stella. Um, is this a bad time?"

"A bad time, no not at all," she followed by buttoning the top button on the men's dress shirt she had thrown on quickly. "Jim, what's this about?"

"There's footage of a couple fooling around by the old power plant. Camera footage has your SUV parked at the State Parking lot not far away at the same time."

"Well, I was at the park today and I did meet someone."

"Is that his car out front?"

"Babe, I told you not to leave you car there. I thought you moved it when we got back."

"Sorry, babe, I wasn't leaving the Jag by the road. Seemed safer around the side of the house."

"The Jag, can you believe this guy? But you know, he's nice. Your Jag is fine anywhere around here. He's not from around here. We talked, we walked, and well, when things got interesting and I told him what I did, I took him near the old stomping grounds."

"Ma'am, I think we're going to have to take you to the precinct."

"Back off, rookie. Stella, you know those grounds are off limits."

"I know," she dropped her head, "I know." She looked up, bit her lip and continued, "Why do you think we were over there? I didn't know there were cameras. I mean, that place has been shut down for so long, I just figured they were waiting till everything died. We just went for a role in the hay, er or whatever is left of the land over there."

"All right, well, since I know you, we'll just call this a first time offence and leave you with a warning."

"But sir?"

"First time offense, son."

"Yes, sir."

"Have a good day St..."

"Stella, everything okay? You coming back in here or am I coming to get you?"

"Bye guys... and don't worry next time, I'll control myself until we get back to my place." She shut the door and headed toward the bedroom. "Okay, so who are you really?"

"I told you. I'm a friend of Jonathan's. Did he find it? Did you help? I heard them say you were trespassing. Where? By the old nuclear power plant I'm guessing?"

"Wait, who, how…"

William was struggling to open the door on the floor. She bent down, "Here, it's like this." She popped the handle and opened it back up.

Jonathan was sitting there, spinning around in a chair. He looked up and saw William with his shirt off and Stella wearing it.

"Well, you guys have fun?"

"Wait, no," she went to take it off, then looked at William, then back at Jonathan, "you do know him right?"

"Yes. We go back. He's on the same team."

"I'm really sorry, we didn't know it was…"

"Stella, relax, I heard everything." He smiled.

"I'll be right back, you guys catch up." She headed toward her bedroom. The door closed.

"William, what are you doing here?"

"Everyone's watching for us. I got word from my connections, everyone is asking for this guy who's looking for the key ingredients to a medication that hasn't been used since clinical trials seven years ago and was pulled from the market because they couldn't ever make it stick in the tests on animals. All the animals die within a few months or a year."

"What? How did you?"

"It's my job. I've even made sure a few key packages and messages for some of these folks got delivered in the last twenty-four hours while I was trying to get here."

"This is crazy."

"No, this is crazy." William pulled out a tablet, tapped a couple quick buttons and handed it to him.

"What is this? This looks like a map of everywhere I, we, we've been these last several weeks."

"Looks that way don't it? That's a map of all the locations between where my colleagues or I have had a request for either a pick up or a delivery."

Jonathan just stood in awe, eyes wide, and began to shake his head. "But I don't understand. Why?"

"Look, this whole small town cop and camera thing could be bigger if it gets seen by the wrong people."

"But who would be interested?"

"Jonathan, if…"

"Hey, you guys want something to drink?"

William was quick to respond. "Some tea would be great!"

"Um, I don't have any made, lemonade, beer…"

"Oh, I just drove half way across the country to get here. Some good southern sweet tea would hit the spot right now."

"Why are you?"

William turned and gave the 'Hush eye' to Jonathan.

"What d'ya say? You mind making us some?"

"All right sure, I guess it is the least I can do."

"Ah, she's a good host."

"Why tea?"

"Because it'll take at least 5 minutes for her to make that. That's all the time I need."

"For?"

"Jonathan, what if Charity really is the only one out there who ever had this procedure done and survived this long, everyone is going to want her. Government research, Zhanger especially. Every drug manufacturer, and scientist who's aware of this thing and catches wind that there's a 'miracle girl' out there is going to be looking for her. They're going to be looking for us. What do we do?"

"William, you said it best. No one delivers a package safely like you. Only now, I need you to deliver us somewhere safe where they won't find us."

"Well, we can't have everyone go to the same place at the same time."

"What else do we need?"

"We have the Cincaberry, and look, we have the Aloe, and we were just making sure it's radiation levels are where we need them to be."

"Ok boys, here are two tall glasses of the Carolina's best southern tea you'll ever find." Stella walked down the stairs and handed a glass to each of them. "You ready?" She checked the meter reading and it seemed to stabilize. "I don't know what you're looking for, but that little drop falls right at a dose measurement of 1 sievert."

William's phone rang.

"Is that a different phone?"

William handed Jonathan a phone. Shaking his hand he handed William his current one. "She has our numbers?"

He nodded and threw the old one on the floor and crushes it.

"Hey!"

"Hello, Tumelo, where are you?"

"I'm on the plane."

"We're on our way."

"Where are we on our way too?" Jonathan questioned

"We need to get to your Doc. And he needs to have what we need when we get there."

"Stella, thank you for your hospitality but we really need to go."

"Where are we going?" She asked

"Um well, we are going to go save a little girl's life and you are going to stay here and pretend nothing happened."

"That's a great idea. Only one problem, I'm on that camera. I need an out. And as a scientist who believes in the healing power of nature, if there is something out there natural that can save a life, I want to learn about it."

"Jonathan, the more of us there are, the more complicated this gets."

"She did help us."

"Okay, let me think."

"You think. I need to make a call."

**

He grabbed the new phone and dialed a familiar number, "Ruth, it's Jonathan."

"Jonathan, what is going on? I had to stop patrolling your home. They're all over it. Everywhere."

"Who?"

"I don't know who exactly, but someone is looking for you and from the looks of it, they aren't all connected. Or at least they aren't directly connected. Where are you?"

"You're going to get a message Ruth. You have a choice. Meet us, or walk away."

William looked up. "Alligators are only cute when they're little."

"Ruth, tomorrow afternoon be ready. And remember. Alligators are only cute when they're little."

"Jonathan, what's happening?"

"And Ruth. You... I, I hope I see you again. Have faith."

"I do have faith."

She looked down at the phone as she heard the click of him hanging up, "... and I have hope."

**

"Okay, I think we've got it. It's going to cost us. Well, more specifically, Jonathan, it's going to cost you."

"I'm going to need access to everything. You need to trust me with everything."

Trust on this level was well beyond anything Jonathan had ever considered. He reached under his waistline behind his pants, took a deep breath, "Here, handing William a USB Drive"

"Everything?"

"Everything you need is there."

"Okay, Stella I need secure web access."

"No one can get to what I have down here. I took a lot of measures to continue my work down here."

"You should take Stella's Jeep and go."

"Where?"

"Where Blackbeard would go, if he were you."

"What?"

Stella shook her head and muttered, *"Blackbeard, treasure, Sapelo?"*

"Go!"

The two headed out quickly. In the Jeep they were driving fairly quickly.

"Slow down."

"Why? It sounds like we need to hurry."

"We do, but we also need to be smart. It's not exactly the time you need to be seen fleeing from your house at eighty miles per hour after a visit from the local sheriff."

"Can we trust William with my stuff?"

"I just trusted him with my entire life and more importantly the life of the only person I have every loved, more than anything... more than anyone even... even myself." Jonathan's head dropped for a moment.

**

"So tell me, where are we going?"

"He said go where Blackbeard would go."

"Yeah, and I heard you say Shapalo?"

She shouted over the wind whipping around them. "Sapelo... Sapelo Island. It's about fifty or sixty miles south of Savannah."

"We're headed for Georgia? And why this Sa-pe-lo Island?"

"Sapelo Island is also known as Blackbeard's Island. Legend is that's where he buried his treasure."

"So, why would we go there?"

"Because your friend... your friend is brilliant, he's..." She paused, shook her head and looked to the sky for a moment, back at the road briefly then toward Jonathan. "Your friend is a genius. He really does know how to deliver a package. I just hope he knows how to get past the wrong folks to get to the right ones. At least I'll be able to help."

"I, I still don't understand."

"The island is home to various entities. One of those is the University of Georgia Marine Institute."

"So, help me out here?"

"Wait, it get's better. It's also home to the Richard Reynolds Wildlife Management Area and the Sapelo Island National Estuarine Research Reserve."

"And like I said, help me out here. Stella, I don't get it."

"Those last two…"

"Yeah?"

"Those last two are both administered by the Georgia Department of Natural Resources."

"And?"

"I don't know if your friend knows it or not, but I attended the University of Georgia. I studied at the Marine Institute. Those organizations I just told you about, know me. The work I did here was largely passed on to them. Even some of the work I was doing in my basement was for those folks. How could he know though?"

"He ran a background on you before he ever got to the house."

"Seriously?"

"Seriously, I don't know anyone as thorough as him. So, how long's the drive?"

"We don't drive." She pulled up to a small marina and threw the jeep into park. "We sail."

A stocky woman walked up as they pulled in.

"Hey Stella, you sure about this?"

"Yep, take the keys."

"Well, there she is."

"Wait, what's happening?"

"I called Lou here just before we left the house."

"Lou?" He looked back and forth between the two ladies.

"Lou Ann Millan, good to meet you. That's my boat. Well, it's Stella's boat now."

"Wait, does it actually say Stella on the side?"

"Yep, that's a story I can share on our way. Message your friend. Let him know where we are and how we'll be getting to the island."

"Lou, can you…?"

"Already on it baby girl. Most everyone still works at the institute and the university and let's just say they're very excited to see you?"

"Really?"

"Sure, I told them you wanted to tour the island for a spot for the big day?"

"Big Day?"

"Look, when people think you're getting married you can do any old crazy thing and nobody ain't gonna ask any questions." She smiled and gave her a hug.

"Thank you, momma."

"Go. I don't know you young man, but I trust that girl and you can too."

"Wait, what just happened? Stella, you are full of surprises. Albeit, some very good surprises."

**

Back at Stella's, William went to work and it wasn't long that each of the team had received a message with clear instructions on what to do and how to stay with the team, or get out after they completed their necessary part in the mission.

**

"I'm gonna need your help. Let's move."

Jonathan looked at his phone. "Stella, I don't suppose you speak any other languages, do you?"

"Portuguese."

"What? Really?"

"Yeah, Portuguese. I studied abroad for a season in Portugal one summer, had to learn the language." She pulled her hair out of the ponytail as they boarded the boat, then turned her head and spun around. "Por que você pergunta?"

"Wow. I didn't see that coming. You really are full of surprises. What did you say?"

"I said, why do you ask?"

"We need an interpreter."

"We do?"

"Yes. I'm guessing everyone on the island who knows you, knows that you speak Portuguese? Any French?"

"No, not at all. Why?"

"Oh, madamouiselle, vous êtes dans l'amour avec un homme français."

"Okay. My turn, what did you say?"

"I said you're in love with a French man. And as your betrothed husband who neither speaks very much English or any Portuguese we fell in love while I was hiking the Appalachian Trail. I have little but all that I have is yours."

"Oh great, a poor French guy."

"We'll say that I am a writer, an aspiring writer who came to the states to write a love story."

"This is going to get interesting."

"Play along. You might find out along the way I'm not so poor."

**

Shu-Ling and Charity are in a small diner near a bus station in Mobile, Alabama. "Shu, I'm tired. I, I really don't feel so good."

"The last couple days have been tough, I know. We'll get us a good hotel tonight somewhere."

"Where? Here?"

A beeping from Shu's phone interrupted their conversation. "What is it?"

Shu-Ling looked down at Charity, "We're going to Georgia. Hope you like peaches."

"I like peaches. How are we getting there?"

"Well, we're already at the Bus Station and so far so good. But I think we may need to get there sooner."

Another beeping from her phone, "What now?"

"It's some numbers."

"What are they?"

"7519"

And, another interruption, "More numbers, 80. Weird."

"Shu, I'm really tired. I need rest."

"I know honey. I know. We just need to figure out what these numbers mean. I think they're important. Maybe a phone number, a zip code, no."

A stranger, an older man in common clothes walked up, "Hello? Do you know how I use this machine?"

"What machine?"

"The machine to get a locker? They have like 80 of them."

"What?" The man was already slowly walking away. She shook her head. "William, how, how do you do this?"

They walked over to the lockers, stepping down to number 80. It required a 4-digit code. She glanced at her phone and entered: 7519. It opened. There was a note and a bag. 'Change everything,' is all it said.

"Rest, yes, I think some rest is good, and if you're up for it a little trip to the Salon."

"Yeah, sure that sounds great!" Charity's eyes lit up.

The two took a walk and stopped at a small spot down the road from the Bus Station. They laughed, got their feet and nails done and then Shu-Ling spoke up. "I think we should do something fun with your hair."

"Really?"

"Sure, look a couple of girls like us, having some fun, let's change it up. What do you have in mind?"

"I just don't know how my dad would feel about it."

"Does your dad ever let you play dress up?"

"Sure, sometimes?"

"Well, let's just say this is a one time thing. We're going to play dress up. Let's both do something fun. I think I'll go blonde."

Charity laughed.

"What…"

"I don't know, I mean the pink and blue suits you."

"Well, you know sometimes, for dress up it's fun to change everything. But just for fun and a short time."

"Okay! I want Pink in Black!"

"Really?"

"Well, really a few light purple streaks would be really fun too!"

"Done!"

A little later, they popped out of the Salon and over to a nice hotel not too far away. They each fell into giant beds that felt like clouds after the hard days prior.

**

William finished what he began, and called Jonathan. "Did she figure it out?"

"Yes."

"I'll be there at noon tomorrow. Let her know we need a room for the afternoon."

"How did you...?" then Jonathan simply added, "Thank you."

Chapter 18 – Hidden Treasure

"So, the woman and a boat with your namesake?"

"Yes, well, Lou and I go way back."

"Yeah, about that Momma thing?"

"Well, when I was in my teens my parents passed quickly one after the other. The first, in a freak response to something they ate, an allergy they never knew about as I understand and the other... well, the other went on the run for a few days. He never returned. I began working for Lou on her boat to make money while he was gone. She reached out to him, and told him to get it together or give her custody so she could at least make sure I was cared for. My parents were good people. My dad was a good man. But my mom and me were all he had, and losing my mom was nearly too much for him. A couple nights later he called Lou, said he was on his way. He had made it quite a way away from here and was driving through the night. Unfortunately he dosed off along the way and was killed when he fell asleep at the wheel and went off the road."

"Oh Stella, I'm so sorry. That's awful."

"Thank you. Well, the one good thing about my dad was he was always prepared. He had already prepared a will and in fact, Lou who it turns out he had known for years, was given custody. She treated me like a daughter but in a different way, more like a favorite niece. I worked for her and when she sold her boat. I was devastated, until..."

"Until?"

"Until she walked me down the marina, pulled out a glass of champagne, just before I was supposed to finish high school and said these words. 'You've worked hard. You'll go on to college and if you ever need her, she'll be here for you.' I was confused, and then she walked me down the slip and pulled the cover from her new boat. On the side it read STELLA."

"Wow."

"Yeah, I told her I couldn't leave. She said then she was

going to give the boat away because the Stella she knew was ready to sail the world, at least metaphorically. She said that's why she had chosen my name for her new boat."

"That's a great story."

**

Just before dawn, William drove up to a pier that had been transformed into a heliport for tours around the outer banks. He parked and walked up to a man standing with a pilot. They exchanged keys. William put on gear, walked over, and got in the passenger seat. Shortly after, he took off.

**

In Camp Lejeune two men are standing around having a conversation.

"Sir, you asked if any unusual activity showed up to let you know."

"Yes Private."

"Well, a helicopter just took off from the Lower OBX Heliport."

"Well, that's common activity."

"Sir, the schedule is every hour on the hour for tours from 10am-5pm."

"And?"

"And this one took off at 9:33am."

"Where's it headed? Can you track it?"

"Yes, it appears to be headed towards Savannah. Should we ground him, live trail him, or just track his route?"

"Let's trail him. I want to make sure if this guy is connected with the trespassing on the old power plant property that we don't have any delays."

"Yes, Sir."

**

As the sun came up over Mobile, there was a knock at the door of Shu-Ling and Charity's room. Shu-Ling pointed towards a closet that had a deep side area where Charity headed to hide. Shu-Ling walked over speaking in Mandarin.

"Wǒmen jiàng zài hòuqí jiǎnchá chū (We'll be checking out late)"

"Kèfáng fúwù bù dàsǎochú (Room service not house cleaning)"

"Nǐ yǒu bīngqílín dàn? (Do you have ice cream with eggs?)"

"Méiyǒu, dàn dǎo shàng chīfàn de kèrén huì ràng tāmen wèi wǒmen (No, but the diner on the island will make them for us.)"

Then switching languages, the man outside continued, "15 Minaṭa daravājā ḍī mēṁ parivahana. (Transport in 15 minutes Door D)"

"Charity, sweetheart, Tumelo will be downstairs to pick us up in 15 minutes." They rushed downstairs and saw a town car waiting. Shu-Ling went around and saw Tumi-1 on the back. Must be his, she thought.

"Hop in." She opened and got in first, something didn't feel right, just as Charity was about to close the door she looked toward the rear view mirror. It was not Tumelo. She tried to push Charity from the vehicle but suddenly a man pushed her in and slammed the door shut.

"Ladies, I'll be giving you a ride. My boss has reason to believe this is a very special little girl." The man sped down 90-East.

"Charity, buckle up!"

"Oh, don't worry, I'm not going to let anything happen to her, you on the other hand..." Suddenly he slammed the gas hard, pushed a couple buttons on the dash and then just as he turned, reached for a gun to pull on Shu-Ling, Charity screamed.

Shu-Ling slammed her feet high into the back of his head. The gun flew into the passenger seat, as his head rammed against the dash to the side of the steering wheel. The car jolted and he grabbed the wheel to keep it steady.

She slammed the rear of the seat so hard that it disengaged from the locks and he slammed again forward this time directly into the steering wheel. Charity looked outside. They were nearing the Mobile River.

"Shu-Ling!"

Shu-Ling repeated her kick, flipped upside down, and wrapped the man's legs between her ankles. "I have this. Can you swim?"

Charity nodded.

She cranked him by the neck sideways against the wheel and the car flew off the bridge. "Hold on," she then turned and hit the window switches and all the windows went down.

"Get ready!" Shu-Ling went into a ball and as the car crashed into the river she expanded her limbs quickly and reached down to Charity's seatbelt and pushed her through the window.

Swimming quickly she brought her up out of the water and Charity released a breath. "What just happened?"

They swam up to the shore, when a hand came out toward them. Shu-Ling looked up. It was Tumelo.

"Where have you been?"

"I came out of the hotel and saw them taking you. I followed you the whole way. What happened?"

"I'll tell you later. How did they know? Who were they?"

"Zhanger's men."

"How do you know?"

"The license plate, I assume you saw it?"

"Yeah, that's what threw me off."

"Quick, let me help you guys up to the car. We need to catch our flight."

"Flight?"

"Yes, I have a plane waiting. I did some translation over the years for a lot of people. Somehow, something along this adventure leaked back to someone who must know them. There's no other way they'd know, nor would they know where I was, and to use part of my name on the plate of that car."

Suddenly the plate floated up to the surface of the river.

"Just as I thought, an over plate just to make it look like it was me. Let's go."

**

"Oh, boy." Stella said.

"What?"

"Coast Guard!"

"Coast Guard? Is that common out here?" Jonathan asked staring out into the water.

"Please pull along side," a voice over a loudspeaker clearly toward them called out.

"What would they want with us?"

"Could be anything, could be nothing." Stella said.

"This is the US Coast Guard, please slow your pace as we pull along side!"

"What do we do?" Jonathan's voice trembled.

"It's like driving a car. You pull over. You're not going to get away from them." The boat slowly began to go around.

"Lovers, huh? About to get married, I assume we are going to sail around the world for you to write a world class story based on our honeymoon adventures?" Stella said with a smile.

"Exactly!"

She hopped onto his hips and they began to kiss.

"Mess up my hair. I'll try to mess up yours." Laughing they began to kiss.

"Ahem," one of the Coast Guard officers said over the loud speaker. "Common boat Stella, what is your intention?"

"Hi, we're just testing the waters, sir."

Jonathan began speaking in French.

Stella put a finger over his lips, "shhh." Stella hopped down and reached for a deck speaker mic. "Gentlemen, I'm headed out on sea to show this lovely man the open waters. We'll be married soon, and well, we're thinking why take a cruise when you can sail the world, just the two of us, for our honeymoon."

"Really?" The officer questioned suspiciously.

"He's a French writer, gentlemen."

"Where exactly are you getting married?"

"Sapelo Island, I studied there. I'm a former botanist, well, that was before I fell in love with this romantic."

"Call it in!" the one on the speakers called to another officer.

Moments later, the young ensign nodded. "I just confirmed they have a couple coming in by boat today to speak about using some space there for a wedding, a former botanist, Stella and her fiancé."

"Okay, move along. But please, move swiftly, there's word of a storm moving in. Try not to get to, um, distracted."

"Yes sir!" Stella saluted the boat and Jonathan pulled her back into his arms and they fell laughing.

The Coast Guard vessel moved off quickly into the distance.

"We should get moving and stay low. And, we should be prepared for anything."

**

Boarding the flight, Shu-Ling saw three men of various dressing styles from a suit, to khakis and a polo shirt, as if fresh from the golf course.

Charity followed her and then Tumelo. Doctor Phillips was on the plane waiting, and he had brought a specialty heart and pediatric surgeon to assist him.

"Doctors, this is Charity. And this is Shu-Ling. Please take a seat. It's time to go." And as one of the Doctors leans forward, Tumelo turned toward them. "And please, no questions. This isn't about any of you."

As they exited the plane, each of them dropped off a generic black brief case in the cargo area. Each contained information that could easily form a case against each of them individually. This was a form of insurance, that none would ever speak of what was about to happen. Where each dropped a briefcase, there was another matching it with their name that contained their payment for their work.

**

As William's helicopter slowly returned landing the OBX

Heliport, the Camp Lejeune based Helicopter set down next to it. A JAG, and supporting Military personnel stepped out as they saw four men exit the other.

Showing their credentials, "We're going to have to ask you men a few questions."

"To what do we owe this special visit sir?"

"Well, really it's simple. We're monitoring the nearby skies for unusual activity. Usually this operation doesn't begin flights until 10am. We heard there was an unscheduled flight prior to regular daily operations." Each of the men introduced themselves, when a man from inside the small building nearby came running out.

"Excuse me, what is this about?"

The military men repeated their explanation.

"Well sir, these men are investors, looking at helping me expand my business from just the outer banks to the entire Mid-Atlantic specialty tourist areas and beyond."

"Gentleman, if you can go inside, we only need about 10 minutes." One by one the men's names came back as clear. Just as they were finishing up, another helicopter was circling back in to land. They each slowly stepped inside.

"We apologize for delaying you good men. Clearly we received some bad information." Then they looked toward the business owner. "What the hell is landing now?"

"Oh, that's from our last tour."

"Are they all the same?"

"Typically, but we have a few different ones we offer. Here's some material in case you ever want to recommend us. Gentlemen, I've prepared the conference room and brunch is here."

"Excellent."

"Good day, gentleman."

William was now on the island. He knew an off-time helicopter flight could look strange to anyone watching so he had organized a flight of businessmen, all clients, and asked a favor that they considered investing in a small excursion opportunity he was familiar with.

Meanwhile, he caught a ride with a nice couple of young ladies whom didn't speak English, and were happy to get a free ride over the Atlantic, he was able to share a little treasure along the way to Black Beard's Island.

He found a nice quiet spot to relax and wait. A couple hours later he saw a small plane flying overhead, and decided it was time to go.

As the plane landed, he met up with them, and a driver of a Jeep.

"Ya'll wanna go over to the University, right? You meeting Stella and her new man, to talk about wedding plans?"

"Yes sir, that is correct." They each stepped off. The man in the suit looked over and got the response, "Oh, hello Pastor. Glad you could make it." The doctor just went with it and nodded.

"Will we be picking them up?"

"Who?"

"Stella and her fiancé?"

"No, no, we have another jeep picking them up when their boat docks."

"Of course," William responded sharing a laugh with the man, as if they'd known each other their whole lives. Just then the men got a message over their radio.

"The boat has docked."

"Okay, great we'll be there soon."

"They docked by Raccoon bluff. I think she wanted to show them the old Quarantine Station. Once a scientist always a scientist, all right, we'll take them there."

Tumelo had stayed behind. He had heard of a small group of persons who had once been part of slave settlement, and still owned a small section of the island. He did what Tumelo did best, decided to see what he could learn and use it.

Just then one of the Gullah decedents drove by, "you looking to see the Reynolds Mansion."

"No," in his best accent to match the West African Geechee and Gullah natives he had encounter in past travels. "I want to see the Quarantine."

"Awful place to go. Many, many ghosts and many stories untold still."

"I need some help. A couple of University men are there with friends. I need to detain them for a few hours and make sure no one knows."

"Why? What do you want with them, with us?"

"I just want to learn more about the Quarantine."

"Are you a reporter? Are you just another one of those trying to take away what is rightfully ours? A taxman, who wants to raise our taxes another five hundred percent!"

"On the contrary." Tumelo pulled out another briefcase, as if he had them stocked on hand, ready and full of cash, "I want to help you keep what is yours and more."

He opened it up, full of money.

"Just to see the Quarantine? That doesn't add up. What else do you want?"

"I want to save a life. But we need a safe place where we can work. We need to know we won't be interrupted. Our government hurt a young girl unknowingly and now she's going to die, because of what they did to her years ago when she was just a baby. Or better spoken, of what they did not do. Sure, in some way they didn't know but now they do and now that it could cost them, make them look bad, they want her for research. But if I can get her to this place, with the right men we can save her."

"Keep your money. You do as you say, and then you send the men who you are helping you to help us. We have a deal?"

Appealing to the good nature of a group of people who knew what it was to be oppressed, fight against others ruling over them, for their lives, and see others die along the way was the most simple and honest way to get the man's help.

They were on their way. Along the way they picked up two additional men. As they arrived to the quarantine they saw Stella docking. Tumelo motioned his new friends toward the boat. They dropped him off and headed off into the trees.

As Jonathan approached him, at the edge of the boat, "Bon Jour Tumelo!" He followed in French, "Il a été longtemps mon ami!" saying "It has been a long time my friend!"

Tumelo responded in kind and then Jonathan introduced Stella, continuing the charade with her, as his fiancé and the excitement to find a place on the island for their small and intimate wedding before sailing the world and working on his latest story.

"Let's meet up with everyone else."

"Ah Tumelo, glad you decided to join us. And I see you found the lovely couple of the day. You must be Stella."

"And you are? Wait let me guess, William."

"Yes! Don't tell me this crazy Frenchman has been talking about me and telling stories again."

"He is quite the storyteller."

"Believe everything and then scale it back a bit. This is Shu-Ling and my daughter Charity."

The local men stepped in. "Looks like you've found a man of the world with friends from everywhere."

"It is so great you were all able to make it. Chris, Ed, thank you so much for your help today." Stella said with a smile.

"Anything for you Stella, it's just great to have you back on the island. But one question, why not have the wedding at the University?"

"Oh, you know me, I have my reasons. There's so much history here and I am marrying a storyteller. It's also going to be very small and intimate. Where's Samantha? I really thought she'd be with you."

"She had a meeting and a class coming for a tour."

Shu-Ling popped up. "Really? Oh, I wish I could go on a tour of the university space here. I bet it's amazing, and I've been considering University of Georgia for my masters."

Chris looked at his watch. "Well, I'm sure we can make it. Stella, we're not supposed to leave you here alone. Ed?"

"I'll tell you what, I have some work to do so I'll ride back with you guys, and bring the jeep back to pick everyone up in a bit. How long do you think you'd like?"

"Oh, maybe an hour or so."

"Are you sure you all don't mind?"

"Of course Shu, please go and enjoy. We'll fill you in later."

Speaking in French, Jonathan went on about how he wanted to search out the spiritual connections in the buildings and get in touch with them. "I was raised in a mixed home, with a very new age father and strong Catholic mother. We must make sure there is nothing evil in our midst. We surely do not want to start our lives in a place of death but in a place of life!"

Tumelo translated and explained. "He seeks life out in everything he does even in the darkest of places."

"Well, good luck with that. We might be a couple of hours. Don't get back on that boat till we're back. I'd say be careful but with Stella here you're probably in better hands than anyone we know."

"Thank you."

"Enjoy the tour Shu-Ling."

Immediately, once the men and Shu-Ling pulled away the rest of them moved toward the buildings. Deep within the buildings there was a single medical room that still had emergency power capabilities and full operating facilities.

While this was operated as the quarantine, they also made it a fully functional small-scale hospital. "I had a lab here for a short time. I enjoyed the connection of the life of earth, to the lives of those who had come through here and believed the treasure that was buried here by Black Beard had nothing to do with Gold."

"Then, what kind of treasure did he bring?"

"Spices, special healing plants, and the remains of some of the most famous men who ever sailed the seas of his time. Explorers, sea captains, and saints."

"Are you saying he killed them?"

"No, no but these men's remains were often considered a treasure in themselves. One other thing that is special here is the soil. When I did carbon dating on the soil and plants it was clear that sometime in the early to mid 1700's there was an incredible change in the land here. If you compare it to other areas of the nearby island soil and plant growth, you'll find that there is a very specifically defined area on the official space of Black Beard Island. And here, near the Quarantine and ends just a short distance beyond here on the northern most part of Sapelo."

William looked up at Jonathan. "I believe this is the package you requested be delivered?" He then pulled a small bag from his messenger-style leather shoulder bag and handed it over.

Stella looked over. "Is he talking about the bag or me?"

William and Jonathan smiled. "We should go. We don't have much time."

"Wait. Am I some sort of package, just manipulated into your plan? I can't be. There's no way... is there?"

Then Charity looked up. "Miss, whatever the reason, if you are here to help save my life, that's all that matters and I am grateful."

At that moment Stella looked down at this young girl who's eyes were growing dark and hair was starting to thin a little. This girl whose skin was growing pale and that had fought to make it to this point, and a tear fell then another and she wiped them away to say, "I am, sweetie that's exactly why I'm here, and you, young lady are very, very wise. Let's go."

As they walked into the building she led them through room after room. Some had been left to resemble, exactly what they looked like as years had gone by. Then, they came through a medical area that was less than modern. The doctors' looks of concern spoke more than a thousand words.

Stella spoke up. "I know it doesn't look like much, but it should have everything you need. And it does get better. Not everyone knows about this, but one late night when I was working away in my lab I learned there's much more to this place than meets the eye." She walked over to a control board and tapped a few keys. Suddenly a wall opened with stairs down to a basement-style room.

Doctor Phillips spoke up quickly, "Now we're talking." Seeing the washroom off to the side he continued, "Gentleman let's wash up. Stella, are you familiar with prepping a patient?"

"Yes."

"Then, get Charity on the table and do what you know. We'll take care of the rest. Then, since you should know as well as anyone, please take the ingredients and combine them in the best way so that we can place 3 separate 5 cc shots directly into Charity's heart. Here is a liquid similar to what we use to help cancer patients accept chemo into their system. Please add enough that it is only 5% of the entire mixture."

"Got it!" Stella responded in excitement, nervousness, care and caution all at once.

"What can we do?"

"Jonathan, the best thing you can do now is to stay out of the way. You've done everything possible to this point. Have your men keep an eye out. You never know what we might need or how long this will actually take."

Stella went to work, stripping the juices of the Cincaberry and combining it with the aloe from the plants. Then, Tumelo handed her what was provided by the small herbal store he had visited.

"What is that?" Doctor Phillips asked as he came away from the washroom.

"I learned of it when I was looking for the radioactive aloe. It grows alongside a mountain near a waterfall west of Guarapari Brazil. Guarapari is known to have very high radiation levels naturally, and it appears some of this comes from nearby mountains and into some of the water and grows into the plants. While I couldn't find any of the Aloe, I did find out about this. Cura lado da montanha or the healing hand of the mountain, because as it grows it extends in long thin finger like leaves of five as if someone is reaching out from the mountain. Each extended leaf is a pod with these little beans.

The healers there say when the small aloe plants do appear in nearby areas during just a few weeks of the year the medicine men in the village rush to harvest them and use them together on the sickest of those in their care."

"Stella, can you examine it? Stella?" They realized she already had it under lenses, and running through machines in her old lab space on site.

"It's safe."

Jonathan jumped in, "Are you sure? How can you be sure?"

"Jonathan, it's what I do. I have run tests after tests with these machines and with these eyes and hands and if there is even the slightest risk I'd catch it. Does she have any allergies, anything at all?"

"No, she has never been allergic to anything."

"What about plants? Poison ivy, oak, anything?"

"No, we've done many hikes and things out doors and she's never…"

"Jonathan," she cut him off. "It's safe. At the worst, outside of the slightly added radiation, which we may want to adjust for with the aloe and it's different as it comes in a natural form not like that of the power plant, it otherwise has no negative appearance. Much like many plants you can eat and live off. They may not taste so good but they aren't going to hurt you."

"Okay, do it."

One of the doctors had a small case. He opened it, pulled out a small clear bag with liquid and connected it with a drip to act as an anesthesia.

"Dad…"

"You're going to be okay. And I'm going to be here the whole time, just as I've always been, just as I'll always be."
She smiled and then her head turned as she drifted off.

"Let's do this."

As the men went to work to check her heart and run some basic tests of vital signs, Stella grinded the powder of the third plant into the mix as directed by Doctor Phillips based on the information Tumelo had been given. Then he added some liquid provided by one of the other doctors. This was designed to break it all down so that it will easily enter the blood stream and from there apply to the heart directly and naturally as it grafts to the weakening areas."

**

Back at the University grounds, a woman comes up to talk to the man standing next to Shu-Ling.

"Chris! How are you? I heard Stella was going to be coming for a visit. Has she made it yet?"

"Oh, actually she's showing some friends the old quarantine buildings. I was just about to head back there after wrapping up some work."

"I'd love to take the visiting students who are here for a tour to see it as well, plus it'd be a bonus for them to meet a former student whom we love and loved it here so much."

"Well, I'll tell you what, we brought one of her friends here who's interested in studying with us to join you.
After you all are done, let me know, and I can take you over. It's getting late too, Shu-Ling was it?"

"Yes, sir."

"Have you eaten?"

"No actually, I'm starving!"

"Samantha, would you mind getting her something while walking about the grounds? I think the food court is open today, correct?"

"It is. Come with me. And tell me, what is it that has you pursuing our school and more about your interest in studying with us?" The two walked away, talking.

**

Stella handed three syringes to the doctors on a small silver tray.

"Thank you. Okay, everyone. Here we go."

They slowly inserted the first one to the upper right third of the area affected. Her heart rate increased, as it worked to adapt and as the radiation and fluid impacted the blood stream.

"Is that normal?"

"I don't know."

Stella took Jonathan's arm. Tumelo and William each placed a hand on his shoulders. Watching her readings closely and seeing how she responded, one of the doctors spoke up a few moments later. "It's time for the second one."

Doctor Phillips responded, "Okay." He then began inserting the second dose.

This time her body began to react more quickly. "Heart rate is increasing, 98, 107, 115…"

"Check her temperature."

"Rising 99, 99.5, 100."

Under his breath Doctor Phillips started to question the operation. "What's different, what's different?"

Doctor Barone, who had mostly been observing overheard him. "Her mother!"

"What?"

"Her mother. That's what is different Doctor Phillips. She isn't here. Her blood. That's what is different."

"Oh my, Doctor Barone you're right. It's the one thing we didn't account for."

William couldn't help but ask, "What blood type is she?"

"She's O positive."

Doctor Barone stopped them and explained, "We brought a small amount of blood, in case it was needed to replace any lost. However, it's a bit more complicated than that for these purposes. It needs to be a close enough match to her that it can actually take.

It needs to come from her family line, as close to her as possible."

"Doctor her heart rate is stabilizing, but it's in the 130s and her temp is holding at 100.5."

Slowly her body began twitching at the toes.

"I'm getting worried Jonathan."

"Test me first!"

"Test you?"

"It appears there's a chance that one of us here can help her. Start with me. No matter what you need, all that I have is for her."

"Jonathan, you heard Doctor Barone, it's not that simple, we have blood."

"You DON'T HAVE MINE! Test it! I'm O positive also. So there's at least that, you might need it."

Doctor Barone nodded. "It can't hurt."

Stella brought over two small strips and a couple of tubes for collecting blood from each. She ran them through a machine she usually used to test for consistency between plant structures. "Doctor Phillips, Doctor Barone, you may want to see this."

The other doctor remained to watch the vitals and alert them if needed.

"Do you see what I do Michael?" referring to Doctor Phillips.

"Stella, can you take three more tubes from Jonathan. We have to move fast."

276

Slowly they began providing the blood into a tube they had running into Charity's aorta.

"Her heart rate is slowing."
"Let's hope not too much."
"It's stabilizing at 92, 88, 85. It's holding at 85. Temperature is down to 99.7."
Everyone took a deep sigh of relief, then she began to shake a bit. "Tumelo, William, hold her. Quick we need to insert the blood from the second tube as we also give her the third dose of the medicine. Here we go. Let's hope this works."
Slowly they began to add both. "Doctor, steady, steady."
"Right with you Michael."
As her heart began to receive the foreign fluid into her blood stream her body began to convulse. "She's having a seizure. Her heart rate is racing."
"Let's all remember this is very different than using another person to move this through. There's no filter. We're relying on Jonathan's blood to filter it."

**

"Chris! We're all ready to go!"
"Great, I just wrapped up. I'd rather not surprise her with twenty folks. Mind if I go ahead of you? I'll radio you as soon as I'm there and have confirmed she's okay with the group coming over. Shu-Ling would you like to come along?"
"Yes, that'd be great. Miss Samantha, it was great talking with you."
"So, you enjoyed your visit?"
"Yes, very much!" The two hopped into the Jeep and headed down the road back to the northern end of the island. Halfway there, they came across a large tree fallen across the road.
"What is this?"
"Oh, well, you see, there is a group of people who live here who feel we have taken this land away from them. Sometimes they make it a little difficult for us. You might call it a protest."

"Mind helping me move…"

"Shu-Ling? Shu-Ling?"

"Oh no." Chris jumped from the Jeep and tied a rope to the front and around the tree and began to move it.

**

Back at the operating table, the tension grew with every passing moment.

"136, 142. Temperature is up to 101."

"Do you have anything cold?"

"There are some ice packs with the testing specimens in the freezer hold on." Stella grabbed them and went back and placed two at Charity's feet and one on her forehead.

"We need to shock her heart."

"Won't that make it worse?"

"No. It appears the medicine and fluids are getting stuck you might say, we need to thin them with a light shock that will cause the heart to expand. Not with electricity but with air."

Doctor Barone opened her mouth and breathed a large dose of air into her lungs. As they expanded, Doctor Phillips pinched the tube to her heart and released it so an air bubble moved in. Her heart expanded slightly and her body stopped shaking.

"Her heart rate is stabilizing at 147."

Everyone sighed, as beads of sweat were across everyone's head.

**

"Shu-Ling? Where did you go?" Chris began to walk the perimeter, stepping slightly into the woods, searching for her but being cautious of what might be waiting for him also.

**

"Her temperature is coming down. And so is her heart rate."

"How is her heart looking?"

"It's taking to the graft of fluids. It's adapting exactly as it would have before."

"We're running out of time. How long until we can get out of here?"

"We need at least 15 minutes. If it remains stable for another 15 minutes, I think we're in the clear. We'll be able to tell if it took. We'll have to follow up in a few days, to know if it worked though. You can go to any doctor and just say she's complained of chest pains and ask to have heart checked. If it worked it should appear near normal in 24-48 hours."

**

Meanwhile, Chris hopped back in the Jeep and began to drive. "Are you kidding? A flat! Come on guys! I can't see you but I know you're there." He picked up the radio. "Samantha. We have trouble. I think we have some protesters slowing me down and the girl has disappeared. I don't think they're the type to take her, but you know there could just be that one that's gone mad."

"Message received, I'll send help."

**

"Okay, let's start cleaning this place up. Keep an eye on those vitals and an ear on her heart."

"Doctor Phillips, something doesn't look right."

"What is it?"

"It appears her heartbeat is weakening. Listen." Charity's heartbeat was not only slowing but the beats were more drawn out.

"It's working hard."

"Do you think the blood is thickening in the arteries near the heart from the medicine?"

"I'm not sure."

"What do we do?" Jonathan nearly screamed.

"Jonathan. We have to monitor her. We may have to go in."

"Doc, I don't think we have that kind of time."

"We may not have anytime if we leave and she's not ready."

"Stella, can you buy us more time?"

"I can try. William, weren't you saying how you'd do whatever it takes to take me away from Jonathan?"

"That's right." He played along with a smile, "Jean Pierre, she is mine!"

She was already running out of the building.

"Let's get to work. Let's open her." Quickly the Doctors moved to action.

Jonathan cringed and turned his head, hurting for her. Tumelo came behind him and said, "I just saw Stella and William storm out screaming how she would never go back with him. What exactly is going on?"

"They're buying us time in case the University folks come back."

"Oh, I see. I thought this was a minimally evasive procedure."

"It was... until..." Jonathan dropped his head. Tumelo put his arm around Jonathan.

"Doctor Barone, it's the tissue, it's tearing apart."

"Quickly, we have to move quickly."

The men tear apart. "Can I do anything Doctors?"

"We need a graft. The medicine is working, but it's too late to actually hold and develop the tissue. It was too thin."

"So, can you use anything else?"

"Heart tissue is unlike other tissue in our body. It's a mix of blood and artery type tissue and well, it's hard to explain."

"Can you take some from another part of her heart?"

"If she was healthy, if she was older, and it was fully developed and if there was less of a risk, yes. But in this case, no."

"Then what?"

"Let me think, Jonathan."

"We're running out of time. Me, use mine."

"Jonathan you know it's not that simple."

"I know that my blood seemed to work with the medicine. I know she had my heart from the moment I looked into her eyes. And..."

"Jonathan..."

"And, I know this will work.

And I know if we don't try, I'll lose her."

"Jonathan… Doctor, can you pull up a second table? We're going to need all eyes on this and be sharp."

**

"Chris?"

"Um, yes?"

"I'm Captain Davis. I'm tracking a man whom I think may have come to the island earlier today. Can we help you to where you may be going?"

"Did Samantha send you?"

"Let's just say, she said you were being held up by some protesters. We can help."

"Captain, I hate to tell you this but it appears your men are either gaining weight or you have a flat as well."

"How far are we from your destination?"

"A little less than a mile I'd guess."

"Let's go for a walk then. It shouldn't take us much more than 10 minutes or so?"

**

Jonathan's head began to drift to the side as the anesthesia set in.

"We don't have much time."

"I'm making the first incision." Slowly the doctors got started, taking just a small piece of Jonathan's tissue from his heart and laying it upon Charity's, where it was nearly pulling apart.

They used a light bandaging agent that would work similar to glue and then dissolved through her system. They also applied what was nearly the last of the serum to help it work more quickly.

Already one of the other Doctors had started to sew up Jonathan. "Doctor Rivera, watch his vitals. Watch that heart."

"On it."

**

"Ouch!" Chris fell to the ground. "Captain!"

"What happened? I don't know. I caught my leg on something."

"Can you walk?"

"Let me try. Ouch!" Chris let out the scream of a banshee with a shrill reaching throughout the woods.

Shaking his head, Captain Davis told the man with him, "Let's get him back to the Jeep. We'll go ahead and change the tire and get him back to the University."

"Captain, I'm sorry."

"It's okay. After we get you back, we'll get back to the Quarantine."

**

A short time later, Tumelo came down to check on the operation. "The others are on watch, can I help?"

"Actually, can you get Stella and keep watch with William?" Tumelo rushed out, and moments later Stella came into the operating room.

"We've already started cleaning up. We need your help. What are the musts to get this place back where no one notices we were here?"

Stella went to work alongside them. "How are we getting them out of here?"

"I have a plan. Everyone else take the boat. I'm going with William."

"Who else here knows how to handle the boat?"

"Tumelo, he's experienced at the sea. You'll be fine."

"Is there a bedroom or a place where they can rest?"

"Yes, below deck. Let's hope for steady waters… and a strong wind."

**

"Alright, Chris, you're going to be fine. We're heading back to the Quarantine."

"Chris, what happened?"

"Hi Samantha, hi Ed, I fell."

282

"Oh, man. I thought you were going back to get Stella?"

"I was and then this happened. Captain Davis here met up with me on his way to see one of the men that were here to meet her."

"Can we join you on the ride back?"

"I'm not sure that's a good idea."

"Well, one of us should go to look over things and meet up with Stella before she goes."

"This Stella seems to be pretty well respected by you all."

"Oh, yes. She's taken some time away from her passion for plants and studies, but everyone here at the University has always loved her ever since she first came to study here."

"Hmm, well that gives her and her friends I guess a bit more of credibility then. Still, we'd like to check on them directly and make sure none of them are dangerous or that there is any reason for concern."

"Sure, we'll be happy to assist you."

"Let's go. This time let's keep our eyes out for those so called protesters, which appeared to have hindered us before."

**

"Okay, let's get Jonathan and Charity below deck."

"Can I help?" a familiar voice called.

"Shu-Ling?"

"I ditched the stiff and some of those friends whom I'm sure Tumelo met here on the island, evidently helped slow them down."

"Stella is wrapping up some cleaning down stairs. Do you mind helping her?"

"Of course!" Immediately Shu headed in.

"Shu-Ling!" Stella hugged her. "We're almost done. So glad you're here but…"

"Don't worry, I'm not sure where The Professor is, but he isn't here with me. Still, we should get out of here."

Tumelo guided William as they moved toward the boat.

"Careful, careful, let's put him on the bed to the left… whoa, my left William."

"Okay, let's get Charity."

"How's he doing?"

"Doctor Phillips, he seems to be perfectly fine. Heart sounded good and his breathing appeared normal. Doctor Rivera is with him now."

"Let's get Charity."

"Be very careful. Any unnecessary stress or pull at where we operated could cause permanent damage. We took our one shot and we need to finish steady getting her to safety."

"Understood."

Using the bed sheet she was on, they cradled her similarly to a girl just lying in a hammock, and they took her to the boat. Everyone else followed them onto the boat preparing to set sail.

"Easy, easy."

As they began to set Charity into the bed, Stella was inside replacing the sheet with the aid of Shu-Ling. They put the finishing touches as to leave no trace behind them. As they came up, they realized they heard what sounded like a car in the distance.

"GO!"

"But?"

"Shu-Ling, go get out of here…" She dashed toward the boat.

Tumelo pulled up the ropes that held the boat at the pier. "Where will we find you?"

"I'm in love with a French man. Where else would we go?" William shouted out as he jumped and slid down a rope from the boat that Tumelo immediately released following. "Go run with the Jaguars! I'll make sure there is a plane waiting."

"Thank you friend."

Slowly Tumelo raised the sails and placed the engine at low speed as to not raise awareness that they were pulling away.

**

"Stella! Stella!"

"Ed! Samantha!" Stella ran toward the oncoming Jeep hoping it kept the boat out of sight. "Oh, Samantha I didn't think I was going to get to see you!"

"Well, here I am! And here you are! Getting married?"

"Yes, well…"

"And, to such a good looking man, I see. Hello sir."

"Bon Jour."

"Oh, William. Stop it."

"What happened to your fiancé?"

"Oh, Ed this is her fiancé!"

"No, no there was another man. This is one of his friends."

"Stella, look at you! What kind of girl have you become since you left the university?"

"No, no… William here has been after me ever since Jean Pierre and I met. But I've told him…" He reached for her and she pushed him away. "I still tell him, I'm already taken!" She laughed and he reciprocated.

"So where is this Jean-Pierre?"

"And, you are?"

"Captain Davis. I thought I was looking for this man here, as he had taken an unexpected trip over here to the island but I get the feeling this is all just a wild goose chase. I can tell you this. Jerry Zhang will not have his way with the military and neither will the Governor of Georgia! The men of Camp Lejeune do not have time for games."

"Ok, Captain. We understand."

Ed continued, "Still Stella, I think we're all curious, where did everyone go?"

"Well, I told you, Jean Pierre is a writer. He tends to make stories he can recreate in fiction at a later time. A bit dramatic for some yes, but he keeps me dreaming. Walk with me."

As they walked a few feet toward the Quarantine she pointed out over the water. "Shortly after his other friend, I think they call him, Tumè, asked if he could see the boat, everyone else asked the same. Then after a while Jean Pierre and I had just been out here meditating and looking around at where we could have the wedding, and well, maybe a few other things happened inside."

"Stella!"

"I said maybe… anyway, He said, 'I better go check on our friends.' Then, I looked over and the ropes were being pulled up and with his friend translating, he shouted out, 'William will know where to find me if you cannot!' He shouted, 'Viva La France' and let the boat sail away."

"He left you?"

"No! He started a new chapter in our story." She sighed and with her eyes opened wide toward the boat then to the sky, like she was in some sort of fairy tale, she continued, "One where now that he has chased me, he wants me to chase him, then we can return here to wed, or go wherever the next chapter leads us."

"Oh my, I can see the stars in her eyes gentleman."

"Well, let's get you back, there's a helicopter from OBX Tours landing soon. I already checked and they were only picking up a couple of folks so you two can go with them."

Captain Davis shook his head. "And, I guess we're your taxi."

"Thank you Captain."

"Yes, thank you Captain."

He continued to shake his head. "Get in."

Chapter 19 – Daylight

Darkness fell as the boat sailed away. "Jaguars? What Jaguars? Well, one thing is sure, we can't go far and she can't get on a plane, at least not tonight."

"How long can this boat handle being at sea?"

Shu-Ling opened up a cabinet. "I found food, so we can survive the night for sure. Not many places to sleep, but a few of us should stay up anyhow, to keep an eye on things and watch the two of them."

"I'll stay up through the night. If I get tired I can still give direction to the rested."

Doctor Phillips responded, "Good idea Tumelo. Doctor Barone, can you take the first shift of three?"

"Of course, I'll wake Doctor Rivera in a few hours. You'll need to be the most rested if anything happens. You know more than any of us about this girl and this procedure."

"I guess I do. I think I may have even learned more than I expected."

Tumelo began searching the boat for supplies and in a drawer found an unopened pre-paid cell phone, he opened it, and plugged it into a spare battery charger he'd been carrying for himself, it lit up. He pulled out his phone, and then used the one he found to dial. "We have them."

"How are they? And why isn't he calling me? What number is this? Are you on the run?"

"It's okay. I don't know where we are going to be tonight or even tomorrow. But I have a feeling this ends in New Orleans."

"New Orleans?"

"Yes."

"I want to… I need to know. I want to be there wherever this all ends."

"I need a secure line to reach you."

"Honey, I'm part of NYPD International now, this is as secure as it gets."

"I'll find a way to get you a message. You find a way to make even more sure that the line is safe."

"I will, safer than a quarterback behind the G-Men's offensive line."

Tumelo hung up. "G-Men?"

"You talking to a Giants fan?"

"Yes, I guess so Doctor. Wait, the Giants. That's New York football right?"

"Yes?"

"Is there a team with the Jaguars as their mascot?"

"Sure, Jacksonville."

"Of course! William was trying to make sure we headed for Jacksonville. We'll go slow and then dock at sunrise."

Through the night, each person took their shift except Tumelo, who remained faithfully watching over the boat and its safety, making sure to keep it as smooth as possible so his friend and his little girl could rest and recover.

As morning dawned everyone had already awoken. Nerves will do that to you.

"Dad? Dad? Doctor Phillips?! Shu-Ling?!"

"I'm right here. And so am I, we're all here."

"Am, am I going to be alright?"

"It appears so. We just need to get you somewhere, where we can, well, we can see inside. And my dad?"

"Oh, my head…" Jonathan tried to rise up. "Oh, not good." Quickly he lied back down. "My chest hurts…"

"Dad?"

"Charity!" Jonathan lit up, wanting so bad to reach out with a hug but he fell back on the pillow.

"Go easy you two. We're pulling into Jacksonville. There's a small clinic near the marina, operated by a friend I studied with in Medical School. He said I could bring you both in. I just told him we were on vacation and you both had chest pains."

"Sounds a little fishy," Jonathan let out with a grunt. "I mean two people with chest pains from your trip out to sea? Wouldn't it likely just be gas?"

"Or, if you my friend had a problem, say an allergic reaction to some seafood, it wouldn't be surprising if it was hereditary."

"Well played, Doc."

"I don't think you understand Jonathan. I think Charity is your daughter."

"Well of course she's my daughter Doc. You know the story."

"Wait, dad. I think the doctor is saying he thinks you're my real dad."

"Wait? How?"

"Of course, we'll have to run some tests but it makes sense, since your blood types are both Type O just as Maria was. Two persons with Type O will have children with Type O."

"But is that enough?"

"Jonathan, your heart tissue didn't create a negative reaction at all, it was as if it was her very own. Only explainable by a blood relative, one with a match so close that the body would accept it. All that being said, it's still just speculative. We'll have to run some tests. You have both rested very well. I suggest you continue to do so."

As they arrived to the marina, a SUV arrived and took most of them to the clinic.

"Doctors Barone and Rivera, go with Shu-Ling to the taxi station."

"Michael, it's good to see you."

"You as well, Doctor Alvarez."

"Okay, let's see what we have here."

"Doctor, I need a favor. I need to be alone with them."

"Michael, that's highly unusual I mean…" Then he saw the look on Michael's face. It was the look of a Doctor who knew he held life and death in his hands, and as a fellow Doctor, he needed him to help give life. "Sure Mike. Go ahead. I was getting a bit hungry and the deli next door makes great sandwiches. Could be a while before I decide what I want."

"Thanks, Jose. I can't thank you enough."

"Just be careful. I just got this machine." They exchanged smiles and tapped one another on the shoulders before Doctor Alvarez exited.

"Okay, lay down. I'm going to begin by taking a small amount of blood from each of you for a quick testing. My friend has many new machines and well, they could be of great help to us." Slowly he began to check over them.

The only one at his side was Tumelo.

"You're a good friend."

"You as well, Doctor."

"I wish I could have done more for Maria."

"You are still doing all you can for her."

Doctor Phillips took a deep breath and began to check each of them. "All vitals are normal. That's an excellent start. I'm going to do an ultrasound on each of them. It should allow me to see what I need to see."

Slowly he worked the transducer across the chest and looked at Jonathan's heart. "It's strong. I really think you are going to be fine. I don't have any concerns for you. Charity, are you ready?"

"Yes, sir. Is it going to hurt?"

"No, it might be a little cold and tickle but try to hold still, okay?"

"I will."

"Tumelo, can you get Jonathan a towel and a wet wash cloth over there?" He pointed toward the sink area near by.

Tumelo responded as always, with action and service.

Doctor Phillips repeated the process with Charity.

"Looks good, looks good. I'm going to apply some light pressure to see how it responds. If it hurts let me know immediately." Slowly as he pushed in various areas like a balloon animal maker he saw one end, or the other bulge just slightly and watches it on the screen.

He asked her to breathe in a variety of ways. He then, held her hands up, then her legs up and each time asked her to move just slightly side to side. "I want to make sure no matter the angle and the work the heart is doing that it doesn't change how it is working. Well, at least that it continues to work steadily. Pumping blood without stress in any one area or struggling to do its job."

"What do you think Doc?"

"I think you're going to be fine. And, I think it's time to look at your blood test results."

"What does that machine do, Doc?"

"Well, you remember how Stella told us she could quickly match up plants, and you might even remember amidst the chaos yesterday she initially used something like that machine to help us determine if your blood might have a shot at working with Charity's to help the medicine take hold?"

"Yes, of course."

"You gave me blood dad?"

"Yes, that's how the Doctor knew we had the same blood type."

"Well, this machine does a rapid match test, among other things including look for imperfections. If something got into your system that shouldn't have from the medicine or the blood given to you we'd know about 90-95%. Please, lie down and rest." Doctor Phillips began to analyze it, and the readings that were coming out on a computer connected to it too.

After waiting, patiently resting, and waiting, Doctor Alvarez returned. "If any of you are hungry I brought food!"

Charity didn't hesitate. "I'm starving!"

"Well then, let's eat!"

Everyone sat and began to eat.

"Jose, I believe this is your specialty. Would you mind reviewing something with me?"

"Of course Michael, what is it?"

"Walk with me." They reviewed the test results again, now having even more time to be scanned. They revealed the same results as before.

"Yes. Yes, it appears that is the case. But, are they ready? I mean they've been through so much. Maybe you should just let them enjoy things as they are."

"It certainly isn't the kind of thing you expect to find when doing these tests, but no, I think it's important they know what lies ahead for them, more importantly where they have come from."

"Well Michael, they are your patients. You have to make that call."

"Thank you, old friend."

The two doctors returned and found Jonathan and Charity eating, they looked over to see Tumelo asleep on the couch.

"He dosed off half way into his sandwich."

"Well, he has been pushing quite hard, even for a man of his strength and character. Jonathan, I have something to share with you and Charity from the results of the blood tests. I even had Doctor Alvarez review them to make sure there was no mistake."

"What is it?"

"Yes, what is it?" Charity repeated after Jonathan.

"Well, it's something that could change things, but I believe with all that is in me it will change nothing. I'm glad to be sharing this with both of you. Charity, after all, you've fought for a very long time, maybe even when you didn't know you were. Your body was fighting and I think you deserve to know. This is your real father. Charity *is* your daughter."

"But, how? I mean I don't even understand how."

"Jonathan, you once told me of your past. And my guess is you didn't remember her, but when the time came, she came looking for you. Evidently she knew something about you that you didn't even know about yourself."

Jonathan's face fell into his hands in tears. With his strength building he slid out of the bed and leaned over against the one where Charity now sat up and they embraced.

"Dad… you're really my DAD! I mean you've always been my dad, but you're really my DAD!"

"I know, I know. Somehow I think I always knew, here." He placed her hand on his heart.

"Me too," she said as she reached to his other hand and places it on her chest in response.

"Gentlemen, I thank you for everything but I just realized we have to get somewhere. Tumelo, where's William?"

Tumelo was awakened a bit startled by the question. "What?"

"Where's Stella?"

"They're meeting us."

"Where?"

"You don't remember do you?"

"Ha... It's a good thing your friends know you well. We have a plane to catch." Just then he pulled his phone from his pocket. A text Tumelo had sent had just gone through: Dinner French Hell's Kitchen Get on the next plane out.

**

On the plane Jonathan looked at Tumelo. "How did you know?"

"When you shouted Viva La France... I knew. You have always loved French culture, French cuisine, everything about it. And William said your favorite restaurant in New York is Marseille."

Jonathan chuckled. They talked, they rested, and they flew through the clouds. Shortly thereafter, they were getting off the plane in Marseille, France.

"Jonathan! Charity!" Two women came running with William directly behind them.

"Stella! Ruth!"

"Stella?" Ruth responded.

"Ruth?" William responded.

"William, I didn't even see you, where were you?"

"Making sure all the packages were delivered. And I'm thinking you have an extra unexpected package here." He said glancing in Ruth's direction not aware that Tumelo had reached out to her.

"Well, I'm not sure I would have recognized you anyway."

"I'm going to let you all catch up," he handed each one of them a plane ticket. "Jonathan, I'm not sure you'll need this, but if not, cash it in. This one's on me."

"And everything else?"

"We'll settle up later. This is going to be one tricky invoice." Everyone hugged and went their separate ways, except for four of them still standing. "Ruth, it is so good to see you."

"Jonathan, you too. And, this is Stella?"

"Yes. Stella was able to help us with caring for Charity."

"That's great, really, really great. Thank you Stella. She's an amazing girl."

"It was nothing. I think I'm going to study science again. Um, does anyone know where my boat is?"

"Jacksonville!" Charity shouted

"Great, that makes sense. I was wondering, why in the world did William give me a plane ticket to Jacksonville. Goodbye, Jonathan." She kissed him on the cheek.

"Stella, will I ever see you?"

"I hope so."

"I think I want to be a scientist too! 'Cause I think I want to study plants. Plants that heal people!"

"Okay, well sweetie, my lab is your lab. I think you'd be wonderful. You are a very strong, very smart girl." She kissed Charity on the cheek. "Ruth, it was very nice to meet you. Jean-Pierre, I get it. Now, I get it."

Flight 1582 to Jacksonville, departing in 20 minutes.

"I better go. That's me. I can't leave my boat for long, Lou will kill me if she finds out I left her alone across an entire ocean!"

Jonathan laughed with her as she walked away. Then he turned to see Ruth and Charity hugging. "Ruth, I need to tell you something."

Charity jumped in, "Well, we need to tell you something!"

"What, what is it?"

"He's my dad!"

She spoke calmly like it was no big deal, with her cute smile, and an endearing sparkle in her eye toward him. "I know he's your dad, sweetie."

"No Ruth. It's true. She's really my daughter. I mean, we mean, she's really my daughter and I really *am* her dad."

"Wait, how? So all that you went through to adopt her and she's…"

"Yep!"

"I've got to hear this story but first things first, where do we go from here?"

"Well, family is where home is. And I'm looking at my family."

"Oh, and that woman, Stella was it?" Ruth rose up from Charity, and looked Jonathan in the eye.

"So, what exactly did she '*get*'?"

"We had an encounter and quite the experience, even sailed on her boat. And yes, we met at a bar."

"Oh, you did? No surprise."

"I ordered a Stella."

"And, you got one."

"You know, sometimes you get what you order but it isn't what you want."

"But you eat it anyway, don't you?"

"Ruth, you know me real well. Put me in that scenario."

There was a long pause and Charity looked up with a smile. Ruth looked back; head half cocked and remembered this was not the Jonathan of years gone by, and then spoke to him. "Not you. You turn it away and say, that's ok I'll go somewhere else. Somewhere where they have what I really want."

"That's right."

"Somewhere like…"

"Marseille."

Charity looked up at each of them, embraced them in one big hug with arms outstretched, "Home *is* where family is. And it looks like we are finally, all, at home."

Author's Note and Acknowledgements

I wrote Charity when I was thinking about 1 Corinthians 13:13. Some translations say Faith, Hope and Love. I was always intrigued however, with how some translate Love as Charity.

"And now abideth faith, hope, charity, these three; but the greatest of these is charity."

Several years ago, as I was reading this verse once again, I thought immediately about a girl named Charity who would bring both Faith and Hope to someone who thought they had it all but came to realize they had nothing. That someone turned out to be the character of Jonathan Harris.

I hope you have enjoyed reading Charity – What's in a name? I hope in some way it inspires you to have Faith and Hope as well.

I dedicate this book to my wonderful wife Lisa. Thank you for your love and support every day. And I dedicate it to my Peanut, Marilyana. In your eyes I am able to, each day, see life through a new lens.

Thanks to every person who has been a part of the process, Family and Friends, who have encouraged me and shared in my excitement as the story developed into what you now hold in your hands.

Bradly Williams,
    Enjoy the Story...

"Charity" Sketch Art by Jeff Martinez – October 2014

Sapelo Island

Courtesy of the U.S. Geological Survey

www.ingramcontent.com/pod-product-compliance
Lightning Source LLC
Chambersburg PA
CBHW031111030726
47496CB00002BA/486